The Fall of Hyperion

Visionary Epic of Dreams,
Art & the Lofty Ambitions of Humankind

A Modern Translation
Adapted for the Contemporary Reader

Henry Wadsworth Longfellow

Translated by Tim Zengerink

Table of Contents

Preface
Message to the Reader

Rebuilding the Greatest Library in Human History

Thousands of years ago, the Library of Alexandria was the heart of global knowledge — a sanctuary where the wisdom of every known civilization was gathered and shared freely.

And then, it was lost.

Now, we're rebuilding it — and you are invited to join us.

At the Library of Alexandria, we've set out to make every book available to every person on Earth — not just in print, but in every language, every format, and for every reader.

Here's how we do it:

- **Deluxe Print Editions at True Printing Cost** - Order any book as a high-quality paperback, elegant hardcover, or stunning boxset — and only pay what it costs to print. No markups. No middlemen.
- **Unlimited Access to the Greatest Works** - Enjoy thousands of timeless classics — from Plato to Shakespeare to Tolstoy — in beautiful, modern eBook and audiobook editions. Read and listen without limits — for every reader, everywhere.
- **Modern Translations for Every Language & Dialect** - We're reimagining the classics in clear, accessible language — and translating them into every dialect imaginable. Everyone deserves to understand humanity's greatest ideas.

When you visit **LibraryofAlexandria.com**, you're not just accessing books — you're joining a global movement to restore, preserve, and share the wisdom of civilization.

Join us today at LibraryofAlexandria.com

Together, we'll ensure the light of human wisdom never fades again.

With gratitude,

The Modern Library of Alexandria Team

Visit:
www.libraryofalexandria.com
Or scan the code below:

Introduction

Dreams, Art, And The Epic Imagination

The Fall of Hyperion is an ambitious and visionary work that stands as one of the most evocative explorations of human aspiration, imagination, and the transcendent power of art. While the title may suggest a simple retelling of mythic events, the text operates on multiple levels: as a meditation on the role of the artist, as a dream-epic in which visionary encounters test the boundaries of human understanding, and as a philosophical reflection on the nature of time, mortality, and the pursuit of beauty. Henry Wadsworth Longfellow, one of America's most beloved poets of the 19th century, uses the framework of myth and dream to create a narrative that speaks to both the personal struggles of the artist and the collective aspirations of humankind.

The poem's title evokes the classical mythology of Hyperion, the Titan god of the sun, whose downfall symbolizes the shift from an old order to a new one. This mythic backdrop allows Longfellow to examine themes of change, loss, and renewal. Much like the Romantic poets he admired—John Keats, Percy Bysshe Shelley, and Lord Byron—Longfellow infuses his work with a sense of longing for the sublime, a yearning to capture truths that lie beyond ordinary experience. Yet *The Fall of Hyperion* is not merely a Romantic imitation; it is a uniquely American epic, reflecting Longfellow's engagement with both European literary traditions and the emerging cultural identity of the United States.

The poem's dream framework places the narrator (often interpreted as a stand-in for Longfellow himself) in a visionary landscape where divine or semi-divine figures challenge his understanding of art, suffering, and human destiny. In this realm, the poet is not merely a passive dreamer but an active seeker, compelled to confront the responsibilities that come with artistic insight. The narrative suggests that true poetry is born not from escapism but from a deep engagement with the realities of life— pain, struggle, and the inexorable passage of time. Longfellow's exploration of these ideas elevates *The Fall of Hyperion* beyond a simple mythological narrative to a profound philosophical and artistic statement.

Themes Of Vision, Sacrifice, And Human Aspiration

One of the central themes of *The Fall of Hyperion* is the relationship between art and sacrifice. Longfellow, like many of his contemporaries, believed that the true poet or artist must endure personal suffering in order to achieve lasting greatness. This idea is dramatized through the poem's dream sequences, in which the narrator undergoes trials that test not only his imaginative powers but also his moral and emotional strength. These trials serve as metaphors for the creative process itself, which requires both inspiration and discipline, vision and endurance.

The poem also reflects on the nature of time and the inevitability of change. The downfall of Hyperion, the sun god, represents the passing of one era into another, a theme that resonates with the broader historical context of the 19th century— a period marked by rapid industrialization, social upheaval, and shifting cultural values. Longfellow's treatment of this theme is both elegiac and hopeful: while *The Fall of Hyperion* signals the end of a golden age, it also clears the way for new forms of beauty and understanding to emerge.

Dreams play a crucial role in the poem, functioning not only as a narrative device but also as a symbol of the subconscious mind and its connection to the divine. In Longfellow's vision, dreams are not mere illusions but gateways to higher truths, offering glimpses of the eternal and the transcendent. The dream-epic form allows him to explore the tension between the material world and the realm of the spirit, between the fleeting nature of human life and the enduring power of art.

Another important theme is the communal and universal nature of human aspiration. While the poem's narrator embarks on a deeply personal journey, his experiences reflect the broader struggles of humanity—the quest for meaning, the desire to leave a lasting legacy, and the hope of transcending the limitations of mortality. Longfellow's language, rich in imagery and allusion, invites readers to share in this collective journey, reminding us that the pursuit of beauty and truth is not the province of a single individual but a shared human endeavor.

Longfellow's Style And Legacy

Henry Wadsworth Longfellow's style in *The Fall of Hyperion* combines the narrative sweep of epic poetry with the lyrical beauty for which he is best known. His use of rich, evocative imagery brings the dream landscapes of the poem vividly to life, while his mastery of rhythm and meter lends the work a musical quality that enhances its emotional impact. Longfellow's diction, though rooted in the literary traditions of his time, remains accessible, allowing readers to engage with both the surface narrative and the deeper philosophical themes.

Longfellow's engagement with myth and classical imagery reflects his belief in the universality of certain human experiences. By drawing on the figure of Hyperion and the fall of the Titans, he situates his narrative within a timeless framework that transcends cultural and historical boundaries. At the same time, his treatment of these themes is distinctly modern, emphasizing the role of the individual imagination in shaping our understanding of the world.

The influence of *The Fall of Hyperion* can be seen in both American and international literary traditions. Longfellow's blending of epic structure with personal introspection anticipated the work of later poets who sought to bridge the gap between individual experience and universal themes. His exploration of the artist's role in society, and of the sacrifices required to achieve true creative vision, continues to resonate with writers, artists, and thinkers today.

For modern readers, *The Fall of Hyperion* offers not only a rich narrative experience but also a profound meditation on the nature of art and the human condition. It challenges us to consider the ways in which our dreams and ambitions shape our lives, and to reflect on the enduring power of creativity to illuminate the darkest and most difficult aspects of existence. As you embark on this visionary epic, allow yourself to be drawn into Longfellow's world of dreams and symbols, where the fall of gods becomes a metaphor for the struggles and triumphs of the human spirit.

Book I.

Opening Quote

"Who never ate his bread in sorrow,
Who has never experienced the sorrowful, midnight hours
Weeping, he has sat upon his bed,
"He doesn't know you, heavenly powers."

Chapter I. The Hero.

In John Lyly's Endymion, Sir Topas is made to say, "Do you know what a Poet is? Why, fool, a Poet is as much as one should say— a Poet!" And you, reader, do you know what a hero is? Why, a hero is as much as one should say—a hero! Some romance writers, however, say much more than this. Indeed, the old Lombard, Matteo Maria Bojardo, set all the church bells in Scandiano ringing simply because he had found a name for one of his heroes. Here, too, church bells shall be rung, but more solemnly.

The loss of a great hope is like watching the sun set. The brightness in our lives fades away. Evening shadows gather around us, and the world appears as nothing more than a faint reflection— a vast shadow of what it once was. We gaze ahead into the approaching, solitary night. Our soul retreats inward. Then the stars emerge, and the night becomes sacred.

Paul Flemming had gone through this experience, even though he was still young. His childhood friend had died. The branch had snapped "under the weight of the unripe fruit." And when, after some time had passed, he lifted his eyes again from the darkness of his grief, everything seemed like an illusion. Like the man whose vision had been miraculously restored, he saw people as if they were trees walking around. His cherished belongings were destroyed. He had no place to call home. His emotions cried out from his empty soul, but no response came from the hectic, chaotic world surrounding him. He didn't choose to surrender to his grief. He fought to stay positive—to remain strong. But he could no longer bear to look at the familiar faces of his friends. He could no longer live by himself in the place where he had lived with her. He traveled overseas, hoping the ocean might separate him from the grave. Unfortunately! between him and his sorrow there could be no ocean, except the one created by time.

He had already spent many months wandering alone, and was now making his way along the Rhine, through southern Germany. He had traveled this same route before, during happier times and in a brighter season, in the springtime of his life and in the month of May. He knew the beautiful river by heart—every rock and ruin, every echo, every legend. The ancient castles, dark and weathered, that seemed to have grown from the cliffs themselves—they all belonged to him; for his thoughts lived within them, and the wind whispered stories to him.

He had spent a sleepless night at Rolandseck and had gotten up before dawn. He opened the balcony window to listen to the rushing waters of the Rhine. It was a humid December morning, and clouds drifted across the sky—thin, misty clouds whose snow-white edges were "often spotted with golden tears, which men call stars." The day broke slowly, and in the blend of daylight and starlight, the island and monastery of Nonnenwerth appeared as one broad, dark shadow on the silver surface of the river. In the distance, the peaks of the Siebengebirg rose up. Solemn and dark, like a monk, the Drachenfels stood in its hood of mist, and behind it stretched the Curtain of Mountains, extending back to the Wolkenburg—the Castle of the Clouds.

But Flemming wasn't thinking about the scene in front of him. Overwhelming sorrow weighed on his spirit during that solitary hour; and, covering his face with his hands, he cried out loud;

"Ghost from the past! Don't look at me so sadly with those large, tear-filled eyes! Don't touch me with that cold hand! Don't breathe on me with that freezing breath from the tomb! Stop singing that mournful song of grief throughout the long, quiet hours of the night!"

Sorrowful voices from the distance seemed to respond, "Treuenfels!" and he recalled how others had endured pain, and his heart became calm.

Slowly the landscape grew brighter. Down the rushing stream came a boat with its white sails spread, darting like a swallow through the narrow pass of God's-Help. The boatmen were singing, but not the song of Roland the Brave, which was heard long ago by the weeping Hildegund as she sat within the walls of that monastery, which now gazed out in the pale morning from among the bare linden trees. The faded traditions of those ancient gray times arose in the traveler's memory; for the ruined tower of Rolandseck still looked down upon the Kloster Nonnenwerth, as if the sound of the funeral bell had transformed the faithful Paladin to stone, and he was still watching to see the form of his beloved emerge, not from her cloister, but from her grave. In this way the bronze clasps of the book of legends were opened, and on the page illuminated by the misty rays of the rising sun, he read once more the tales of Liba, and the sorrowful bride of Argenfels, and Siegfried, the mighty dragon slayer. Meanwhile the mists had lifted from the Rhine, and the entire air was filled with golden mist, through which he saw the sun hanging in heaven like a drop of blood. Just so the sun shone within him, amid the winter vapors rising from the valley of the shadow of death, through which flowed the stream of his life—sighing, sighing!

———————

Chapter II. The Christ of Andernach.

Paul Flemming continued his journey alone. The morning remained foggy, though the air was warm. Beyond the Rhine, the sun pushed through the reddish mist, and the wide river stretched out soft and silver-white, its surface smooth without a single ripple or any sign of the constantly flowing current beneath. A small boat with a single loose sail floated at anchor, positioned hull to hull with another vessel that lay directly beneath it like its own reflection, and everything was quiet, peaceful, and beautiful.

The road was mostly empty, since few travelers journey along the Rhine during winter. Peasant women worked in the vineyards, climbing up the slick hillsides like pack animals with large baskets of fertilizer strapped to their backs. At one point during the morning, a group of apprentices carrying backpacks walked past, singing, "The Rhine! The Rhine! a blessing on the Rhine!"

Oh, the pride that fills the German heart when they think of this magnificent river! And they have every right to feel this way, because among all the rivers on this beautiful planet, none can match its beauty. There's barely a mile along its entire journey, from where it begins in the snow-covered Alps to where it ends in the sandy lowlands of Holland, that doesn't have its own special appeal. By God! If I were German, I would feel proud of it as well; and of the thick clusters of grapes that dangle around its banks as it winds forward through the vineyards in a victory parade, like Bacchus himself, wearing a crown and intoxicated.

But I won't try to describe the Rhine; it would make this chapter far too long. And to do it properly, one would need to write like a god; and let his style flow forward majestically with pauses and flourishes, like the waters of that majestic river, and let ancient, charming, and Gothic times be mirrored in it. Unfortunately! this evening my style doesn't flow at all. Flow, then, into this smoke-colored glass, you blood of the Rhine! out of your prison-house,--out of your long-necked, tapering bottle, shaped much like a church spire among your native hills; and, from the crystal bell tower, let the cheerful tinkling bells ring loudly, while I drink a toast to my hero, whose heart holds sadness, and whose ears hear the bells of Andernach ringing noon.

He is making his way alone through a narrow alley, and now up a flight of stone steps, and along the city wall, toward that old round tower, built by Archbishop Frederick of Cologne in the twelfth century. It holds a romantic appeal in his eyes; for he still carries in his mind and heart that beautiful sketch by Carové, in which a day on the tower of Andernach is described. He finds the old keeper and his wife still there; and the old keeper closes the door behind him slowly, as he always has, so he won't slam it too hard on the poor souls in Purgatory, whose fate it is to suffer in the cracks of doors and hinges. But alas! alas! the daughter, the maiden with long, dark eyelashes! she is sleeping in her little grave, under the linden trees of Feldkirche, with rosemary in her folded hands!

Flemming walked back to the hotel feeling disappointed. As he made his way through the narrow streets, his mind wandered to many different thoughts, but mostly to the keeper's daughter who lay sleeping in the churchyard of Feldkirche. All at once, as he rounded the corner of an old, dark church, something caught his eye—a small chapel tucked into a corner of the wall. It was nothing more than a tiny thatched roof, resembling a bird's nest, beneath which stood a crude wooden figure of the Savior on the Cross. A real crown of thorns rested on his head, which was tilted downward as if in the throes of death, and drops of blood trickled down his cheeks and from his hands, feet, and side. The face appeared gaunt and ghastly beyond description, bearing an expression of indescribable physical suffering. The rough sculptor had managed to capture this much, but his skill could extend no further. The magnificence of death in a dying Savior, the fading divine nature of Jesus of Nazareth, was absent from the work. The artist had drawn no heavenly inspiration from his subject. Everything about it was crude, harsh, and disturbing to anyone with a delicate sensibility, and Flemming turned away with a shudder as he noticed this terrible image staring at him with its motionless and half-closed eyes.

He quickly arrived at the hotel, but that agonized face continued to haunt him. He couldn't help but mention it to an elderly woman who sat knitting by the dining room window in a tall-backed, old-style armchair. I think she was the innkeeper's grandmother. In any case, she was certainly old enough to be one. She removed her large, round spectacles and, while cleaning the lenses with her handkerchief, said;

"Dear Heaven! Is it possible! Did you never hear of the Christ of Andernach?"

Flemming said no.

"Dear Heaven!" the old woman continued. "It's a truly wonderful story, and a true one, as every good Christian in Andernach will tell you. And it all happened before my blessed husband died four years ago—let me think—yes, four years ago this Christmas."

Here the elderly woman fell silent but continued with her knitting. Different thoughts appeared to fill her mind. She was probably thinking about her blessed man, as German widows refer to their deceased husbands. However, since Flemming had expressed an eager desire to hear the remarkable story, she shared it using words very similar to these.

There was once a poor old woman in Andernach whose name was Frau Martha, and she lived all alone in a house by herself, and loved all the Saints and the blessed Virgin, and was as good as an angel, and sold pies down by the Rheinkrahn. Her house was very old, though, and the roof tiles were broken, and she was too poor to buy new ones, so the rain kept coming in, and no Christian soul in Andernach would help her. But Frau Martha was a good woman who never harmed anybody, and she went to mass every morning and sold pies by the Rheinkrahn. One dark, windy night, when all the good Christians in Andernach were in bed and asleep under their covers, Frau Martha, who slept under the roof, heard a great noise over her head, and in her room, drip! drip! drip! as if the rain were dropping down through the broken tiles. Dear soul! and sure enough it was. Then there was a pounding and hammering overhead, as if somebody were working on the roof; and she thought it was Pelz-Nickel tearing the tiles off, because she had not been to confession often enough. So she began to pray; and the faster she said her Pater-noster and her Ave-Maria, the faster Pelz-Nickel pounded and pulled; and drip! drip! drip! it went all around her in the dark room, until the poor woman was frightened out of her wits, and ran to the window to call for help. Then in a moment all was still—death-still. But she saw a light streaming through the mist and rain, and a great shadow on the house across the street. And then somebody came down from the top of her house by a ladder, and had a lantern in his hand; and he took the ladder on his shoulder and went down the street. But she could not see clearly, because the window was streaked with rain. And in the morning the old broken tiles were found scattered about the street, and there were new ones on the roof, and the old house has never leaked to this blessed day.

"As soon as mass was over, Frau Martha told the priest what had happened, and he said it wasn't Pelz-Nickel, but without a doubt, St. Castor or St. Florian. Then she went to the market and told Frau Bridget everything about it; and Frau Bridget said that two nights before, Hans Claus, the cooper, had heard loud pounding in his shop, and in the morning found new hoops on all his old barrels; and that a man with a lantern and a ladder had been seen riding out of town at midnight on a donkey, and that the same night the old windmill at Kloster St. Thomas had been repaired, and the old gate of the churchyard at Feldkirche made as good as new, though nobody knew how the man got across the river. Then Frau Martha went down to the Rheinkrahn and told all these stories over again; and the old ferryman of Fahr said he could tell something about it; for the very night that the churchyard gate was mended, he was lying awake in his bed because he couldn't sleep, and he heard loud knocking at the door, and somebody calling to him to get up and take him across the river. And when he got up, he saw a man down by the river with a lantern and a ladder; but as he was going down to him, the man blew out the light, and it was so dark he couldn't see who he was; and his boat was old and leaky, and he was afraid to take him across in the dark; but the man said he had to be in Andernach that night; and so he took him across. And after they had crossed the river, he watched the man until he came to an image of the Holy Virgin, and saw him put the ladder against the wall, and go up and light his lamp, and then walk along the street. And in the morning he found his old boat all sealed up, and watertight, and painted red, and he couldn't for the life of him tell who did it, unless it was the man with the lantern. Dear soul! How strange it was!"

And so this continued for quite some time; whenever people spotted the man carrying the lantern walking through the streets at night, they could be certain that by morning, some kind deed had been performed for the benefit of a deserving person; everyone knew he was responsible for these acts; yet no one could discover his identity or determine where he made his home;-- because, whenever anyone approached him, he would extinguish his light and turn down a different street, and if they pursued him, he would vanish suddenly in a way that no one could explain. Some people claimed it was Rübezahl; others believed it was Pelz-Nickel; and still others thought it was St. Anthony-on-the-Health.

"Now one stormy night a poor, sinful woman was wandering through the streets, carrying her baby in her arms, and she was hungry and cold, and not a soul in Andernach would give her shelter. When she reached the church, where the great crucifix stands, she saw no light in the little chapel at the corner; but she sat down on a stone at the foot of the cross and began to pray, and prayed until she fell asleep, with her poor little baby on her chest. But she didn't sleep long; for a bright light shone directly in her face; and when she opened her eyes, she saw a pale man, holding a lantern, standing right in front of her. He was almost naked; and there was blood on his hands and body, and great tears in his beautiful eyes, and his face was like the face of the Savior on the cross. He didn't say a single word to the poor woman; but looked at her with compassion, and gave her a loaf of bread, and took the little baby in his arms, and kissed it. Then the mother looked up at the great crucifix, but there was no figure there; and she screamed and collapsed as if she were dead. And there she was found with her child; and a few days later they both died, and were buried together in one grave. And nobody would have believed her story, if a woman, who lived at the corner, hadn't gone to the window when she heard the scream, and seen the figure hang the lantern up in its place, and then set the ladder against the wall, and climb up and nail itself to the cross. Since that night it has never moved again. Oh! Dear Lord!"

Such was the legend of the Christ of Andernach, as the elderly woman wearing spectacles recounted it to Flemming. The story left a distressing mark on his troubled and melancholy spirit; and for the first time he truly understood the immense power that popular superstition holds over people.

The post-chaise had arrived at the door, and Flemming was quickly on his way to Coblentz, a city situated on the Rhine at the point where the Mosel flows into it, across from Ehrenbreitstein. The journey from Andernach to Coblentz wasn't particularly long, and the sole event that happened to break up the monotony of the trip was encountering a plump, ruddy-faced man riding horseback, moving at a leisurely trot toward Andernach. When they passed each other, the eccentric little postilion playfully struck him with his whip and burst into an outburst that revealed his origins in Münster;

"Jesmariosp! my friend! How is the Man in the Custom-House?"

Now to any reasonable person this would seem like a fair enough question; but the red-faced man on horseback didn't think so; for he became extremely angry, and replied, as the carriage rushed past;

"The devil take you, and your Westphalian ham, and pumpernickel!"

Flemming called out to his servant, and the servant called to the postilion, seeking an explanation for this brief exchange; the explanation they received was that on the bell tower of the Kaufhaus in Coblentz stands an enormous head, complete with a bronze helmet and beard; whenever the clock chimes, with each strike of the hammer, this giant's head opens its massive jaws and clashes its teeth together, as though, like the bronze head of Friar Bacon, it wished to declare; "Time was; Time is; Time is past." This figure is recognized throughout the surrounding countryside as "The Man in the Custom-House"; when a friend from the country encounters a friend from Coblentz, rather than asking, "How are all the good people in Coblentz?"--he asks, "How is the Man in the Custom-House?" In this way the giant plays an important role in the town; and so concluded the first day of Flemming's Rhine journey; the only charitable act he had performed was giving money to a poor beggar woman, who raised her shaking hands and cried out;

"You blessed baby!"

———————

Chapter III. Homunculus.

After all, a journey up the Rhine during the misty and solitary December days isn't as unpleasant as readers might think. You have the entire road and river all to yourself. No one else is traveling; there's barely another soul on the journey. The ruins remain unchanged, along with the river and the silhouettes of the hills. There are hardly any people moving through the landscape to interrupt your contemplation, disturb your thoughts, or kick up dust around you.

So our traveler thought as he continued his journey the next day. The sky was overcast, with clouds threatening rain or snow. Why did he stop at the small village of Capellen? Because directly above him on the high cliff, the magnificent ruins of Stolzenfels gazed down at him with hollow eyes, beckoning with a massive finger as if saying, "Come up here, and I will tell you an ancient story." So he got off his horse and walked up the narrow village lane, climbed the stone steps, and made his way up the steep path until he reached the ancient ruins, catching his breath as he listened to the soft sound of falling snow, like the footsteps of angels coming down to earth. And the ancient ruin spoke to him in its hollow voice, saying:

"Beware of dreams! Beware of the illusions of fantasy! Beware of the solemn deceptions of your vast desires! Below me flows the Rhine, and like the stream of Time, it flows among the ruins of the Past. I see myself reflected in it, and I know that I am old. You, too, will be old. Be wise while you can. Like the stream of your life runs the stream beneath us. Down from the distant Alps—out into the wide world, it bursts forth, like a young person leaving their family home. Broad-chested and strong, and with serious efforts, like adulthood, it carves itself a path through these difficult mountain passes. And finally, in its old age, it stops, and its steps are tired and slow, and it sinks into the sand, and through its grave, passes into the great ocean, which is its eternity. This is how it will be with you."

"In ancient times there lived within these halls a follower of Jesus of Jerusalem—an Archbishop in the church of Christ. He surrendered himself to dreams; to the illusions of imagination; to the enormous desires of the human soul. He searched for the impossible. He searched for the Elixir of Life—the Philosopher's Stone. The wealth that should have fed the poor was melted in his crucibles. Within these walls the Eagle of the clouds drank the blood of the Red Lion, and received the spiritual Love of the Green Dragon, but sadly! was childless. In solitude and complete silence did the disciple of the Hermetic Philosophy work from day to day, from night to night. From the place where you stand, he looked at evening upon hills, and valleys, and waters spread beneath him; and saw how the setting sun had transformed them all to gold, by an alchemy more skillful than his own. He saw the world beneath his feet; and said in his heart, that he alone was wise. Sadly! he read more eagerly in the book of Paracelsus, than in the book of Nature; and, believing that 'where reason has experience, faith has no place,' would gladly have made for himself a child, not as Nature teaches us, but as the Philosopher taught—a poor homunculus, in a glass bottle. And he died poor and childless!"

Whether it was worthwhile to climb the Stolzenfels to hear such a sermon as this, some people might perhaps question. But Paul Flemming had no doubts. He took the lesson to heart; and it would have spared him many hours of sorrow, if he had learned that lesson better, and remembered it longer.

In ancient times, three statues of Minerva stood in the citadel of Athens. The first statue was made of olive wood and, according to popular belief, had fallen from heaven. The second statue was made of bronze, celebrating the victory at Marathon; and the third was made of gold and ivory—a magnificent work of art from the age of Pericles. Similarly, in the citadel of Time stands humanity itself. In childhood, we are formed from soft and delicate wood, having just fallen from heaven; in adulthood, we become a bronze statue, celebrating our struggles and victories; and finally, in the maturity of old age, we are perfectly crafted in gold and ivory—a true work of art!

Flemming had already experienced the golden age of youth. He was transitioning into the bronze age, entering his early adulthood; and in his hands the flowers of Paradise were transforming into the sword and shield.

And this brings to mind that I haven't yet described my hero. I'll do so now, as he stands gazing down at the magnificent landscape—but I'll keep it brief. In both appearance and personality, he was like Harold the Fair-Hair of Norway, who is portrayed in the ancient Icelandic Death-Song of Regner Hairy-Breeches as "the young leader so proud of his flowing hair; he who spent his mornings with young women; he who enjoyed talking with beautiful widows." This was a charming flaw, and it occasionally got him into trouble. Imagination ruled his mind completely. His thoughts came in pairs: the thought itself, and its symbolic reflection in the physical world. So through the calm, peaceful waters of his soul, each image drifted in duplicate, "swan and shadow."

These character traits—a good heart and a poetic imagination—filled his life with joy and made the world beautiful. But eventually Death struck down the sweet, blue flower that bloomed beside him, wounding him with that sharp sickle so deeply that he bowed his head and wished he could have been gathered up in the same bundle with that sweet, blue flower. After that, the world seemed less beautiful to him, and life became serious. It would have been better if he could have forgotten the past, so he wouldn't have lived so sorrowfully within it, but instead could have enjoyed and made the most of the present. However, his heart refused to do this. As he drifted on life's great ocean, he constantly looked down through the clear waters, dappled with sunlight and shadow, into the vast chambers of the mighty depths where his happier days had sunk and where they still lay visible, like golden sand, precious stones, and pearls. Half in despair and half in hope, he reached down toward them again, only to pull back his hand filled with nothing but seaweed and dripping with salty tears! Between him and those golden sands, a glowing figure floated like the spirit in Dante's Paradise, singing "Ave-Maria!" And as it sang, it sank downward, slowly fading away.

The truth is that in everything he did, he acted more on impulse than on established principles, which is typical of most young men. His principles barely had enough time to develop, since he constantly uprooted them, just like children do with the flowers they've planted when they want to check if they're growing. However, there was much good in him, because beneath the surface beauty of poetry and the solid principles that could have flourished if he had given them time, there existed a foundation of strong and healthy common sense. This foundation was nourished by natural springs of emotion and enriched by many disappointed hopes that had settled upon it like fallen leaves.

Chapter IV. The Landlady's Daughter.

"Come on, Fuchs! Come on, let's go!" shouted the impatient postilion to his horses, his voice echoing like the wild sounds from the Lurley Felsen, bouncing from one side of the river to the other—speaking in words that switched between French and German. The truth was, he had grown tired of waiting; and when Flemming finally got back into the post-chaise, the poor horses had to make up for all the time that had been lost while dreaming on the mountain. This happens far more often than most people realize. Half the world has to sweat and struggle so that the other half can dream. It would have been nearly impossible for either the traveler or his postilion to convince the horses that these dreams were somehow for their benefit.

The next stop was the small tavern called the Star, located in a remote corner of the town of Salzig. It sits along the banks of the Rhine River, and rising directly in front of it from the water's edge are the steep mountains of Liebenstein and Sternenfels, each crowned with its crumbling castle. These are the Brothers from ancient legend, still staring at each other across the divide, and below them in the valley sits a monastery—a humble symbol of the orphaned child they both loved so deeply.

In a small, flat-bottomed boat, the landlady's daughter rowed Flemming "across the Rhine-stream, rapid and roaring wide." She was a beautiful sixteen-year-old girl with black hair, dark, lovely eyes, and a face that seemed to hold a story waiting to be told. How remarkably different faces are in this respect! Some faces don't speak at all. They're like books with nothing written inside except perhaps a date. Others resemble great family bibles, containing both the Old and New Testament within them. Some are like Mother Goose and nursery tales, while others appear to be tragic dramas or slapstick comedies. Still others, like the face of the landlady's daughter at the Star, are sweet collections of love poetry and songs about deep feelings. It was for this reason that Flemming spoke to her as they glided out into the swift current:

"My dear child! Do you know the story of the Liebenstein?"

"I memorized the story of the Liebenstein when I was a little child," she replied.

And here her large, dark, passionate eyes looked into Flemming's, and he had no doubt that she had learned the story far too soon, and far too well. He longed to hear that story, as if it were unknown to him; for he knew that the girl, who had memorized it as a child, would tell it as it should be told. So he asked her to repeat the story, which she was more than happy to do; for she loved and believed it, as if it had all been written in the Bible. But before she began, she paused for a moment with her oars, and taking the crucifix that hung from her neck, kissed it, and then let it fall back into her chest, as if it were an anchor she was lowering into her heart. Meanwhile her moist, dark eyes were turned toward heaven. Perhaps her soul was walking with the souls of Cunizza, and Rahab, and Mary Magdalen. Or perhaps she was thinking of that Nun, of whom St. Gregory says, in his Dialogues, that, having greedily eaten a lettuce in a garden, without making the sign of the cross, she found herself soon after possessed by a devil.

The probability, however, is that she was looking up at the ruined castles only, and not toward heaven, because she soon began her story, telling Flemming how, many, many years ago, an old man lived in the Liebenstein with his two sons. She explained how both young men loved Lady Geraldine, an orphan under their father's care, and how the elder brother left in despair while the younger became engaged to Lady Geraldine. She described how they were as happy as Cinderella and the Prince. Then the holy Saint Bernard came and took away all the young men to war, just as Napoleon did later, and the young lord went to the Holy Land while Lady Geraldine sat in her tower and wept, waiting for her lover's return, as the old father built the Sternenfels for them to live in when they married. When it was finished, the old man died, and the elder brother returned and lived in the Liebenstein, taking care of the gentle Lady. Before long, news came from the Holy Land that the war was over, and the gentle Lady's heart beat with joy, until she heard that her faithless lover was returning with a Greek wife—the wicked man! Then she entered a convent and became a holy nun. So the young lord of Sternenfels came home and lived in his castle in great splendor with the Greek woman, who was a wicked woman and did what she should not do. But the elder brother was angry about the wrong done to the gentle

Lady and challenged the lord of Sternenfels to single combat. While they were fighting with their great swords in the valley of Bornhofen behind the castle, the convent bells began to ring, and Lady Geraldine came forth with a procession of nuns all dressed in white, and made the brothers friends again, telling them she was the bride of Heaven and happier in her convent than she could have been in the Liebenstein or the Sternenfels. When the brothers returned, they found that the false Greek wife had gone away with another knight. So they lived together in peace and were never married. And when they died—

"Lisbeth! Lisbeth!" shouted a harsh voice from the shore, "Lisbeth! Where are you taking the gentleman?"

This brought the poor girl back to reality, and she realized how quickly they had been carried downstream. While telling her story, she had forgotten everything else, and the fast-moving current had swept them down to the tall walnut trees of Kamp. They came ashore in front of the Capuchin Monastery. Lisbeth walked ahead through the small village, then turned right and pointed up the picturesque, secluded valley that leads to the Liebenstein, even offering to accompany him up there. But Flemming gently touched her cheek and shook his head. He walked up the valley by himself.

―――――――

Chapter V. Jean Paul, The Only-One.

The character in the play who longed for "some forty pounds of lovely beef, placed in a Mediterranean sea of brewis," could have nearly satisfied his enormous appetite at the table d'hôte of the Rheinischen Hof in Mayence, where Flemming had dinner that day. At the head of the table sat a gentleman with a smooth, broad forehead and large, intelligent eyes. He came from Baireuth in Franconia and spoke about poetry and Jean Paul to a pale, romantic-looking lady seated to his right. Music played throughout the entire meal at the far end of the hall—a harp, a horn, and a voice—so much of the stout gentleman's conversation with the pale lady was lost to Flemming, who sat across from her and could gaze directly into her large, melancholy eyes. However, what he managed to hear fascinated him so deeply—indeed, the mere mention of the beloved Jean Paul's name would have been sufficient—that he decided to join their conversation and asked the German whether he had known the poet personally.

"Yes; I knew him well," the stranger replied. "I'm from Baireuth, where he spent the finest years of his life. In my view, the man and the writer are inseparably connected. I can't read a single page of his work without hearing his voice and seeing him standing before me. There he sits, with his magnificent, towering forehead, his gentle blue eyes, and his elegantly shaped nose and mouth; his large frame dressed loosely and carelessly in an old green coat, with book corners sticking out of the pockets, and perhaps the end of a loaf of bread and the neck of a bottle;--a straw hat with green lining resting nearby; a massive walking stick in his hand, and at his feet a white poodle with pink eyes and a string around its neck. You would have mistaken him for a master carpenter rather than a poet. Is he one of your favorite authors?"

Flemming said yes.

"But a foreigner must find it extremely difficult to understand him," said the gentleman. "It's certainly not an easy task for us Germans."

"I've always noticed," Flemming responded, "that truly understanding and appreciating a poet depends more on personal character than on national identity. When there's a connection between the writer's mind and the reader's mind, the limitations and obstacles of a foreign language are quickly overcome. Once you grasp an author's character, understanding their writings becomes straightforward."

"Very true," the German replied, "and Richter's character is too distinctive to be easily misunderstood. His most notable qualities are tenderness and strength—traits that are rarely combined to such a remarkable degree as they are in him. Everything he observes, everything he writes, is bathed in the warm light of a joyful spirit—the glow of endless human love. Every expression of human happiness and human grief finds a profound echo within his heart. In every person, he cherishes only their humanity, not their sense of superiority. The declared purpose of all his literary work was to restore the weakened faith in God, virtue, and immortality; and, in a self-centered, revolutionary era, to rekindle our human compassion, which has grown cold. And equally limitless is his love for nature—for this external, beautiful world. He holds it all close to his heart."

"Yes," Flemming replied, practically finishing the stranger's thought, "because in his mind everything becomes idealized. He appears to be describing himself when he portrays the hero of his Titan as a child, swaying in strong winds on the branches of an apple tree in full bloom. As the tree's top was swept around by the wind, sometimes it plunged him into deep green shadows, and other times it lifted him high into brilliant blue sky and gleaming sunlight. In his imagination, that tree stood enormous—it grew alone in the universe, as though it were the tree of eternal life. Its roots reached down into the depths below; white and red clouds hung like blossoms on its branches; the moon served as its fruit; tiny stars twinkled like dewdrops, and Albano rested in its endless crown. A storm rocked the treetop from Day into Night, and from Night back into Day."

"Yet the spirit of love," interrupted the Franconian, "wasn't weakness, but strength. It was combined in him with great courage. The sword of his spirit had been shaped and hammered by poverty. Its strength had been tested by a thirty years' war. It wasn't broken, not even dulled; but instead strengthened and sharpened by the blows it delivered and endured. And, having this noble spirit of humanity, perseverance, and self-sacrifice, he made literature his calling; as though he had been divinely appointed to write. He appears to have cared for nothing else, to have considered nothing else, than living peacefully and creating books. He says that he felt it his responsibility, not to enjoy, nor to gain, but to write; and declared proudly that he had created as many books as he had lived years."

"And what do you Germans consider the prominent characteristics of his genius?"

"Without question, his wild imagination and playfulness stand out most. He casts a strange and magical light over everything. You're struck by the boldness and beauty of his metaphors and examples, which are scattered everywhere with reckless abundance—countless, like the blossoms of early summer—and just as fragrant and beautiful. Among a thousand wild flourishes are mixed ten thousand beauties of thought and expression, which spark the reader's imagination and carry it forward in a daring flight, through the glow of sunrise and sunset, and the dewy coolness and starlight of summer nights. He is hard to understand—complex, strange—drawing his examples from every hidden corner of science, art, and nature—a comet among the bright stars of German literature. When you read his works, it's as if you were climbing a high mountain with cheerful companions to watch the sun rise. Sometimes you're wrapped in mist—the morning wind rushes past you with a roar—you hear the distant rumbling of thunder. Wide below you stretches the landscape—field, meadow, town, and winding river. The ringing of distant church bells, or the sound of a solemn village clock, reaches you—then rises the sweet and varied fragrance of flowers—the birds begin to sing—the mists roll away—up comes the glorious sun—you rejoice like the lark in the sunshine and bright blue sky, and everything becomes a delirious dream of soul and sense—when suddenly a friend at your side laughs out loud and offers you a piece of Bologna sausage. As in real life, so in his writings—the serious and the comic, the sublime and the grotesque, the touching and the ridiculous are blended together. Sometimes he is wise, energetic, simple; then again, unclear and wordy. His thoughts are like mummies preserved in spices and wrapped in elaborate coverings; but within these wrappings the thoughts themselves are kings. Sometimes joyful, beautiful images and airy forms move past you, graceful and harmonious—sometimes the glaring, wild-looking ideas, chained together by hyphens, brackets, and dashes, noble and base, high and low, all in their colorful costumes, go sweeping down the dusty page, like the galley slaves who sweep the streets of Rome, where you might happen to see the nobleman and the peasant shackled together."

Flemming smiled at the German's warmth, which seemed to be enhanced by both the lady's presence and the Laubenheimer wine, and then said;

"It's better to be an outlaw than to live without freedom!"— These are his exact words. And this is how he transforms himself whenever he chooses. Like Thor, the god from ancient Norse mythology, he sometimes displays the seven brilliant stars shining in the bright sky above us, and other times he conceals himself within the clouds, striking away with his mighty hammer.

"And yet this isn't pretense on his part," the German replied. "It's his nature, it's Jean Paul. And the images and decorative elements of his writing style, wild, imaginative, and often surprising, like those found in Gothic cathedrals, are not simply what they appear to be, but solid cornerstones and supports that hold up the structure. Take them away, and the roof and walls collapse. And through these gargoyles, these wild faces carved on spouts and gutters, flow out, like collected rainwater, the brilliant, plentiful thoughts that have fallen from heaven."

"Everything he does is carried out with a kind of serious playfulness. He is a sea monster, enjoying himself on the vast ocean; even his play is earnest; there is something majestic and serious about it. In everything there is strength, a rough good-nature, all sunshine overhead, and underneath the heavy moaning of the sea. Well may he be called 'Jean Paul, the Only-One.'"

With such conversation the dinner hour passed; and after dinner Flemming went to the Cathedral. They were singing vespers. A beadle, dressed in blue, with a cocked hat, and a crimson sash and collar, was strutting, like a turkey, along the aisles. This important gentleman led Flemming through the church, and showed him the choir, with its heavily-carved stalls of oak, and the beautiful figures in brown stone, above the bishops' tombs. He then guided him, through a side-door, into the old and ruined cloisters of St. Willigis. Through the low gothic arches the sunshine poured upon the pavement of tombstones, whose images and inscriptions are mostly worn away by the footsteps of many generations. There stands the tomb of Frauenlob, the Minnesinger. His face is carved on an entablature in the wall; a fine, strongly-defined, and serious face. Below it is a bas-relief, depicting the poet's funeral. He is carried to his grave by ladies, whose praise he sang, and thereby earned the name of Frauenlob.

"So this," Flemming said, "is the grave, not of Praise-God Bare-bones, but of Praise-the-Ladies Meissen, who wrote songs 'somewhat of lust, and somewhat of love.' But where does the dust of his rival and enemy rest, sweet Master Bartholomew Rainbow?"

He intended this as a casual remark; but the turkey-cock overheard it and responded;

"I don't know. He wasn't from this parish."

It was already nighttime when Flemming crossed the Roman bridge spanning the Nahe River and entered the town of Bingen. He stopped at the White Horse inn, and before retiring for the evening, he gazed out from his window into the faint starlight toward the Rhine. His heart soared as he observed what appeared to be the dramatic silhouette of nearby hills crowned with Gothic ruins—which in the morning turned out to be nothing more than a tall, slate-covered roof adorned with elaborate chimneys.

The morning was bright and crisp, with frost covering everything, and the river reflected vibrant colors from the rising sun. A gentle, light mist drifted through the air. The frost sparkled in the sunlight like silver stars, and Paul Flemming traveled triumphantly down a long tree-lined path where wet branches drooped and scattered droplets like pearls in front of him.

I won't drag out this journey any longer, since I'm tired and worn out from traveling, and I'd really like to reach Heidelberg with my readers and my hero. Night had already fallen when he arrived at the Manheim gate and drove down the long main street so slowly that it felt endless to him. The shops were lit up on both sides of the street, and he could see faces in the windows here and there, along with figures moving through the lamplight, visible for just a moment before disappearing into the darkness. The thoughts filling his mind were peculiar, as are always the thoughts of a traveler entering a strange city for the first time. This small world had been continuing for centuries before he arrived, and it would continue for centuries after he was gone. He knew nothing about any of the thousands of people who lived there, and what did they know or think about the stranger who, in that cramped carriage, exhausted from travel and chilled by the evening wind, was slowly rumbling over the cobblestone street! Indeed, this world can carry on without us, if only we would accept that fact. If it had been a hearse instead of a carriage, it would have meant nothing different to the people of Heidelberg—though it certainly would have meant something very different to Paul Flemming.

But at the far end of the city, near the Castle and the Carls-Thor, one warm heart was waiting to welcome him; and this was the German heart of his friend, the Baron of Hohenfels, with whom he would spend the winter in Heidelberg. As soon as the carriage had stopped at the iron-grated gate, and the postilion had blown his horn to announce a traveler's arrival, the Baron appeared among the servants at the door; and, moments later, the two long-separated friends were embracing each other, and Flemming received a kiss on each cheek, and another on the lips, as the promise and symbol of the German's friendship. They clasped each other's hands for a long time, and gazed into each other's faces, and saw themselves reflected in each other's eyes, both literally and figuratively; literally, because the images were actually there; and figuratively, because each was wondering what the other thought of him after the passage of several years. Through friendly hopes and questions and answers, the evening slipped away at the supper table, where many more topics were explored than just the roasted hare and the Johannisberger; and they remained awake late into the night, discussing the thoughts and emotions and pleasures that fill the hearts of young men who have already experienced joy and sorrow, and hoped and faced disappointment.

Chapter VI. Heidelberg and The Baron.

High and weathered on the forehead of the Jettenbühl stands Heidelberg Castle. Behind it rise the oak-crowned hills of the Geissberg and the Kaiserstuhl; and in front, from the broad stone terrace, you could almost throw a stone onto the roofs of the city, so close do they lie beneath. Above this terrace rises the wide front of the chapel of Saint Udalrich. On the left stands the slender eight-sided tower of the clock, and on the right, a huge round tower, battered and shattered by the hammer of war, supports with its broad shoulders the beautiful palace and garden terrace of Elisabeth, wife of Pfalzgraf Frederick. In the back are older palaces and towers, forming a vast, irregular quadrangle—Rodolph's ancient castle, with its Gothic pavilion and fantastical gables; the Giant's Tower, guarding the drawbridge over the moat; the Rent Tower, with linden trees growing on its summit, and the magnificent Great Hall of Otho-Henry, Count Palatine of the Rhine and grand seneschal of the Holy Roman Empire. From the gardens behind the castle, you pass under the archway of the Giant's Tower into the great courtyard. The varied architecture of different eras catches the eye, along with curious sculptures. In niches on the wall of Saint Udalrich's chapel stand rows of knights in armor, all broken and dismembered; and on the front of Otho's Great Hall, the heroes of Jewish history and classical legend. You enter the open and desolate chambers of the ruin; and on every side are medallions and family coats of arms; the Globe of the Empire and the Golden Fleece, or the Eagle of the Caesars, resting on the shields of Bavaria and the Palatinate. Over the windows and doorways and fireplaces are sculptures and moldings of exquisite craftsmanship; and the eye is overwhelmed by the abundance of caryatids, and arabesques, and rosettes, and fan-like flutings, and garlands of fruits and flowers and acorns, and bulls' heads with draperies of foliage, and muzzles of lions, holding rings in their teeth. The skilled hand of Art was busy for six centuries, raising and adorning these walls; the armored hands of Time and War have defaced and overthrown them in less than two. Next to the Alhambra of Granada, Heidelberg Castle is the most magnificent ruin of the Middle Ages.

In the valley below, the rushing waters of the Neckar River flow swiftly. Rising directly from its banks on the far side stands the Mountain of All Saints, topped with the crumbling remains of an old convent, while the mountain wall of the Odenwald extends up the valley. The hills that close off the valley to the east are so numerous and tightly packed that the river appears more like a lake. However, toward the west, the valley opens wide onto the expansive Rhine plain, resembling the flared mouth of a trumpet; and like a trumpet's powerful blast, the winter wind sometimes roars through this narrow mountain passage. The blue hills of Alsace rise in the distance beyond, and on a flat terrace of land situated between the Neckar River and the mountains, directly beneath the castle, lies the city of Heidelberg; as the old song declares, "a pleasant city, when it has done raining."

Paul Flemming witnessed something like this when he got up the next morning and gazed out his window. The morning was warm and misty, with a battle taking place between the fog and the rising sun. The sun had claimed the hilltops, but the mist still held control of the valley and the town. The spire of the great church pierced through a thick mass of snow-white clouds, and to the east, on the hills, the faint vapors rolled across the windows of the ruined castle, resembling the fiery smoke of a massive fire. To him, it appeared as a symbol of the sun of Truth rising over a world lost in darkness; its light poured through the ruins of centuries, and down in the valley of Time, the cross on the Christian church captured its beams, even though the priests were chanting in mist and darkness below.

In the cozy breakfast room, he discovered the Baron waiting for him. The Baron was reclining on a sofa, dressed in a morning robe and purple velvet slippers, both decorated with floral patterns. He held a guitar in his hand while keeping a pipe between his lips, simultaneously smoking, playing music, and humming his beloved song by Goethe.

"The water rushed, the water swelled,"

A fisherman sat nearby.

Flemming could barely keep himself from laughing when he saw his friend, telling him that the sight brought to mind a street musician he had once encountered in Aix-la-Chapelle, who performed on six instruments simultaneously. The musician wore a helmet adorned with bells on his head, carried a Pan's pipe in his cravat, held a fiddle in his hand, balanced a triangle on his knee, had cymbals attached to his heels, and bore a bass drum on his back that he played with his elbows. To be honest, the Baron of Hohenfels was quite an eclectic young man, something of a Renaissance soul. He threw himself into everything with enthusiasm, though only for brief periods: music, poetry, painting, pleasure, even studying the Pandects. His emotions were intensely responsive to life's pleasures. His greatest weakness was that he loved humanity too deeply. However, through the strength of his imagination, the earthbound goat transformed into the brilliant constellation Capricornus—no longer a mere animal on the ground, but a pattern of stars in the heavens. His relaxed and easygoing nature made him gentle and innocent in his behavior, and ultimately, the appeal of his character, like that of a precious opal, stemmed from a flaw in its structure. He was tall and slender in build, with light-colored hair and blue eyes as lovely as a woman's. His voice carried something impossibly soft and charming, and he spoke German with the melodious, gentle accent of his homeland in Courland. While his bearing might not have possessed Antinous's effortless grace, he certainly had his own natural elegance. This, in brief, was Flemming's closest friend.

"And what do you think of Heidelberg and the old castle up there?" he said, as they sat down at the breakfast table.

"Last night the town felt incredibly long to me," Flemming responded; "and regarding the castle, I've only caught a brief glimpse of it through the fog. People tell me there's nothing more magnificent of its kind, except for the Alhambra of Granada; and I'm sure I'll discover that's true. I just wish the stone were gray instead of red. But whether red or gray, I can already see that I'll spend many long hours wandering through its empty halls. Tell me, does anyone actually live up there these days?"

"Nobody," replied the Baron, "except the man who shows visitors the Heidelberg Tun, and Monsieur Charles de Grainberg, a Frenchman who has been there sketching since eighteen-ten. He has also written an absolutely magnificent description of the ruins, in which he states that during the day only birds of prey disturb the silence with their sharp cries, and at night, screech-owls and other nocturnal creatures. Those are his exact words. You should purchase his book and his sketches."

"Yes, your quotation and the way you're speaking will definitely convince me to do that."

"Take his work or nothing at all, my friend, because you won't find any others. And honestly, his drawings are really good. There's one hanging on the wall over there that's beautiful, except for that awkward figure sprawled among the bushes in the corner."

"But isn't there a ghost or a haunted room in the old castle?" Flemming asked after quickly glancing at the picture.

"Oh, absolutely," the Baron replied; "there are two. There's the ghost of the Virgin Mary in Ruprecht's Tower, and the Devil in the Dungeon."

"Ha! That's wonderful!" Flemming exclaimed, his delight clearly visible. "Tell me the entire story, quickly! I'm as curious as a child."

"This is a story from the time of Louis the Debonnaire," the Baron said with a smile, "a dusty old legend from a gullible era. His brother Frederick lived here in the castle with him and had a romantic affair with Leonore von Luzelstein, a lady of the court, whom he later scorned and who consequently despised him with all her heart. For political reasons, he was equally detested by certain minor German tyrants who, seeking to destroy him, accused him of heresy. But his brother Louis refused to hand him over to their rage, so they decided to accomplish through trickery what they could not achieve through scheming. Therefore, Leonore von Luzelstein, dressed as the Virgin Mary, and the Elector's father confessor, costumed as Satan, appeared in the Elector's bedroom at midnight and terrified him so completely that he agreed to surrender his brother to two Black Knights who claimed to be ambassadors from the Vehm-Gericht. They went together to Frederick's chamber, where fortunately old Gemmingen, a courageous soldier, stood guard behind the tapestry. The monk entered first in his Satanic outfit, but as soon as he stepped into the prince's bedroom, the brave Gemmingen drew his sword and said simply, 'Die, wretch!' and so he perished. The others fled and were never seen again. And now the spirits of Leonore and the monk haunt the place where they committed their midnight crime. You can find the story in Grainberg's book, embellished with a kind of red-leather and burnt-cork grandeur, complete with great melodramatic rattling of chains, hooting of owls, and other theatrical nonsense!"

"After breakfast," said Flemming, "we'll head up to the castle. I need to get to know this mirror of owls, this modern Till Eulenspiegel. Look at what a beautiful morning we have! This is truly an amazing winter! What summer-like sunshine; what gentle Venetian mists! How the playful, deceptive air flirts with the old gray-bearded trees! Weather like this makes the grass and our beards grow quickly! But we have an old English saying that winter never rots in the sky. So it will eventually come down in its old-fashioned, powdery coat. We'll have snow in spring; and the blossoms will all be snowflakes. And then a summer that won't really be summer, but, as Jean Paul says, just a winter painted green. Isn't that right?"

"Unless I'm seriously mistaken about Heidelberg's weather," the Baron responded, "we won't have to wait long for snow. We experience sudden weather changes here, and I wouldn't be surprised if it started snowing before nightfall."

"All the more reason to make good use of the morning sunshine, then. Let us hurry to the castle, which my heart longs for."

———————

Chapter VII. Lives of Scholars.

The Baron's predictions came true. During the afternoon, the weather shifted. A western wind started blowing, and its breath pulled a curtain of clouds across the sky, like breath fogging up a person's face in a mirror. Before long, snow started falling. It swept across the distant landscape like white mist. The storm wind arrived from the Alsatian hills and struck the thick clouds at an angle as they moved through the air. The snow fell faster and faster, a thundering cascade from those towering clouds. The setting sun blazed fiercely from the hilltops and disappeared like a burning ship lost at sea, destroyed by the storm. Evening arrived this way, and winter stood at the doorway shaking his white and shaggy beard, like an old musician singing an ancient song: "How cold it is! how cold it is!"

"I love storms like this," said Flemming, standing at the window and gazing out into the tempest and the deepening darkness. "The quiet descent of snow strikes me as one of nature's most profound experiences. Falling autumn leaves don't move me nearly as much. But a driving storm like this is magnificent. It shocks me awake; it stirs something deep within me. It's wild and sorrowful, just like my own spirit. I can't stop thinking about the ocean; how the waves surge and throw their arms around, and how the wind plays those enormous harps created by ship rigging and masts. Winter has truly arrived! Listen to how that old rascal howls and whips the snow around! Sleet and rain are coming down as well. The trees are already decorated with icicles, and those two wide branches on that pine tree over there look exactly like the white mustache of some old German Baron."

"And tomorrow it will look even more wintry," said his friend. "We'll wake up and discover that the frost spirit has been working all night, creating Gothic cathedrals on our windows, just as the devil built the Cathedral of Cologne. So draw the curtains, and come sit here by the warm fire."

"And now," said Flemming, after doing what his friend had asked, "tell me about Heidelberg and its University. I imagine we'll live just as solitary and scholarly a life here as we did back in little Göttingen, with nothing to entertain us except our own daydreams."

"Pretty much so," the Baron replied, "which should definitely please you, since you're seeking peace and quiet. As for the University, it's one of the oldest in Germany, as you know. Count Palatine Ruprecht founded it in the fourteenth century, and in its first year it had more than five hundred students, all busily memorizing, in the old scholastic manner, the grammar rules put into verse by Alexander de Villa Dei, and the excerpts that Peter the Spaniard compiled from Michel Psellus's Synopsis of Aristotle's Organon, along with the Categories and Porphyry's Commentaries. Honestly, I'm not surprised that Erigena Scotus was killed by his students with their penknives. They must have been driven to the absolute brink of desperation."

What a fascinating picture a university presents to the mind. The lives of scholars in their quiet seclusion—literary figures with withdrawn habits, and professors who study sixteen hours a day, and never see the world except on a Sunday. Nature has, undoubtedly, for some wise purpose, placed in their hearts this love of literary work and isolation. Otherwise, who would tend the eternal flame of thought? Without such people as these, a gust of wind through the gaps and openings of this old world, or the waving of a conqueror's flag, would extinguish it forever. The light of the soul is easily put out. And whenever I think about these things I become conscious of the great significance, in a nation's history, of the individual reputation of scholars and literary figures. I fear that it is far greater than the world is willing to recognize; or, perhaps I should say, than the world has considered recognizing. Erase from England's history the names of Chaucer, Shakespeare,

Spenser, and Milton alone, and how much of her glory would you erase with them! Remove from Italy such names as Dante, Petrarch, Boccaccio, Michelangelo, and Raphael, and how much would still be missing from the completeness of her glory! How would the history of Spain appear if the pages were ripped out, on which are written the names of Cervantes, Lope de Vega, and Calderon! What would be the fame of Portugal, without her Camões; of France, without her Racine, and Rabelais, and Voltaire; or Germany, without her Martin Luther, her Goethe, and Schiller!—Indeed, what were the nations of old, without their philosophers, poets, and historians! Tell me, do not these people in all ages and in all places, decorate with bright colors the coat of arms of their country? Yes, and far more than this; for in all ages and all places they give humanity confidence in its greatness; and say; Do not call this time or people completely barbarous; for this much, even then and there, could the human mind accomplish! But the turbulent world has barely considered acknowledging all this. In this it has shown itself somewhat ungrateful. Otherwise, where would come the great criticism, the general contempt, the loud mockery, with which, to take a familiar example, the monks of the Middle Ages are viewed! That they slept their lives away is completely false. For in an age when books were scarce—so scarce, so valuable, that they were often chained to their oak shelves with iron chains, like galley-slaves to their benches, these people, with their hardworking hands, copied onto parchment all the knowledge and wisdom of the past, and passed it down to us. Perhaps it is not too much to say that, without these monks, not one line of the classics would have reached our time. Surely, then, we can forgive something to those superstitious ages, perhaps even the mysticism of the scholastic philosophy, since, after all, we can find no harm in it, only the confusing of the possible for the real, and the high aspirations of the human mind after a long-sought and unknown something. I think the name of Martin

Luther, the monk of Wittenberg, alone sufficient to free all monkhood from the accusation of laziness! If this will not, perhaps the massive volumes of Thomas Aquinas will—or the countless manuscripts, still preserved in old libraries, whose yellow and wrinkled pages remind one of the hands that wrote them, and the faces that once leaned over them.

"An eloquent homily," said the Baron laughing, "a most touching appeal on behalf of suffering humanity! As for me, I'm no supporter of this complete withdrawal from the world. It has a very harmful effect on a scholar's mind. The Chinese proverb rings true; a single conversation across the table with a wise person is better than ten years of simply studying books. I've known some of these literary men who shut themselves away from the world like this. Their minds never engage with those of their fellow human beings. They read very little. They think extensively. They are nothing but dreamers. They don't know what is new or what is old. They often stumble upon lines of thought that were written down by good authors a century or so ago, and are even commonly spoken by people around them. But they don't realize this; and they imagine they are presenting something very original when they publish their thoughts."

"It reminds me," Flemming responded, "of what Dr. Johnson said about Goldsmith when he suggested traveling overseas to bring back improvements—'He will return home with a wheelbarrow and call that an improvement.' Unfortunately, the same thing happens with some of these scholars."

"And the worst part," said the Baron, "is that when you're alone, a single obsessive thought can take hold in your mind and grow until it dominates everything you think about. All your opinions eventually bend to this one idea; no new thought can enter your mind without being shaped by this fixed notion. It stays there and keeps growing. It's like the story of the watchman's wife in the tower of Waiblingen, who became so enormous that she couldn't fit down the narrow staircase anymore; and when her husband died, his replacement had no choice but to marry the enormous widow who was trapped in the tower."

"I remember an old English comedy," said Flemming, laughing, "where a scholar is portrayed as someone who can light a fire in the morning with his tinderbox, put on a pair of lined slippers, sit thinking until dinner, and then go eat when the bell rings. He's described as someone who has a particular talent for coughing and permission to spit. Or, if you want him defined by what he can't do, he's someone who can't bow properly and can't eat a bowl of soup without making a mess. What do you think of that?"

"That's exactly how people are always portrayed in English comedy," said the Baron. "The portrait is exaggerated—turned into a caricature."

"And yet," Flemming went on, "just yesterday, in the preface of a work by Dr. Rosenkranz, Professor of Philosophy at the University of Halle, I read this passage."

He opened a book and read.

"Here in Halle, where we have no public garden and no Tivoli, no London Exchange, no Paris Chamber of Deputies, no Berlin or Vienna theaters, no Strasbourg Cathedral, nor Salzburg Alps— no Greek ruins nor elaborate Catholicism, in short, nothing that can entertain and refresh a person after finishing their daily work, without them knowing or caring how—I find the sight of a proof sheet just as delightful as a walk in Vienna's Prater. I fill my pipe very calmly, take out my inkwell and pens, settle myself in the corner of my sofa, read, correct, and now for the first time really begin to think about what I have written. To witness this birth of a book, this transformation of manuscript into print, is a joy to which I surrender myself completely. You see, this bittersweet pleasure, which would have provided the late Voss with worthy material for more than one blessed pastoral poem—especially since on such occasions, I am usually dressed in a morning gown, though I regret to say, not a silk one with large flowers—this bittersweet pleasure had already developed here in Halle into a sweet, scholarly habit. Since I began my solitary life here, I have been printing; and as long as I remain here, I shall continue printing. In all likelihood, I shall die with a proof sheet in my hand."

"This," said Flemming, closing the book, "is no caricature by a comedy writer, but a portrait painted by a man's own hand. We can see from it how easily, under certain circumstances, one might slip into habits of isolation, and in a kind of casual, careless boldness, with a pipe and a proof-sheet, challenge the world. Scholars have too often fallen into this state; thus providing some basis for the common opinion that scholarship and rusticity cannot be separated. To me, I admit, it is painful to see the scholar and the world so often take a hostile stance, and set themselves against each other. Surely, it is a defining trait of a great and generous mind that it recognizes humanity in all its forms and conditions. I am a student—and always, when I sit alone at night, I recognize the divinity of the student, as she reveals herself to me in the smoke of the midnight lamp. But, because solitude and books are not unpleasant to me—indeed, they are wished-for, sought after—shall I say to my brother, You fool! Shall I grab the world by the beard and say, You are old, and mad!—Shall I look society in the face and say, You are heartless!—Heartless! Beware of that word! Life, says very wisely the good Jean Paul, Life in every shape, should be precious to us, for the same reason that the Turks carefully collect every scrap of paper that comes their way, because the name of God may be written upon it. Nothing is more true than this, yet nothing more neglected!"

"If it's painful to witness this misunderstanding between scholars and the world," the Baron said, "I believe it's even more painful to observe the private suffering of professional authors. How many have wasted away in poverty, how many have died with broken hearts, how many have lost their minds from excessive stress and crushed dreams! How educational and heartbreakingly fascinating their lives are! They contain so many flaws—so much that needs forgiveness—so much that deserves sympathy—so much that commands respect! I think the person wasn't entirely wrong who claimed that, aside from the Newgate Calendar, the Biography of Authors represents the most disturbing chapter in human history."

Chapter VIII. Literary Fame.

Time keeps a record book like the Doomsday Book, continuously writing down famous names on its pages. However, whenever a new name gets written, an old one vanishes. Only a select few appear in glowing letters that can never be erased. These represent nature's true aristocracy—the masters of humanity's shared realm of ideas. Future generations will never doubt their rightful place. But those whose reputation exists only in the foolish opinions of unwise people will soon be forgotten as completely as if they never existed. Most people must face this great erasure from memory. It's better, therefore, that they accept this reality early on, understanding that just as their bodies will eventually return to dust and their graves will tell no stories about them, their names will also be completely forgotten, and their most treasured thoughts, goals, and beliefs will no longer exist as individual contributions among humanity. Instead, these will dissolve and merge into the vast universe of human thought. If our imagination can follow the noble remains of heroes until we discover them plugging a beer barrel, and realize that

"Imperial Caesar, dead and turned to clay,

"May stop a hole to keep the wind away;"

it can also track the noble ideas of great thinkers until it discovers them crumbling into ordinary everyday talk, used to silence people's arguments and fill gaps in theories to cover up weaknesses in beliefs. Examples of this include all popular sayings and wise proverbs, which have now dissolved into the general pool of human thought; their creators are forgotten, and they no longer exist as individual contributions among people.

It's better, then, for people to quickly accept that they'll be forgotten and search around them or inside themselves for a higher purpose in their actions than seeking human approval, which is fame. Instead, they should focus on their duty and work steadily and quietly in their own areas, paying no attention to results and letting their reputation take care of itself. This must certainly be difficult given our flaws, and perhaps impossible to accomplish completely. However, the determined and unyielding human will can accomplish a great deal—sometimes even this victory over oneself—when convinced that fame only comes when it's earned, and when it does, it's as unavoidable as fate, because it is fate.

It's often said that brilliant minds are always ahead of their time, and this is true. There's something equally true, though less commonly recognized: among these brilliant individuals, the finest and most courageous are ahead not just of their own era, but of all eras. As the German prose-poet observes, every possible future lies behind them. We cannot imagine that a time will ever arrive when the world, or any significant part of it, will catch up to these great minds enough to fully understand them.

And oh! how magnificently they move through history; some shine like the sun, surrounded by all its radiant glory; others are shrouded in darkness, yet as glorious as a star-filled night. Through the otherwise silent shadows of the past, the spirit can hear their slow and solemn steps. Forward they continue, like those ancient elders witnessed in the sublime vision of an earthly Paradise, with attending angels carrying golden lights ahead of them, and above and behind, the entire sky painted with seven distinct colors, as if from the trail of brushes!

And yet, on earth, these men were not happy—not completely happy in the external circumstances of their lives. They lived in poverty and pain, and knew prison bars well, along with the damp, weeping walls of dungeons! Oh, I have looked with amazement at those who, despite sorrow and hardship, physical discomfort and illness—which is death's shadow—have continued working toward the completion of their great goals; laboring extensively, enduring greatly, achieving much; and then, with broken nerves and weakened bodies, have laid themselves down in the grave and slept the sleep of death—while the world speaks of them as they sleep!

It truly appears as though all their suffering has only made them more sacred! It's as if the angel of death, while passing by, had brushed them with the edge of his robe and made them holy! It's as if the hand of illness had reached out to them only to mark the sign of the cross upon their spirits! And just as we can see the great stars shining in the sky during a solar eclipse, so in this eclipse of life these people have witnessed the lights of the great eternity, burning solemnly and forever!

This was what Flemming was daydreaming about. His thoughts were interrupted by the Baron's voice, who suddenly called out;

"An angel is soaring above the house! Here, in this cup that's as fragrant as Hymettus honey and as sweet-smelling as the wildflowers in Angel's Meadow, I raise a toast to the sacred nature of your dreams."

"This is pure perfection," said Flemming as he drank. "The wine of the Prince, and the Prince of wines. By the way, have you ever read that brilliant Italian dithyramb, Redi's Bacchus in Tuscany? It's an ode that seems to have been poured straight from the author's soul, like wine flowing from a golden pitcher,

Filled with the wine
Of the Vine
Benign,
"That flames so red in Sansavine."

"He calls the Montepulciano the king of all wines."

"Prince Metternich," said the Baron, "is more powerful than any king in Italy; and I'm surprised that this excellent wine has never motivated a German poet to compose a Bacchus on the Rhine. We have many short songs on this subject, but none particularly remarkable. The finest are Max Schenkendorf's Song of the Rhine, and the Song of Rhine Wine, by Claudius, a poet who never drank Rhine wine without sugar. We will drink a toast in his honor to the Rhine."

And once more the crystal lips of the wine glasses touched each other, creating a musical chime that sounded like evening bells ringing during harvest time from the villages along the Rhine. Honestly, I'm not at all surprised that the German poet Schiller enjoyed writing by candlelight with a bottle of Rhine wine sitting on his table. I'm also not surprised by the respected schoolmaster Roger Ascham, when he writes in one of his letters from Germany to Mr. John Raven of John's College: "Tell Mr. Maden I will share a drink of wine with him now; and I wish to God he had a vessel of Rhenish wine; and perhaps, when I return to Cambridge, I will arrange things here so that every year I will have a small supply of Rhenish wine." Finally, I'm not surprised by the German Emperor whom he mentions in another letter to the same John Raven, saying, "The Emperor drank better than anyone I have ever seen; he kept his head in the glass five times longer than any of us, and never drank less than a full quart at once of Rhenish wine." These were scholars and gentlemen.

"But to return to our old topic of scholars and where they should live," said the Baron, with an unusual warmth, caught no doubt from the golden sunshine, trapped, like the student

Anselmus, in the glass bottle; "where should the scholar make his home? In solitude or in society? In the peaceful quiet of the countryside, where he can hear nature's heartbeat, or in the dark, gray city, where he can hear and feel the pulsing heart of humanity? I will answer for him, and say, in the dark, gray city. Oh, how greatly mistaken are those who believe that the stars are all the poetry that cities possess; and therefore that the poet's only home should be in woodland solitudes, beneath the green canopy of trees. Beautiful, without question, are all the forms of Nature, when transformed by the miraculous power of poetry; villages and harvest fields, and brown waters, flowing endlessly under the forest, vast and shadowy, with all the sights and sounds of country life. But after all, what are these except the decorations and painted backdrops in the great theater of human existence? What are they but the raw materials of the poet's song? Magnificent indeed is God's world around us, but more magnificent is God's world within us. There lies the Land of Song; there lies the poet's homeland. The river of life, flowing through bustling streets, carrying along so many brave hearts, so many ruins of humanity;--the countless homes and households, each a small world unto itself, revolving around its hearth, like a central sun; all forms of human joy and suffering, brought into that confined space;--and to exist in this and be part of this; acting, thinking, celebrating, grieving, with his fellow human beings;--such, such should be the poet's existence. If he wishes to describe the world, he should live in the world. The scholar's mind, too, if you want it broad and generous, should encounter other minds. It is better that his armor should be somewhat dented by rough confrontations, than hang forever rusting on the wall. Nor will his subjects be few or insignificant, because apparently confined between the walls of buildings, and having only the ornaments of street scenery. A destroyed character is as striking as a ruined castle. There are dark chasms and gaping abysses in the human heart, which can be made passable only by spanning them with iron nerves and sinews, as Challey bridged the Savine in Switzerland, and Telford the sea between Anglesea and England, with chain bridges. These are the great subjects of human thought; not green grass, and flowers, and moonlight. Besides, the mere outward forms of Nature we make our own, and carry with us into the city, through the power of memory.

"I'm concerned, though," Flemming interrupted, "that city life makes people's souls grow arrogant. Sometimes a person needs to be sent out into the countryside, like that ancient Assyrian king, to become 'a strange outcast without weeds,' eating wild plants and being humbled and disciplined by rainstorms and harsh winter weather. What's more, cities pose the risk of souls becoming addicted to pleasure and forgetting their noble purpose. There have been souls devoted to heaven since childhood, protected by guardian angels like sacred retreats for holy thoughts, prayers, and all virtuous intentions; where devout wishes lived like nuns, and every mental image was saintly; yet through life's ups and downs, through betrayal by circumstances, through the overwhelming passions found in great cities, these souls have become corrupted and sinful. They're like those monasteries along the Rhine River that have been turned into taverns; their devout residents left long ago, and in their hallways travelers' footsteps have worn away the images of buried saints, and their walls are now covered with crude jokes and strangers' names, and they no longer echo with sacred songs, but with wild partying and loud voices."

"Both the city and the countryside have their dangers," the Baron said, "and so, no matter where a scholar chooses to live, he must never lose sight of his noble calling. Other artists dedicate themselves completely to mastering their craft. It becomes almost like a religion to them. Most of the time, especially when they're young, they live in places where beauty fills the very air around them; the atmosphere is so thick with it, like moisture in the air, that their entire being becomes infused with the spirit of their art. This is what an artist's life is like in Italy, for instance."

"I agree with you," Flemming declared enthusiastically; "and that's how poets should be everywhere; because he carries his Rome, his Florence, his entire radiant Italy within the four walls of his library. In his books, he possesses the ruins of an ancient world and the splendors of a modern one—his Apollo and Transfiguration. He must never forget or diminish his calling; instead, he should thank God that he is a poet; and everywhere remain true to himself, and to 'the vision and the faculty divine' that he feels within him."

"But, at any rate, city life is filled with the most events," the Baron went on. "Those who write or compile the biographies of poets and scholars always complain that these lives lack interesting incidents. Nearly every literary biography starts with this kind of apology, which is unwisely offered. I admit, though, that this complaint has some basis in truth—if by incidents we only mean those shocking events that suddenly redirect the flow of time and alter world history in a single hour. There's definitely a sameness in literary life, whether pleasant or unpleasant, that usually makes today feel like yesterday's twin. But if by incidents you mean events in the development of human thought (and why shouldn't we?), quiet events that don't leave visible scars on the world's face like battles do, yet still transform it just as much, then certainly the lives of literary figures are the most eventful of all. Both the complaint and the apology are foolish. I don't understand why a successful book shouldn't be considered as significant an event as a successful military campaign—they're simply different types of achievements that can't easily be compared."

"Indeed," interrupted Flemming, "the complaint isn't strictly accurate in any sense, though it may sometimes appear to be. There are plenty of events if they were all recorded. A life that's worth writing about at all deserves to be written about in detail.

Furthermore, not all literary figures have lived in silence and isolation—not all in quiet circumstances, not all in obscurity. Many have lived during turbulent times, amid the harsh and challenging circumstances of their state and era, and could say with Wallenstein,

Our life was nothing more than a battle and a march;
And, like the wind's blast, never-resting, homeless,
We charged across the war-torn earth.

History has recorded many such examples: Dante, Cervantes, Byron, and others—men of steel who dared to face the powerful force of public opinion head-on, sailing directly into the wind like ghost ships. Others were extinguished by the first opposing breeze that came their way, left dishonored and grief-stricken because they couldn't satisfy others. Indeed, "the tears live in an onion, that should water such a sorrow." If they had been true men, they would have turned these setbacks into their greatest allies and learned from them the essential lesson of depending on themselves.

"To be honest," the Baron continued, "the lives of writers, with their dreams and letdowns, their conflicts and disasters, show us a sad portrait of human strength and frailty. For exactly that reason, the scholar can use them as sources of inspiration, comfort, and caution."

"And after all," Flemming continued, "perhaps the greatest lesson that the lives of literary men teach us can be summed up in a single word: Wait! Every person must patiently wait for their time to come. They must wait. This lesson is especially important in countries like my homeland, where life's pulse beats with such feverish and impatient rhythms. Our national character lacks the dignity of calm reflection. We seem to live in the middle of a battlefield—there's such noise, such constant rushing back and forth. On the streets of a busy city, it's hard to walk slowly. You feel the crowd rushing around you, and you rush along with it. In the pressure of our daily lives, it's difficult to stay calm. In this storm of wind and tide, all professions seem to lose their anchors and get swept out to sea. The voices of the present say, Come! But the voices of the past say, Wait! With calm and steady steps, the rising tide pushes against the rushing current upstream and forces back the hurrying waters. With equally calm and steady steps, and just as certainly, a great mind stands firm against public opinion and pushes back its rushing current. Therefore, every person should wait—should bide their time. Not in lazy idleness, not in pointless activities, not in complaining depression, but in constant, steady, cheerful efforts, always willing and ready to fulfill and accomplish their work, so that when the opportunity comes, they'll be ready for it. And if it never comes, what does it matter? What does it matter to the world whether I, or you, or someone else did such a deed or wrote such a book, as long as the deed and book were done well! It shows unwise and troublesome ambition to care too much about fame—about what the world thinks of us. To always look into other people's faces for approval, to always worry about the effect of what we do and say, to always shout just to hear the echo of our own voices! If you look around, you'll see people who are wasting their lives in feverish anxiety about fame, and the last thing we'll ever hear about them will be the funeral bell that calls them to their early graves! Unhappy and unsuccessful people! Because their goal isn't to accomplish their work well, but to grab the "trick and fantasy of fame," and they go to their graves with unfinished purposes and unfulfilled wishes. It would be better for them, and for the world through their example, if they had known how to wait! Believe me, the secret of success is nothing more than doing what you can do well, and doing well whatever you do—without thinking about fame. If fame comes at all, it will come because it's deserved, not because it's chased after. And furthermore, there will be no doubts, no disappointment, no hasty, feverish, exhausting excitement."

Thus ends the First Book of Hyperion. I won't describe the winter months. Paul Flemming immersed himself in books—old, dusty volumes. He devoted himself to studying Germany's ancient poetic traditions, beginning with Frankish legends of Saint George and Saxon verse chronicles, then moving through the Nibelungenlied and heroic tales, songs of the Minnesingers and Mastersingers, Ships of Fools, tales of Reynard the Fox, Dances of Death, and Lamentations of Damned Souls, finally arriving in the bright, sunlit realm of abundance, where modern poets walk among golden wheat and blue cornflowers, creating their songs.

Book II.

Opening Quote

"The heart must have something to treasure,"
Must learn love, joy, and sorrow;
Something with passion clasp, or perish,
"And in itself to ashes burn."

———————

Chapter I. Spring.

It was a beautiful song that the children of Rhodes used to sing long ago in springtime, carrying a swallow in their hands as they went from house to house, using it as a symbol to announce the arrival of the new season;

"The Swallow has arrived!"
The Swallow has arrived!
O beautiful are the seasons, and bright
Are the days that she brings,
With her dark wings,
"And her bosom snowy white."

A beautiful song is also the one that Hungarian boys on the Danube islands sing to welcome back the stork in spring;

"Stork! Stork! poor Stork!"
Why is your foot so bloody?
A Turkish boy has torn it;
Hungarian boy will heal it,
"With fiddle, fife, and drum."

But what child feels like singing in our unpredictable climate, where Spring arrives from the ocean carrying wet, heavy clouds like sails, with the misty banner of the East wind attached to its mast! Even so, right here in our stormy March weather, there are still bright, warm mornings when we throw open our windows to breathe in the sweet air. Pigeons dart back and forth, and we can hear the rushing sound of their wings. Old flies emerge from crevices to bask in the sunshine, believing summer has arrived. They perish in their delusion; and our hearts do the same when the cold ocean breeze sweeps in from the eastern waters; and once more,

"The driving hail"
Upon the window beats with icy flail.

The red-flowering maple blooms first, its stunning purple flowers opening two weeks before the leaves appear. The moose-wood comes next, displaying rose-colored buds and leaves, followed by the dogwood, dressed in the white of its own pristine blossoms. Then the sudden rainstorm arrives, and the birds dart back and forth, crying out. Where do they take shelter during such storms? At what hearths do they dry their feathered coats? At the hearth of the great, welcoming sun tomorrow, not before—they must remain in their wet clothing until then.

Spring is beautiful in every climate. In the South, it becomes intoxicating and drives a poet to ecstasy. The birds start singing— they release a few joyful notes, then pause for a response in the quiet woods. Those green-dressed musicians, the frogs, celebrate in the nearby marshes. They also belong to Nature's orchestra, whose enormous theater opens once again, even though the doors have been locked with icicles for so long, and the scenery has been draped with snow and frost like spider webs. This serves as the prelude that signals the rising of the vast green curtain. The grass is already sprouting. Water rushes with an exciting pulse through the earth's veins; sap flows through the veins of plants and trees;

and blood courses through human veins. What an exciting thrill springtime brings! What happiness there is in existing and moving! People work in their gardens, and the air carries the scent of fresh soil. The leaf buds start to expand and turn pink. The white cherry blossoms hang on the branches like snowflakes, and before long our neighbors next door will be completely concealed from view by the thick green leaves. The May flowers open their gentle blue eyes. Children are released into the fields and gardens. They hold buttercups beneath each other's chins to discover if they enjoy butter. The little girls decorate themselves with dandelion chains and curls, pluck the yellow petals to learn if the schoolboy cares for them, and blow the fluffy seeds from the bare stem to determine if their mothers need them at home.

And at night, so clear and so peaceful! There's no sound from any living creature—no rustling of leaves or swaying branches—no breeze stirring—no noise on the ground or in the sky! Above stretches the blue heavens, fresh with dew and gentle, glowing with countless stars, like the upturned cup of some blue blossom, dusted with golden powder, and releasing sweet scent. Or when the sky is covered with clouds, it's not a fierce tempest of wind and rain; instead, clouds that dissolve and descend as gentle showers. You don't want to fall asleep; you stay awake to listen to the delightful sound of the falling rain.

It was in this way that Spring arrived in Heidelberg.

―――――――――

Chapter II. A Colloquy.

"And what do you think of Tiedge's Urania," said the Baron with a smile, as Paul Flemming closed the book and placed it on the table.

"I think," said Flemming, "that it's very much like Jean Paul's grandfather—extremely poor and pious."

"Excellent!" the Baron exclaimed. "That's the finest critique I've heard about that book. Personally, I dislike it just as much as Goethe did. It was extremely popular at one time and could be found lying around in every living room and bedroom. This irritated the old gentleman tremendously, and I can't blame him for that. He complained that for a while, people talked and sang about nothing but this Urania. He believed in immortality but wanted to hold onto his belief in peace and quiet. He once told a friend that he had learned one thing from all the chatter about Tiedge and his Urania: that saints, just like nobility, form their own kind of aristocracy. He said he encountered foolish women who were proud simply because they believed in immortality along with Tiedge, and he had to endure quite a few mysterious interrogations and drawing-room lectures on the subject. He would cut them short by saying that he had no problem whatsoever with entering another state of existence in the afterlife, but he only prayed that he might be spared the honor of meeting any of those people there who had believed in it here on earth. If he did encounter them, the saints would swarm around him from every direction, crying out, 'Weren't we right? Didn't we tell you so? Hasn't everything turned out exactly as we predicted?' With such self-satisfied chatter ringing in his ears, he thought that within six months, he might die of boredom even in Heaven itself."

"The good old ladies must have been absolutely shocked," Flemming said.

"Without question, their nerves were somewhat frayed; but the young women adored him even more for his clever and mischievous nature; and they believed that if only they could wed him, they would be able to change his ways."

"Bettina Brentano, for instance."

"Oh no! That took place much later. Goethe was already a silver-haired elderly man of sixty at that time. She had never met him and only knew him through his writings; she was a romantic seventeen-year-old girl."

"And yet she was deeply in love with the sixty-year-old man. And certainly a more wild, fantastical, and, forgive me, German passion had never emerged in a woman's heart. She was a flower that worshipped the sun."

"She later married Achim von Arnim and is now a widow. What makes this situation particularly strange is that, having grown older and hopefully wiser, she chose to publish the letters that she and Goethe exchanged."

"Especially the letter where she describes her first trip to Weimar, and her meeting with the previously unseen god of her fantasies. The elderly man placed her on his lap, and she dozed off with her head resting on his shoulder. This brings to mind Titania and Nick Bottom, though I apologize for comparing your All-sided-One to Nick Bottom. Oberon must have brushed her eyes with the essence of Love-in-idleness. Nevertheless, this book of Goethe's Correspondence with a Child offers a truly unique and precious glimpse into the emotions he stirred in women's hearts. You mentioned she later wed Achim von Arnim?"

"Yes; and he and her brother, Clemens Brentano, published that wonderful book, the Boy's Wonder-Horn."

"The Boy's Wonder-Horn!" Flemming said after a brief pause, as the title seemed to send him into deep thought. "I know that book almost by heart. Of all the German books I've read, it's the one that has the most wild and magical effect on my imagination. I have a real passion for ballads!"

"And who hasn't?" said the Baron with a smile. "They are the wandering children of song, born beneath green hedges, in the tree-lined lanes and side paths of literature—in the warm summertime."

"Why do you say summer-time instead of just summer?" Flemming asked. "That phrase brings to mind your ancient Minnesingers—Heinrich von Ofterdingen, Walter von der

55

Vogelweide, Count Kraft von Toggenburg, and probably your own ancestor, Burkhart von Hohenfels. They were constantly singing about the gentle summer-time. They appeared to have lived poetry just as much as they sang it, like birds that build their nests for love in the lush, abundant trees."

"Is that from Shakespeare?"

"No; from Lope de Vega."

"You have extensive knowledge of ancient traditions and the Dawn Songs and Night Watch Songs of the old Minnesingers. What are your thoughts on the cobbler poets who followed them, with their trade guilds and singing academies? It amuses me to imagine how the mighty German Helicon, reduced to a small stream, flows babbling and splashing over the rocky names of Zwinger, Wurgendrussel, Buchenlin, Hellfire, Old Stoll, Young Stoll, Strong Bopp, Dang Brotscheim, Batt Spiegel, Peter Pfort, and Martin Gumpel. And then there's the Guild of the Twelve Wise Masters, with their blunt rhymes and ringing rhymes, along with Hans Tindeisen's rosemary melody, Joseph Schmierer's flowery paradise melody, and Frauenlob's yellow melody, blue melody, frog melody, and mirror melody!"

"Oh, I beg you," Flemming exclaimed with laughter, "don't call those men poets! You're taking me back to charming old Nuremberg, where I can picture Hans Sachs crafting shoes and Hans Folz shaving the mayor."

"By the way," the Baron interrupted, "have you ever read Hoffmann's beautiful story about Master Martin, the Cooper of Nuremberg? I'll read it to you tonight. It's the most wonderful picture of that era you could imagine. But look! the sun has already disappeared behind the Alsatian hills. Let's go up to the castle and search for the ghost in Prince Ruprecht's tower. Oh, what a magnificent sunset!"

Flemming gazed at the evening sky, and a shadow of sadness crossed his face. He didn't share with his friend the sorrow that weighed heavily on his heart; instead, he kept it to himself alone. He understood that the time that comes to everyone—the time to endure pain and remain silent—had arrived for him as well; and he said nothing. How true it is that there is no grief like the grief that cannot be expressed.

Chapter III. Owl-Towers.

"There sits old Frau Himmelhahn, perched up in her owl-tower," the Baron said to Flemming as they walked along the Hauptstrasse. "She peers down through her round spectacles from her nest up there and watches everyone who passes by. I wonder what trouble she's stirring up now? Do you know she's almost destroyed your reputation in town? She claims you have a roguish appearance because you carry a walking stick and your hair is curly. Your gloves are also a shade too light for a truly virtuous man, according to her."

"It's very thoughtful of her to look after my reputation so carefully, especially since I'm new to this town. She's probably well-versed in the philosophy of clothing."

"And completely unaware of everything else. She asked a friend of mine recently whether Christ was Catholic or Protestant."

"That is really too absurd!"

"Not too ridiculous to be believable. And despite her ignorance, she manages to cause quite a bit of trouble throughout the year. In fact, the ladies are already calling you Wilhelm Meister."

"They're free to call me whatever they want. But you, who know me better, understand that I am something more than what they suggest with that label."

"She also says that American women sit with their feet hanging out of windows and don't carry handkerchiefs."

"Excellent!"

They walked across the marketplace and climbed up under the magnificent terrace into the castle's courtyard.

"Let's go up and sit beneath the large linden trees that grow on top of the Rent Tower," Flemming suggested. "From that spot, like from a watchtower, we can look down into the garden and observe the crowd below us."

"And entertain ourselves, just like old Frau Himmelhahn does, sitting at her window on Hauptstrasse," the Baron added.

The keeper's daughter unlocked the tower door for them, and after climbing the steep staircase, they sat down on a wooden bench beneath the linden trees.

"Look how beautifully these trees have grown over the old tower! And see what a solid mass of stonework lies in the great ditch down there, knocked from its foundation by a mine explosion! It looks like a rusty helmet split in two, but still crowned with towering plumes!"

"What a diverse crowd fills the garden! Philistines and Sons of the Muses! And there walks the respected Thibaut, taking his evening walk. Do you see him there, with his silver hair flowing over his shoulders, and that kind face, which has spent so many years studying the Pandects. I tell you, he fills me with reverence. And yet he is a cheerful old man, and enjoys his humor, especially when it comes at the expense of Moses and other ancient lawmakers."

Here their attention was drawn to a wild-looking person who walked with long strides under the archway in the moat, directly beneath them, and vanished among the bushes. He was poorly dressed, his hair blowing in the wind, his movements quick and anxious, and the expression on his broad face was wild, strange, and intense.

"Who could that be!" Flemming asked. "He's walking away angrily, like one of Ossian's ghosts?"

"A great philosopher, whose name I have forgotten. Truly a strange owl!"

"He looks like a lion with a hat on."

"He is a mystic who reads Schubert's History of the Soul and spends most of his time lost in the mystical world of the Middle Ages. For him, the spiritual realm remains accessible. He believes in the transmigration of souls, and I wouldn't be surprised if he's currently following the spirit of some deceased friend who has taken the form of that pigeon over there."

"What an odd delusion! I imagine he exists in a realm of shifting shadows and illusions. And just as St. Thomas Aquinas was reportedly lifted from the earth by the intensity of his prayers, so too is he undoubtedly carried away by the passion of his visions."

"He definitely seems to ignore all earthly matters; and, judging by certain signs, since you appear to enjoy religious comparisons, one might say that, like St. Serapion the Sindonite, he owned only a single shirt. But what does he care? He lives in that poetic dreamworld of his thoughts, and dresses his imagined creations in poetry."

"He is a poet, then, as well as a philosopher?"

"Yes; but he's a poet who never puts pen to paper. There's nothing in the natural world that his imagination doesn't transform with poetic beauty. However, he lacks the ability to help others see these same objects through that poetic lens. Still, he's a man with remarkable abilities and deep sensitivity; because, next to actually being a great poet, the greatest gift is the capacity to truly understand one—to discover yourself within their work, as we Germans express it."

Three figures dressed in black emerged from one of the green pathways and paused at the edge of a small fountain that sparkled among the colorful flowers in the garden. The oldest of the three was a woman in that stage of life when early autumn gives summer leaves a richer warmth without yet causing them to fade. Though she had given birth to many children, she remained beautiful—like those trees that bloom in October when the leaves are changing color, bearing both fruit and blossoms on their branches simultaneously. Beside her stood a girl of about sixteen years who appeared to lean on her arm for support. The girl had a delicate figure and a beautiful face, though it was deathly pale, with gentle eyes like nightshade flowers—pale blue but radiating golden light. They were accompanied by a tall young man with foreign features who looked like a young Antinous, complete with a mustache and a nose in the style of Kosciusko. In every other way, he was the perfect romantic hero.

"Unless my eyes are deceiving me," said the Baron, "there's Mrs. von Ilmenau with her pale daughter Emma, and that ever-present Polish Count. He's always hanging around them, playing the role of the miserable exile just to stir up that poor girl's sympathy; he's as wretched as genius and recklessness can make a person."

"Well, he's already married, you know," Flemming replied. "And his wife is young and beautiful."

"That doesn't stop him from being in love with someone else. That question was settled in the Courts of Love during the Middle Ages. So he has sent his beautiful wife to Warsaw. But how pale the poor child looks."

"She has just recovered from a serious illness. During the winter, you know, people thought she might not survive from one hour to the next."

"And she had barely gotten over that illness when she appeared to be facing an even worse threat: a hopeless romantic obsession. However, people don't die from love these days."

"Rarely, maybe," Flemming said. "But it's foolish to pretend that anyone ever completely gets over a broken heart. Those kinds of wounds always leave a mark. There are faces I can never see without feeling something. There are names I can never hear mentioned without nearly jumping!"

"But who do we have here?"

"That's the French poet Quinet, along with his lovely German wife; she's one of the most fascinating women I've ever met. He wrote a very unconventional Mystery, or dramatic prose-poem, where the Ocean, Mont Blanc, and the Cathedral of Strasbourg all play roles; the saints depicted in the cathedral's stained glass windows come to life and speak, while the statues and deceased kings perform the Dance of Death. The work is called Ahasuerus, or the Wandering Jew."

"Or, as the Danes would translate it, the Shoemaker of Jerusalem. That would be an even more fantastical title for his fantastical book. You know I'm not a great admirer of the modern French school of writers. The stories of Paul de Kock, who is, I believe, the most popular of them all, strike me as vulgar tales told at dinner parties after the ladies have left the room. It has been aptly said of him that he is not only popular but appeals to the masses; and it has been equally well said of George Sand and Victor Hugo that their works stand like fortresses, well constructed and well stocked with military supplies; but they prove ineffective against the Grand Army of God, which advances forward as if nothing had occurred. When examining a national literature, the starting point must be national character. This reveals many secrets to you; for instance, Paul de Kock's popularity. The most distinctive feature of the French character is their love of entertainment and excitement; and--"

"I would say it's more about the fear of boredom," Flemming interrupted. "One of their own writers spoke with great truth when he said that the French nobility rush into Paris to escape from boredom, just as in the glorious days of chivalry, the defenseless people of the countryside fled into castles when some pillaging knight or lawless baron approached. They abandon the magical twilight of their native woods for the lavish gardens of royalty. What do you think of that?"

The Baron responded with a smile;

"There is only one Paris; and out of Paris there is no salvation for decent people."

The two friends sat beneath the linden trees on the Rent Tower, talking about many different topics, while the crowd slowly vanished from the garden and the surrounding objects became unclear in the dimming twilight. Against the amber-colored western sky, the thick leaves of the trees appeared heavy and solid, as though they were made of bronze; and the evening stars already hung like silver lanterns in the tall branches of that Tree of Life, which had been brought over two centuries earlier from its original Paradise in America to enhance the beauty of the Palatinate gardens.

"I find a sad kind of joy in looking at that tree," Flemming said as they stood up to leave. "It stands there so upright and towering, with metal bands wrapped around its majestic trunk and branches, in quiet dignity, or murmuring only in its own language, and filling the evening breeze with sorrowful sounds! It makes me think of some captured king from a wild tribe, brought across the enormous ocean to be displayed, and bound in the town's public square, proudly silent, or expressing only in melancholy tones a wish for his homeland forest, a yearning to be free."

"Magnificent!" exclaimed the Baron. "I always feel something similar when I stroll through a greenhouse. The lush tropical plants—those remarkable exotic species, with their stunning, bright pink flowers and enormous, drooping leaves that look like elephant ears—have an unusual effect on my imagination and make me think of a zoo with wild animals kept in cages. But your comparison is better—truly, a wonderful metaphor. Write it down for an epic poem."

———————

Chapter IV. A Beer-Scandal.

On their way home, Flemming and the Baron walked through a narrow lane where a well-known student tavern was located. At the entrance stood a young man whom the Baron immediately recognized as his friend Von Kleist. He was a student and universally acknowledged among his young friends as an extremely handsome fellow, despite having a prominent scar on his cheek and a cream-colored mustache as soft as corn silk. In short, he was famous and a duelist.

"What are you doing here, Von Kleist?"

"Oh, my dear Baron! Is that you? Come in, come in. You're going to witness quite a show. There's some shady business dealings happening, and a proper drinking scandal unfolding."

"Should we go inside, Flemming?"

"Absolutely. I'd like to see how these matters are handled in Heidelberg. You're a Baron, and I'm an outsider. It doesn't matter what you and I do, as the king's jester Angeli told the poet Bautru when he encouraged him to put his hat on at the royal dining table."

William Lilly, the astrologer, writes in his autobiography that when he was confined to the guard room in Whitehall, he felt as though he was in hell because "some were sleeping, others swearing, others smoking tobacco; and in the chimney of the room there were two bushels of broken tobacco pipes, and almost half a load of ashes." I have no idea what he would have thought if he had glimpsed into this Heidelberg student tavern. He certainly wouldn't have believed himself in heaven, unless it was a Scandinavian version of paradise. The windows stood open, yet the air was so thick with tobacco smoke and beer fumes that the tallow candles burned only dimly. A crowd of students sat at three long tables in the large hall—a mixed group of fellows known at German universities by the slang terms Old-Ones, Mossy-Heads, Princes of Twilight, and Pomatum-Stallions. They were smoking, drinking, singing, shouting, and debating the great laws of the Broad-Stone and the Gutter. They also had plenty to say about Besens, Zobels, and Poussades; and if they had been charged for the noise they created, as travelers once were in the old Dutch taverns, they would have faced a much larger bill for that than for their beer.

In a large armchair at the center table sat one of those distinguished individuals known among German students as a Senior, or Leader of a Landsmannschaft. He wore boots and spurs, along with a very small crimson cap, a very tight blue jacket, very long hair, and a very dirty shirt. He served as President of the night, and as Flemming entered the hall with the Baron and his friend, the Senior struck the table with a mighty broadsword and shouted in a loud voice;

"Silentium!"

At that exact moment, a door at the far end of the hall burst open, and a line of newcomers, known as Nasty-Foxes in the college slang, walked in two by two, appearing nervous, inexperienced, and awkward. As they moved forward, they had to walk under a pair of bare swords held crosswise by two Old-Ones, who used pieces of charred cork to draw enormous mustaches on the smooth, pink cheeks of each newcomer as he passed beneath this ceremonial archway. While the procession was making its way into the hall, the President raised his voice once more and started singing the famous Fox-song, with everyone present enthusiastically joining in the chorus.

What's coming down from that hill?
What's coming down from that hill?
What comes there from the leathery hill?
Ha! Ha!
Leathery hill!
What's coming down from that hill?
It is a postilion!

It is a postilion!
It is a leathery postilion!
Ha! Ha!
Postilion!
It is a postilion!
What does the mail carrier bring?
What does the mail carrier bring?
What does the weathered mail carrier bring?
Ha! Ha!
Postilion!
What does the mail carrier bring?
He brings us a fox!
He brings us a fox!
He brings us a tough fox!
Ha! Ha!
Leathery Fox!
He brings us a fox!
Your servant, my Masters!
Your servant, my Masters!
Your humble servant, esteemed Masters!
Ha! Ha!
Much-honored Masters mine!
Your servant, my Masters!
How is Papa doing?
How is Papa doing?
How is the tough old man doing?
Ha! Ha!
Herr Papa!
How is Papa doing?
He reads in Cicero!
He reads in Cicero!
He reads from the leather-bound works of Cicero!
Ha! Ha!

Cicero!
He reads in Cicero!
How is your mother doing?
How is your mother doing?
How is the tough old mother doing?
Ha! Ha!
Frau Mama!
How is your mother doing?
She makes tea for Papa!
She makes tea for Papa!
She makes Papa tough, bitter tea!
Ha! Ha!
Leathery tea!
She makes tea for Papa!
How is Miss Sister doing?
How is Miss Sister doing?
How is the tough old Sister doing?
Ha! Ha!
Mamsell Sœur!
How is Miss Sister doing?
She knits stockings for Papa!
She knits stockings for Papa!
She knits leather stockings for Papa!
Ha! Ha!
Leathery stockings!
She knits stockings for Papa!
How is the Rector doing?
How is the Rector doing?
How is the tough old Rector doing?
Ha! Ha!
Herr Rector!
How is the Rector doing?
He calls the scholar, Boy!

He calls the scholar, Boy!
He calls the scholar, leathery Boy!
Ha! Ha!
Leathery Boy!
He calls the scholar, Boy!
And smokes the Fox tobacco?
And smokes the Fox tobacco?
And smokes the tough Fox tobacco?
Ha! Ha!
Fox tobacco!
And smokes the Fox tobacco?
A little, my Masters!
A little, my Masters!
A little, much-honored Masters mine!
Ha! Ha!
Much-honored Masters mine!
A little, my Masters!
Then let him fill a pipe!
Then let him fill a pipe!
Then let him fill a leather pipe!
Ha! Ha!
Leathery pipe!
Then let him fill a pipe!
O Lord! It makes me sick!
O Lord! It makes him sick!
O Lord! It makes me absolutely sick!
Ha! Ha!
Leathery sick!
O Lord! It makes me sick!
Then let him throw it off!
Then let him throw it off!
Then let him throw it off completely!
Ha! Ha!

Take off that leather!
Then let him throw it off!
Now I am well again!
Now he is well again!
Now I am completely well again!
Ha! Ha!
Leathery well!
Now I am well again!
So the Fox becomes a student!
So the Fox becomes a student!
So the cunning Fox becomes a student!
Ha! Ha!
Fox a Bursch!
So the Fox becomes a student!

At last the song came to an end. During this time, large clumps and strips of paper had been twisted into the hair of the Branders, which is what they called students who had already spent one semester at the University, and then at a predetermined signal these papers were lit on fire, and the Branders rode around the table on sticks while everyone roared with laughter. When this ritual was over, the President stood up from his chair, and in a serious tone delivered a lengthy speech that mixed old university jokes with fatherly guidance for young men beginning their adult lives, and the entire address was liberally decorated with carefully chosen passages from the Old Testament. Then everyone took their seats at the table and the serious beer-drinking began, just like among the Gods and Heroes of ancient Northern mythology.

"Brander! Brander!" shouted a young man, his face red and heated from dinner and beer; "Brander, I'm telling you! You're a Doctor! No—a Pope—you're a Pope, by—"

These words were spoken to a pale, quiet-looking man who sat across from them, busily trying to make a miserable, shaved poodle sit upright on its hind legs in a chair beside its master and hold a short clay pipe in its mouth—a trick the poodle clearly had no interest in performing.

"You are challenged!" replied the pale Student, turning from his dog, who dropped the pipe from his mouth and leaped under the table.

Seconds were selected immediately, and the weapons were arranged: six large goblets, or Bassgläser, filled to the top with foaming beer. Three goblets were positioned in front of each participant.

"Grab your weapons!" shouted one of the seconds, and each fighter took hold of a goblet.

"Strike!"

And the glasses clinked together, creating a sound like swords clashing in salute.

"Get to work!"

Each person raised the goblet to their lips.

"Out!"

Each man poured the liquid down his throat as though he were emptying it through a funnel into a beer keg. The remaining two glasses came one after another in rapid succession, with barely enough time to take a deep breath between them. The pale Student emerged victorious. He was the first to empty the third glass completely. He held it upside down for a moment to let the final drops fall out, then set it gently on the table, looked his opponent directly in the eye, and said;

"Hit!"

Then, with complete composure, he glanced under the table and whistled for his dog. His opponent froze halfway through his third drink. Every blood vessel in his forehead appeared ready to burst; his eyes were wild and bloodshot, his grip on the table slowly weakened, and he collapsed and crumpled like a sheet of metal. He was drunk.

At that moment, a commanding figure came striding down the table like a ghost through the hazy, smoke-filled air. He had removed his coat, his neck was exposed, his hair was disheveled, his eyes were wide open, and he stared straight ahead as if he could see some beckoning hand in the air that no one else could perceive. His left hand rested on his hip, while his right hand gripped a drawn sword that he held extended and pointed downward. Ignoring everyone around him, he stood upright and marched with military precision directly along the center of the table, smashing glasses and knocking over bottles with every step. The students pulled back as he approached, until finally one who was either more intoxicated or more daring than the others threw a glass full of beer into his face. Complete chaos broke out, and the student with the sword jumped down to the floor. It was Von Kleist. He was performing it. Through all the commotion, the offensive words could still be heard;

"Arrogant! Ridiculous! Rude! Foolish boy!"

That night, von Kleist returned home facing no fewer than six duels. He fought every single one over the course of just as many days, walking away with only a cut slicing through his upper lip and another gash through his right eyelid, both courtesy of a skilled Swabian swordsman.

Chapter V. The White Lady's Slipper And The Passion-Flower.

That night Emma of Ilmenau went to her room feeling deeply saddened, and her dark eyes were filled with tears. She was one of those tender souls who seemed made only to love and be loved. A touch of sadness softened her nature. She avoided the harsh brightness of daylight and social gatherings, preferring to be by herself. Like the evening primrose, her heart only opened after the sun went down, but it flourished through the dark hours of night with sweet fragrance. Her mother, in contrast, displayed herself boldly in the bright spotlight of society. There was no understanding between them. Their spirits never came close, never truly knew each other, and harsh words were often said that cut deeply. And so Emma of Ilmenau went to her room that night with tears in her eyes.

She was followed by her French chambermaid, Madeleine, who was born in Strasbourg and had grown old while serving the family. In her youth, she had been poor and virtuous because she had never faced temptation; now that she had aged and seen no immediate reward for her virtue, like most weak-minded people, she had lost faith in Providence and regretted that she had never been tempted. While this unfortunate woman was lighting the wax candles on the dressing table, pulling the bed curtains closed, and chattering as she moved about the room, Emma collapsed into an armchair and crossed her hands in her lap, letting her head drop to her chest as if lost in thought.

"Why was I given these tender feelings!" she thought to herself. "Why was I born with all these passionate emotions—these intense desires for what is good—if they only bring pain and letdown? I want to love someone—love him completely and forever—dedicate myself entirely to him—live for him—die for him—exist only for him! But sadly, in this entire vast world there is no one to love me the way I want to be loved—no one I can love the way I'm capable of loving. How hollow, how lonely the world around me appears! Why did Heaven give me these emotions, only to have them wither and die!"

Sadly, poor child! You too must learn, just like everyone else, that the magnificent mystery of divine providence continues in silence and offers no explanation of itself—no answer to our impatient questions!

"Good heavens, child, what's wrong with you?" Madeleine exclaimed, noticing that Emma wasn't paying any attention to her casual chatter. "When I was your age--"

"Don't talk to me right now, dear Madeleine. Please leave me, I want to be alone."

"Well, here's something," the maid continued, pulling a letter from her dress, "that I hope will cheer you up. When I was your age--"

"Quiet! Quiet!" Emma said, taking the note from Madeleine's rough hand. "I'm asking you again, please leave me! I want to be alone!"

Madeleine picked up the lamp and slowly walked away, wishing her young mistress many good nights and pleasant dreams. Emma broke open the seal on the letter. While she read, her face turned deathly pale, and then, as quickly as lightning, a deep red flush appeared on her cheek, and her hands began to shake. Affection, compassion, love, wounded pride, the frailty and strength of womanhood, were all mixed together in her expression, shifting and moving across her beautiful face like shadows from passing clouds. She collapsed back into her chair, burying her face in her hands, as though she wanted to hide it from herself and from Heaven.

"He loves me!" she said to herself. "He loves me, and yet he's married to someone else—someone he doesn't love! And he has the nerve to tell me this! Oh, never—never—never! But still, he's so friendless and alone in this cold, uncaring world. He's an exile, homeless! I can't help but feel sorry for him—yet I hate him, and I won't see him anymore!"

This brief daydream of love and hatred was interrupted by the sound of a clear, rich voice that, in the complete silence of the moment, seemed almost like the voice of a ghost. It was a voice, unaccompanied by any instrument, singing those beautiful lines of Goethe;

"Under the tree-tops is quiet now!"
In all the forests you hear
Not a sound!
The small birds are sleeping in the trees,
Wait! Wait! And soon, just like these,
"Are you sleeping!"

Emma recognized the voice and jumped with surprise. She hurried to the window to shut it. The evening was gorgeous, with stars twinkling serenely above the All-Saints mountain. The Neckar's murmur was gentle and quiet, while nightingales sang from within the dark shadows of the forest. The enormous crimson moon glowed like a precious ruby within the broad circle of the horizon, and shimmering golden strands of light appeared woven together with the flowing waters of the river. The white statues on the bridge stood tall and ghostlike. The contours of the hills, the castle, the bridge's arches, and the church spires and town rooftops were so sharply defined they looked as though they had been cut from cardboard. Within this enchanted landscape, a small boat drifted quietly downstream. Emma quickly shut the window and pulled the curtains tightly closed.

"I hate him, but I'll still pray for him," she said as she rested her tired head on the pillow where, just a few months earlier, she believed she would never lift it again. "Oh, if only I had died then! I don't dare love him, but I will pray for him!"

Sweet child! If the deceiver's face appears so frequently between you and Heaven, I fear for your destiny! The plant that grew from Helen's tears destroyed serpents—if only from yours might grow peace of mind—some plant, at least, to destroy the serpents in your heart. Believe me, only along the banks of heavenly streams do those healing herbs grow that can cure heartache!

The silent stars witnessed this scene from their place in the heavens above, yet they kept what they saw to themselves. Mrs.

Himmelhahn also observed these events from her bedroom window, but unlike the silent stars, she was not nearly as discreet.

———————

Chapter VI. Glimpses Into Cloud-Land.

"There are many things that, lacking physical evidence, can only be perceived and understood through the reasoning powers of the mind. Therefore, the unclear nature of matter can only be grasped through imperfect opinion. Matter serves as the foundation of all physical bodies and bears the imprint of various forms. Fire, air, and water originate and derive their essence from the scalene triangle. However, earth was formed from right-angled triangles, where two sides are of equal length. The sphere and pyramid embody the form of fire, while the octahedron was designed to represent air, and the icosahedron to represent water. The right-angled isosceles triangle creates a square from itself, and this square produces a cube, which is the distinctive shape of earth. The form of a beautiful and perfect sphere was given to the most beautiful and perfect world, so that it would lack nothing but contain everything, embracing and encompassing all things within itself, and thus would be excellent and wonderful, consistent with and harmonious to itself, always moving in a musical and melodious way. If I employ unfamiliar language, please forgive me. As Apuleius states, forgiveness must be extended to new words when they help clarify the mystery of things."

These words came from the lips of the lion-like philosopher, who has been mentioned before in these pages. He was sitting with Flemming, smoking a long pipe. As the Baron said, he was indeed a strange owl; for the owl is a serious bird; a monk, who sings midnight mass in the great temple of Nature;--a hermit,--a pillar saint,--the very Simeon Stylites of his neighborhood. Such, likewise, was the philosophical Professor. Solitary, but with a mighty current, flowed the river of his life, like the Nile, without a tributary stream, and making fertile only a single strip in the vast desert. His temperament had been in youth a joyful one; and now, amid all his sorrows and hardships, for he had many, he looked upon the world as a happy, bright, glorious world. On the many joys of life he gazed still with the eyes of childhood, from the far-gone Past upward, trusting, hoping;--and upon its sorrows with the eyes of age, from the distant Future, downward, triumphant, not despairing. He loved solitude, and silence, and candlelight, and the deep midnight. "For," said he, "if the morning hours are the wings of the day, I only fold them about me to sleep more sweetly; knowing that, at its other end, the day, like the birds of the air, has an epicurean morsel,--a parson's nose; and on this rich midnight my spirit revels and is glad."

The Professor had been speaking in a barely comprehensible manner for over two hours. The Baron had dozed off completely in his chair, but Flemming remained alert, listening with his imagination stirred, as the Professor went on with the following words, which, as far as his listener could recall, appeared to be gathered from various passages in Fichte's Destiny of Man and Shubert's History of the Soul.

"Life is one, and universal; its forms many and individual. Throughout this beautiful and wonderful creation there is never-ceasing motion, without rest by night or day, ever weaving to and fro. Swifter than a weaver's shuttle it flies from Birth to Death, from Death to Birth; from the beginning seeks the end, and finds it not, for the seeming end is only a dim beginning of a new out-going and endeavour after the end. As the ice upon the mountain, when the warm breath of the summer sun breathes upon it, melts, and divides into drops, each of which reflects an image of the sun; so life, in the smile of God's love, divides itself into separate forms, each bearing in it and reflecting an image of God's love. Of all these forms the highest and most perfect in its god-likeness is the human soul. The vast cathedral of Nature is full of holy scriptures, and shapes of deep, mysterious meaning; but all is solitary and silent there; no bending knee, no uplifted eye, no lip adoring, praying. Into this vast cathedral comes the human soul, seeking its Creator; and the universal silence is changed to sound, and the sound is harmonious, and has a meaning, and is comprehended and felt. It was an ancient saying of the Persians, that the waters rush from the mountains and hurry forth into all the lands to find the Lord of the Earth; and the flame of the Fire, when it awakes, gazes no more upon the ground, but mounts heavenward to seek the Lord of Heaven; and here and there the Earth has built the great watch-towers of the mountains, and they lift their heads far up into the sky, and gaze ever upward and around, to see if the Judge of the World comes not! Thus in Nature herself, without man, there lies a waiting, and hoping, a looking and yearning, after an unknown something. Yes; when, above there, where the mountain lifts its head over all others, that it may be alone with the clouds and storms of heaven, the lonely eagle looks forth into the gray dawn, to see if the day comes not! when, by the mountain torrent, the brooding raven listens to hear if the chamois is returning from his nightly pasture in the valley; and when the soon uprising sun calls out the spicy odors of the thousand flowers, the Alpine flowers, with heaven's deep blue and the blush of sunset on their leaves;--then there awakes in Nature, and the soul of man can see and comprehend it, an expectation and a longing for a future revelation of God's majesty. It awakens, also, when in the fullness of life, field and forest rest at noon, and through the stillness is heard only the song of the grasshopper and the hum of the bee; and when at evening the singing lark, up from the sweet-smelling vineyards rises, or in the later hours of night Orion puts on his shining armor, to walk forth in the fields of heaven. But in the soul of man alone is this longing changed to certainty and fulfilled. For behold! the light of the sun and the stars shines through the air, and is nowhere visible and seen; the planets hasten with more than the speed of the storm through infinite space, and their footsteps are not heard, but where the sunlight strikes the firm surface of the planets, where the stormwind strikes the wall of the mountain cliff, there is the one seen and the other heard. Thus is the glory of God made visible, and may be seen, where in the soul of man it meets its likeness changeless and firm-standing. Thus, then, stands Man;--a mountain on the boundary between two worlds;--its foot in one, its summit far-rising into the other. From this summit the manifold landscape of life is visible, the way of the Past and Perishable, which we have left behind us; and, as we evermore ascend, bright glimpses of the daybreak of Eternity beyond us!"

Flemming wanted to interrupt this conversation several times to respond and ask questions, but the Professor continued speaking, becoming increasingly animated and passionate. Finally, there was a brief pause, and Flemming said;

"All these vague longings—these yearnings for something unknown—I have felt and continue to feel within me; but I have not yet found their fulfillment."

"That is because you have not faith," answered the Professor. "The Present is an age of doubt and disbelief, and darkness; out of which shall arise a clear and bright Hereafter. In the second part of Goethe's Faust, there is a grand and striking scene, where in the classical Walpurgis Night, on the Pharsalian Plains, the mocking Mephistopheles sits down between the solemn antique Sphinxes, and boldly questions them, and reads their riddles. The red light of countless watch-fires blazes all around, and shines upon the terrible face of the arch-mocker; while on either side, stern, majestic, solemnly peaceful, we see the gigantic forms of the children of Chimera, half buried in the earth, their gentle eyes staring steadily, as if they heard through the midnight, the swift-rushing wings of the Stymphalides, trying to outrun the speed of

Alcides' arrows! Angry griffins are near them; and not far are Sirens, singing their wonderful songs from the swaying branches of the willow trees! Just like this does a mocking and unbelieving Present sit down, between an unknown Future and a too believing Past, and question and challenge the gigantic forms of faith, half buried in the sands of Time, and gazing forward steadily into the night, while sounds of anger and voices of delight alternately trouble and comfort the ear of man!--But the time will come, when the soul of man shall return again childlike and trusting to its faith in God; and look God in the face and die; for it is an old saying, full of deep, mysterious meaning, that he must die, who has looked upon a God. And this is the fate of the soul, that it should die continually. No sooner here on earth does it awaken to its unique being, than it struggles to see and understand the Spirit of Life. In the first dim twilight of its existence, it sees this spirit, is filled by its energies,--is quick and creative like the spirit itself, and yet falls away into death after having seen it. But the image it has seen, remains, in the eternal creation, as a unified existence, is again renewed, and the apparent death, from moment to moment, becomes the source of kind after kind of existences in ever-rising series. The soul reaches ever onward to love and to see. It sees the image more perfect in the brightening twilight of the dawn, in the ever higher-rising sun. It sleeps again, dying in the clearer vision; but the image seen remains as a permanent kind; and the sleeper awakens anew and ever higher after its own image, until at length, in the full blaze of noonday, a being comes forth, which, like the eagle, can look upon the sun and not die. Then both live on, even when this bodily element, the mist and vapor through which the young eagle gazed, dissolves and falls to earth.

"I'm not sure I understand what you're saying," Flemming replied, "but if I do, you're suggesting that just as the body constantly changes and takes on new characteristics, and isn't the same today as it was yesterday, the soul also sheds its peculiarities and transforms by gaining new abilities, and in this way could be said to die. Therefore, strictly speaking, the soul always exists in the present moment and has no future—because the future becomes the present, and the soul that will live in me then will be a higher and more perfect soul, and this continues forever."

"I mean exactly what I say," the Professor continued, "and I cannot find more suitable words to express my thoughts than those I have already used. But as I mentioned before, you must forgive the unusual nature of my language when it helps clarify things that are difficult to understand. I believe you will clearly see from what I have explained that this earthly life, when viewed later from heaven, will appear like an hour that passed long ago and is only faintly remembered. Despite being long, difficult, and filled with both happiness and sorrow, it will have shrunk to nothing more than a tiny dot, barely visible to the far-seeing vision of the spirit freed from its body. But the spirit itself continues to rise upward. Therefore, death is neither an ending nor a beginning. It is a passage not from one existence to another, but from one condition of existence to another. No connection is severed in the chain of being, just as none is broken when we move from childhood to adulthood, or from adulthood to old age. There are periods of deep thought and contemplation that seem to me similar to death. The soul slowly loses its awareness of what is happening around it and no longer notices nearby objects. For that moment, it appears to have severed its connection with the body. It has moved into a different state of being. It exists in another world. It has traveled across lands and oceans and communicates with those it loves in far-off places on earth and in the even more distant heaven. It sees familiar faces and hears cherished voices that the physical senses can no longer see or hear. This too is death, except that when we die, the soul never returns to the home it has abandoned."

"You seem to assume," Flemming interrupted, "that when we daydream, our soul actually leaves our body and travels to faraway places, rather than creating their likeness within ourselves through the power of memory and imagination!"

"Something I must take for granted," the Professor replied. "We won't discuss that point now. I don't speak without careful thought. Just observe what a magnificent thing human life becomes when viewed in this light, and how magnificent our destiny is. I am; you are; he is! This might seem like nothing more than a schoolboy's grammar lesson. But within these words lies a profound mystery. These simple phrases carry deep meaning. We see all around us one vast unity, where no person can work for themselves without simultaneously working for everyone else; a glimpse of truth that, through the universal harmony of all things, becomes an inner blessing and lifts the soul powerfully upward. This becomes even more true when someone sees themselves as an essential member of this unity. The sense of our dignity and our strength grows powerful when we tell ourselves: My existence isn't meaningless or pointless; I am a vital link in the great chain that stretches from the full awakening of consciousness in the first human being forward into eternity. All the great, wise, and good people throughout history, all those who have benefited humanity whose names I read in the world's history, and the even greater number of those whose good works have outlasted their names—all of them have worked for me. I have inherited their achievements. I walk the green earth where they once lived. I follow in their footsteps, from which blessings continue to grow. I can take on the noble task they once undertook: the mission of making our shared humanity wiser and happier. I can continue building where they were forced to stop, bringing closer to completion the great structure they left unfinished. And eventually I, too, must leave it behind and depart. Oh, this is the most sublime thought of all! I can never complete this noble task;

therefore, as surely as this task is my destiny, I can never stop working, and consequently never stop existing. What people call death cannot interrupt this never-ending task; therefore no limit is placed on my existence, and I am eternal. I raise my head boldly to the threatening mountain peaks, to the thundering waterfall, and to the storm clouds floating in the fiery sea above and declare: I am eternal, and I challenge your power! Crash down upon me! And you, Earth, and you, Heaven, merge in wild chaos! And you elements, foam and rage, and destroy this speck of dust—this body that I call mine! My will alone, with its unwavering purpose, shall soar brave and victorious over the ruins of the universe; for I have understood my destiny, and it is more lasting than you are! It is eternal; and I, who recognize it, am likewise eternal! Tell me, my friend, don't you have faith in this?"

"I have," Flemming replied, and another silence followed. Then he said;

"I have listened to you patiently and without interruption. Now listen to me. You complain about the skepticism of our time. This represents one way the philosophical spirit of our age shows itself. Let me tell you that another form it takes is that of poetic daydreaming. Plato in ancient times had dreams like these, as did the Mystics of the Middle Ages, and their followers still wander in the cloud-filled dreamland of this poetic philosophy. Pleasant and cool upon their souls rest the shadows of the trees under which Plato taught. From their whispering leaves comes a solemn and mysterious sound that drifts across the noise of crowded centuries, which to them represents the voice of the World's Soul. All of nature has become spiritualized and transformed, and wrapped in beautiful, vague dreams of the real and the ideal, they live in this green world like the little child in the German tale who sits by the edge of a woodland lake and hears the blue heaven and the branches overhead argue with their reflection in the water about which is reality and which is the image. I freely admit that such daydreams as these strongly appeal to my imagination. They are visitors and companions to those lofty souls who, soaring ever higher and higher, build themselves nests under the very edges of the stars, forgetting that they cannot live on air but must come down to earth for food. Yet I recognize them as daydreams only, as shadows rather than substantial things. What I mainly dislike about the New Philosophy is the cool arrogance with which an old idea, wrapped in new clothing, looks you in the face and pretends not to know you, even though you have been close friends since childhood. I remember an English author who, when speaking of your German Philosophies, says very wisely: 'Often a proposition of mysterious and frightening appearance, when boldly confronted and torn from its shadowy hiding place and its bristling defenses of strange terminology—and dragged forth into the open light of day to be seen by the natural eye and tested by merely human understanding—proves to be a very harmless truth, familiar to us from long ago, sometimes so familiar as to be obvious. Too often the anxious beginner is reminded of Dryden in the Battle of the Books; there is a helmet of rusty iron, dark, grim, gigantic; and within it, at the farthest corner, is a head no bigger than a walnut.'—Can you believe that these words ever came from the lips of Carlyle! He has himself adopted the strange terminology lately, and many pure, simple minds are greatly offended by it. They seem to take it as a personal insult. They are angry and deny him the just reward of praise. However, it is hardly worthwhile to lose our composure. Let us instead benefit as we can, even from this spectacle, and recognize the monarch in his disguise. For, hooded and wrapped in that strange and ancient garb, there walks a kingly, a most royal soul, just as the Emperor Charles walked among solemn cloisters under a monk's hood— still a monarch in soul. Such things are not new in the history of the world. From time to time they sweep over the earth and blow themselves out quickly, and then there is quiet for a while, and the atmosphere of Truth seems more peaceful. Why would you preach to the wind? Why argue with thunderstorms? Better to sit quietly and watch them pass over like a parade, cloudy, magnificent, and vast."

The Professor smiled with self-satisfaction, but didn't say a word. Flemming continued;

"I will add no more than this: there are many theories in Literature, Philosophy, and Religion that, while enjoyable to explore and backed by distinguished authorities, ultimately lead nowhere significant. They are like those paths in the western forests of my homeland that start out wide and inviting, running beneath the shade of massive trees, but eventually narrow to nothing more than a squirrel's trail that ends up a tree trunk!"

The Professor wasn't sure whether he should laugh or feel insulted by this witty remark; placing his hand on Flemming's arm, he said with a serious tone;

"Believe me, my young friend, the time will come when you will think more wisely about these matters. And I trust that time will arrive soon for you, since it comes more quickly for some people than for others. But what exactly is Time? Is it the shadow on the sundial, the chiming of the clock, the flowing of sand through an hourglass, day and night, summer and winter, months, years, centuries? These are merely arbitrary and external markers—ways to measure Time, not Time itself! Time is the Life of the Soul. If it's not this, then tell me what it is?"

The Professor's loud and excited voice woke the Baron from his sleep. Not clearly understanding what had been said, but thinking the Professor was asking about the time, he innocently called out:

"I think it must be close to midnight!"

This left the Professor feeling somewhat unsettled, and he departed shortly after. Once he had gone, the Baron said;

"Excuse me for treating your guest so dismissively. His transcendentalism irritated me quite a bit, and I sought escape in sleep. One would think, judging by the way this group talks, that they alone can see any beauty in Nature. When I listen to one of them speak, I'm immediately reminded of Goethe's Baccalaureus, when he declares: 'The world didn't exist before I created it; I brought the sun up from the sea; the moon's changing cycle began with me; the day adorned itself for my sake; the earth turned green and bloomed to greet me; at my command on that first night, all the magnificent stars revealed themselves; who but I freed you from all the constraints of narrow-minded, limiting thoughts? I, however, liberated as my mind convinces me I am, happily follow my inner light, boldly moving forward in my own unique ecstasy, with brightness ahead of me and darkness behind!'—Don't you see the similarity? Oh, they could be humble enough to admit that one wandering beam of light might, by chance, reach the blind eyes of even us poor, unenlightened heathens?"

"Oh! how little respect we show!" Flemming said. "I couldn't help ending the conversation with a joke. An inappropriate sense of humor often catches me off guard. Whenever this happens, I remember a scene from the University, where during a serious debate about the possibility of Absolute Motion, a student mentioned that he had witnessed a rock crack open, releasing a toad that couldn't possibly have any understanding of the outside world, and therefore its movement must have been absolute. The distinguished Professor who was leading that discussion was barely more shocked and amazed than our distinguished Professor was just five minutes ago. But come on; wind your watch, and let's go to sleep."

"By the way," said the Baron, "did you notice what an unusual head he has? There are two crowns on it."

"That's a sign," Flemming replied, "that he will eat his bread in two kingdoms."

"I think the poor man would be very grateful," said the Baron with a smile, "if he could always be certain of eating it all at once. He is what the Transcendentalists call a god-intoxicated man; and I advise him, as Sauteul advised Bossuet, to go to Patmos and write a new Apocalypse."

Chapter VII. Mill-Wheels and Other Wheels.

A few days later, the Baron received letters from his sister informing him that her doctors had recommended several weeks at the Baths of Ems, and she was urging him to join her there before the fashionable season began.

"Come," he said to Flemming, "take this short trip with me. We'll spend a few enjoyable days at Ems and explore the other spa towns of Nassau. It will chase away those gloomy daydreams that trouble you. Maybe your future wife is waiting for you right now at the Serpent's Bath, feeling vague premonitions and unexplained yearnings."

"Or some widow from Ems, with a cork leg!" said Flemming, smiling; and then added, in a tone of voice half joking, half serious, "Certainly; let us go in pursuit of her;--
Whoever she may be,
That woman who is not impossible to find,
That will control my heart and me.
Wherever she lies,
Hidden from human sight,
In shady leaves of destiny.' "

They began their journey to Frankfurt in the afternoon, traveling slowly along the beautiful Bergstrasse, which is famous throughout Germany for its stunning scenery. They passed by the ruins of the house where Martin Luther had hidden after the Diet of Worms, and continued through the village of

Handschuhsheimer, which dates back to the time of King Pepin the Short—a small settlement nestled beneath the hills, almost completely covered in blossoms and green foliage. The mountains of the mysterious Odenwald rose up close by on the right side, while on the left lay the Neckar River, resembling a steel bow stretched across the meadow. Further to the west, a thin, smoky haze revealed where the Rhine flowed, and beyond that river, the blue, rolling hills of Alsace stretched out like a restless sea. The air was filled with birdsong, the sound of evening church bells, and the sweet scent of flowering trees, while the large red sun slowly and quietly descended, partially concealed behind layers of clouds.

"We won't be spending the night at Weinheim," the Baron told the postilion, who had gotten down from his horse to walk up the hill that led to the town. "You can drive to the mill in the Valley of Birkenau."

The postman grabbed one of his heavy horses by the tail and pulled himself back up onto his seat. They clattered through the cobblestone streets of Weinheim, paying no attention to the innkeeper of the Golden Eagle, who stood so welcomingly at the entrance of his tavern; and the remains of Burg Windeck, high above on its mountainous perch, glowered down at them for rushing past without stopping to pay their respects.

"The old ruins look impressive from down here in the valley," the Baron said, "but we should avoid climbing that steep hill. Most travelers behave like children—they feel compelled to touch everything they see. They scramble up to every crumbling remnant of a castle they encounter along their route, enduring a difficult climb and blazing sun for their trouble, only to come back down exhausted and let down. I hope we have better judgment than that."

They crossed the bridge and turned upstream, walking beneath a stone archway that acts as an entrance to this magical Valley of Birkenau. What a cool and beautiful valley it was! Enclosed by towering hills and shaded by alder trees and tall poplars, beneath which flows the Wechsnitz, a rushing mountain stream that frequently lends its powerful force to turn mill wheels, proving it can work just as well as it can sing. They decided to spend the night at one of these mills.

A mill stands as a defining feature of the romantic German countryside, just as it does in romantic German stories. It serves not only as a mill, but also as a tavern and country inn, so the images it brings to mind involve not just work, but enjoyment as well. It sits in the narrow valley pass, with its charming, straw-covered roof; peasants gather there on holidays, and rustic dances take place beneath the trees.

In the fading light of the quickly approaching summer evening, the Baron and Flemming walked together along the banks of the stream. As they listened to it rushing and flowing among the stones and twisted roots, and the large wheel turning in the current with its constant splash! splash! it reminded them of that beautiful, simple song by Goethe, the Youth and the Mill-brook. For a moment, it seemed like a water spirit singing to them through the voice of the flowing water.

"I'm convinced," said Flemming, "that to truly understand and appreciate the folk poetry of Germany, you need to be familiar with the German countryside. Many charming little poems are expressions of spontaneous emotions—words that find their perfect accompaniment in birdsong, the whisper of leaves, and the babbling of fresh streams. Or perhaps I should say they are words that people have set to nature's own music. Can't you hear it right now, this little brook telling you how it flows toward the mill, where at dawn the miller's daughter opens her window and comes down to wash her face in its waters, and her chest is so full and pale that it stirs the flame of love in those cool waters!"

"A truly delightful ballad," said the Baron. "But like many of our simple songs, it needs a poet to feel and understand it. Sing them in the valley and among woodland shadows, beneath the leafy canopies of garden paths, at night, and in solitude, as they were meant to be sung. Don't sing them in the noisy world—for the noisy world mocks such things. It is Mueller who says, in that little song where the maiden wishes the moon good evening;

This song was created to be sung at night,
And anyone who reads it in broad daylight,
Will never understand the mystery correctly;
"And yet it's incredibly simple!"

He has written many beautiful songs that express the fleeting, vague yearnings and impulses of the human soul. He calls them the songs of a Wandering Horn-player. One of them is particularly relevant to our current discussion. In it, he captures the feeling of restlessness and the urge to move that the sight and sound of flowing water often awakens in us. It is titled 'Whither?' and is worth sharing with you.

I heard a small stream flowing
From its rocky spring nearby,
Down into the valley rushing,
So fresh and wonderfully clear.
I don't know what came over me,
Nor who gave the advice;
But I must hurry downward,
All with my pilgrim's staff.
Downward, and ever farther,
And always the brook flowing nearby;
And murmured ever more freshly,
And the tide becomes ever clearer.
Is this the way I was going?
Where are you going, little brook?
You have, with your gentle whisper,
Whispered my senses into oblivion.
What do I say of a murmur?
That cannot be a murmur;

It's the water nymphs that are singing
Their songs and dances beneath me.
Let them sing, my friend, let them murmur,
And wander happily nearby;
The mill's wheels are turning.
In every clear little brook.'

"There you have the poetic reverie," Flemming said, "and the dull prose commentary and explanation in matter of fact. The song is beautiful; and was probably inspired by some scene like this one we're looking at right now. Without a doubt, all your old national traditions emerged in the popular mind just as this song did in the poet's."

"You're absolutely right," the Baron replied; "but all this imaginative poetry doesn't stop me from feeling the cold night air and the sharp pangs of hunger. Let's head back to the mill and see what our hostess has prepared for supper. Did you notice how loud and shrill her voice is?"

"People who live in mills and near waterfalls always have."

The next morning they reluctantly left the green, shadowy valley and traveled along the flat highway to Frankfurt, where that evening they attended Mozart's magnificent Don Giovanni. This opera was Flemming's absolute favorite. What ecstatic soaring melodies! What stirring, moving harmonies! What untamed, exuberant celebration of passion! What intoxication of the senses!--what an expression of torment and sorrow! All the emotions of suffering and celebrating humanity resonated with and found expression in those musical notes. Flemming and the Baron listened with growing enchantment.

"How wonderful this is!" exclaimed Flemming, overwhelmed by his emotions. "How the chorus rises and falls, like a summer breeze! How those mysterious passages seem to sway back and forth, like tree branches moving in the wind; from which suddenly a single sweet voice breaks free like a bird, floating away to revel in the bright, warm sunlight! And then notice! how, within the chorus of a hundred voices and a hundred instruments—flutes, drums, and trumpets—this universal cry and whirlwind of turbulent air, you can still clearly hear the melancholy vibration of a single string, touched by a finger—a mournful, weeping sound! Ah, this is truly human life! where in the rushing, noisy crowd, amid sounds of joy and a thousand mixed emotions, clearly audible to the thoughtful ear, are the beats of some sad string of the heart, touched by an unseen hand."

Then came, in the midst of these excited feelings, the ballet; drawing its magic net about the soul. And soon, from the tangled yet harmonious mazes of the dance, came forth a sylph-like form, her scarf floating behind her, as if she were fanning the air with gauze-like wings. Silent as a feather or a snowflake falls, her feet touched the earth. She seemed to float in the air, and the floor appeared to bend and wave beneath her, like a branch when a bird lands upon it and takes flight again. Loud and enthusiastic applause followed each wonderful step, each graceful movement; and, with a flushed cheek and burning eye, and chest breathing heavily to be free, stood the gracefully majestic figure for a moment still, and then the swift feet of the quick dancing-girls flashed around her, and she was lost again in the crowd.

"This is absolutely beautiful!" the Baron exclaimed, clapping enthusiastically along with the crowd. "What an impressive presence! Such elegance! Such poise! There's so much emotion in every movement! So much meaning in each gesture! I tell you, it affects me the same way a beautiful poem does. It is poetry. Each step is like a word, and everything together forms a complete poem!"

The Baron and Flemming were thrilled by the performance, and they were also greatly entertained by watching an elderly, prudish woman in the neighboring box, who appeared to view the entire magical spectacle with the same disapproval that Michal,

Saul's daughter, felt when she gazed from her window and witnessed King David dancing and jumping in his minimal clothing.

"After all," said Flemming, "the old French priest wasn't so far off the mark when he said, in his rough dialect, that dancing is the Devil's procession; and makeup and decorations are the sharpening of the devil's sword; and the circle formed in dancing is the devil's grindstone, where he hones his blade; and finally, that a ballet is the ceremony and mass of the Devil, and whoever enters it joins his ceremony and mass; for the woman who sings is the Devil's prioress, and those who respond are his clerks, and those who watch are his parishioners, and the cymbals and flutes are his bells, and the musicians who play are the Devil's ministers."

"I'm sure this fine lady sitting near us feels the same way," the Baron replied with a laugh, "but she enjoys it nonetheless."

When the play ended, the Baron asked Flemming to remain seated until the crowd had left.

"I have an odd fascination," he said, "whenever I visit the theater, with seeing how everything ends. After the audience has left and the curtain is raised once more to ventilate the building, with all the lights extinguished except for a few scattered ones backstage, the contrast with what came before is deeply moving. Everything takes on a dreamlike quality. The vacant boxes and seats, the quiet, the hazy dusk, and the magical set now stripped bare create within me an unusual, enigmatic sensation. It resembles a faint reflection of a theater in water, or in a grimy mirror, and brings to mind some of Hoffmann's fantastical Tales. It serves as a tangible moral teaching, a reflection on the performance, and makes the entire experience whole."

It was exactly as he had described, only ten times more bleak, solemn, and striking, creating in the mind the same effect we feel when sleep is suddenly interrupted and dreams blend with reality, leaving us uncertain whether we're still asleep or awake. As they finally made their way through the poorly lit corridor, they overheard a coarse-looking man with a lustful face and unkempt whiskers speaking to some people standing nearby, who appeared to be theater regulars.

"I'll run her for six nights in Munich, and then take her on to Vienna."

Flemming believed he was talking about some cherished horse. He was actually talking about his beautiful wife, the ballet dancer.

Chapter VIII. Old Humbug.

What fascinated our travelers most in the ancient city of Frankfurt wasn't the opera or Dannecker's Ariadne, but rather the house where Goethe was born and the places he visited during his childhood that he still remembered in his later years. These included, for instance, the walking paths that circled the city beyond the moat; the bridge spanning the Main River with its golden rooster perched on the cross, which the poet had gazed upon with wonder as a child; the monastery of the Barefoot Friars, through which he would sneak with reverent fear to sit beside old Rector Albrecht's oilcloth-covered table; and the garden where his grandfather would pace back and forth among the fruit trees and rose bushes, dressed in his long morning robe, black velvet cap, and those antique leather gloves he received each year as Mayor on Piper's Day of Judgment, cutting a figure somewhere between Alcinous and Laertes. This is how your footsteps become sacred, O Genius! And the star shines eternally above the place where you were born.

"Your English critics can complain all they want," said the Baron, as he and Flemming walked back from their stroll through the lush gardens beyond the moat; "but when all is said and done, Goethe was a truly magnificent man. Just consider his life; his passionate youth, swinging between hope and despair, turbulent, reckless, and headstrong;--his romantic middle years, when passion transformed into strength; diligent, meticulous, laboring tirelessly, never rushing, never resting; and his sublime old age,-- that period of peaceful and classical tranquility, where he stands like Atlas, as Claudian depicted him in the Battle of the Giants, supporting the world above his head, the ocean currents frozen solid in his gray hair."

"A perfect example of what the world labels his indifference."

"And do you know, I actually find this indifference quite appealing? Have you ever had the misfortune of living in a community where any parish problem seemed to signal the end of the world? Or have you known one of those supposed benefactors of humanity during the height of their reckless enthusiasm? If you have, I think you'll find something beautiful in the calm and dignified stance that the old philosopher takes."

"It's unfortunate that his admirers didn't possess even a fraction of this philosophical composure. I find it entertaining to read the different labels they attach to him: The Dear, dear Man! The Life-enjoying Man! The All-sided One! The Representative of Poetry upon earth! The Many-sided Master-Mind of Germany! His critics swing to the opposite extreme, hurling harsh accusations like Old Humbug! and Old Heathen! which strike with the force of pistol shots."

"I admit, he was no saint."

"No; his philosophy is the old ethnic philosophy. You'll find it all in a convenient, concentrated, and portable form in Horace's beautiful Ode to Thaliarcus. What I object to most in the old gentleman is his sensuality."

"Oh nonsense. Nothing can be purer than the Iphigenia; it is as cold and passionless as a marble statue."

"That's absolutely true; but you can't say the same thing about some of the Roman Elegies and that terrible book the Elective

Affinities."

"Ah, my friend, Goethe is an artist who views everything simply as subjects for his art. Why shouldn't he be permitted to recreate in words what painters and sculptors recreate with colors and marble?"

"The artist reveals his character through the subjects he chooses to portray. Goethe never created a sculpture of Apollo or painted a Madonna. Instead, he presents us only with fallen Magdalens and wild Fauns. Rather than idealizing his subjects, he brings them to life as they truly are."

"He only copies nature."

"The same was true for the artists who created the bronze lamps of Pompeii. Would you display one of those in your entrance hall? Simply saying that someone is an artist who copies nature isn't sufficient. There are two major schools of art: the imitative and the imaginative. The latter is the more noble and more lasting, and Goethe belonged more to the former. Have you read Menzel's criticism of him?"

"It's absolutely brutal. The Swabian is attacking him with fierce determination. I hope you're not taking his side."

"Absolutely not. He's going overboard. He's criticizing the poet for not being a politician. He might just as well criticize him for not being a missionary to the Sandwich Islands."

"And what do you think of Eckermann?"

"I think he's a sycophant; a sort of German Boswell. Goethe was aware that his portrait was being painted, and he posed accordingly. He works extremely hard to transform an old Jupiter into a Saint Peter, just as the Catholics did in Rome."

"Well, call him Old Humbug, or Old Heathen, or whatever you like; I maintain that, despite all his mistakes and shortcomings, he was a magnificent example of a man."

"He definitely was. Have you ever thought that in some ways he resembled Ben Franklin? Like a poetic version of Ben Franklin?

His practical way of thinking was identical; his passion for science was identical; his kind, philosophical nature was identical; and many of his brief poetic sayings and wise observations appear to be nothing more than the practical wisdom of Poor Richard, put into verse."

"What bothers me most is that now every German fool feels they must take a shot at the dead lion."

"And everyone who passes through Weimar must throw a book upon his grave, just as travelers of old threw a stone upon the grave of Manfredi at Benevento. But of all that has been said or sung, what pleases me most is Heine's Apologetic, if I may call it that; in which he says that the minor poets who flourished under the imperial reign of Goethe 'resemble a young forest, where the trees first show their own size after the hundred-year-old oak, whose branches had towered above and overshadowed them, has fallen. There was no shortage of opposition that fought against Goethe, this majestic tree. Men of the most conflicting opinions united themselves for the battle. The supporters of the old faith, the orthodox believers, were annoyed that in the trunk of the vast tree, no niche with its holy image could be found; indeed, that even the naked Dryads of paganism were allowed to practice their magic there; and gladly, with consecrated axe, would they have imitated the holy Boniface and brought the enchanted oak crashing to the ground. The followers of the new faith, the apostles of liberalism, were annoyed on the other hand that the tree could not serve as the Tree of Liberty, or at least as a barricade. In fact the tree was too tall; no one could place the red cap upon its summit or dance the Carmagnole beneath its branches. The multitude, however, revered this tree for the very reason that it raised itself with such independent grandeur and so graciously filled the world with its fragrance, while its branches, streaming magnificently toward heaven, made it appear as if the stars were only the golden fruit of its wondrous limbs.' Don't you think that beautiful?"

"Yes, very beautiful. And I'm happy to see that you can find something to admire in my favorite author, despite his flaws; or, to use an old German saying, that you can drive the hens out of the garden without trampling down the flower beds."

"Here is the old gentleman himself!" exclaimed Flemming.

"Where!" the Baron shouted, as though he momentarily expected to see the poet's living form walking ahead of them.

"Here at the window—that full-length sculpture. Excellent, isn't it! He's dressed, as always, in his long yellow cotton coat, with a white necktie crossed at the front. What a magnificent head! And what a pose! He stands like a tower of strength. And, by God! He was nearly eighty years old when that was created."

"How do you know?"

"You can see by the date on the pedestal."

"You're absolutely right. But look at how upright he stands, with those broad shoulders pulled back and his hands clasped behind him. He appears as though he's standing in front of a fireplace. I'm almost tempted to place a glowing ember in his hand—it's positioned so invitingly, half-open like that. Gleim's portrayal of him, written shortly after his arrival in Weimar, presents quite a different picture. Do you remember it?"

"No, I do not."

"It is a story that good old father Gleim used to tell with great delight. He was one evening reading the Göttingen Musen-Almanach in a select society at Weimar, when a young man came in, dressed in a short, green shooting-jacket, booted and spurred, and having a pair of brilliant, black, Italian eyes. He in turn offered to read; but finding probably the poetry of the Musen-Almanach of that year rather too bland for him, he soon began to improvise the wildest and most fantastic poems imaginable, and in all possible forms and measures, all the while pretending to read from the book. 'That is either Goethe or the Devil,' said good old father Gleim to Wieland, who sat near him. To which the 'Great I of

Osmannstadt' replied; 'It is both, for he has the Devil in him tonight; and at such times he is like a wild colt, that kicks out in front and behind, and you would do well not to go too near him!'"

"Very good!"

"And now that noble figure has turned to dust. Just a few months ago, those magnificent eyes saw daylight for the final time on a beautiful spring morning. Peaceful, like a deity, the elderly man sat there; and with a smile appeared to say goodbye to the daylight, which he had witnessed for more than eighty years. Books surrounded him, along with the pen that had recently fallen, as if from his dying hands. 'Open the shutters, and let in more light!' were the final words that escaped those lips. Slowly extending his hand, he appeared to write in the air; and, as it lowered back down and became still, the spirit of the old man passed away."

"And yet the world continues. It's strange how quickly, when a great man dies, his position is filled; and so completely, that he no longer seems necessary. But let us go in here. I want to buy that cast and send it home to a friend."

Chapter IX. The Daylight of The Dwarfs, And the Falling Star.

After spending a day or two in Frankfurt, the two friends traveled across through Hochheim to the Rhine, then up into the hills of the Rheingau to Schlangenbad, where they stopped only to bathe and dine before continuing their journey to Langenschwalbach. The town sits in a valley, surrounded by gently sloping hills, with long avenues of poplar trees extending out into the countryside. One endless street divides the town in half, and there are old houses with intricate faces carved on their facades, bearing dates from bygone eras.

Our travelers quickly left their hotel, eager to drink the strengthening waters from the springs. They walked far up the valley beneath the poplar trees. Fresh grain swayed in the fields, birds sang in the trees and through the air, and everything appeared joyful, except for a poor old man who came stumbling out of the woods with a heavy bundle of sticks on his shoulders.

Retracing their path, they walked down through the valley and along the lengthy street until they reached the crumbling old Lutheran church. A set of stone steps led up from the street to the green terrace or platform where the church stood, which in earlier times had served as the churchyard, or as the Germans more reverently called it, God's-acre; where generations lie scattered like seeds, and what is planted in decay shall rise again in eternal life. On the steps stood an elderly man—an extremely elderly man— holding a small girl's hand. He removed his worn cap as they walked by and bid them good day. His teeth were missing; he could barely speak clearly. The Baron inquired about the age of the church. He gave no response; but when the question was asked again, he moved closer to them, and removing his cap once more, turned his ear toward them with attention, and said;

"I have trouble hearing."

"Poor old man," said Flemming. "He's just as much a ruin as the church we're walking into. It won't be long before he's also planted like a seed in this graveyard!"

The little girl ran to a nearby house and returned with a large key. The church door swung open, and after going down several steps, they walked through a low-ceilinged corridor into the church. Everything was in ruins. The tombstones in the floor had shifted from their original positions; the underground burial chambers gaped open; the ceiling overhead was crumbling piece by piece; there were cracks in the ancient tower; and there were hidden passageways and side doors with rickety wooden staircases that led down into the graveyard. Among all this destruction, only one thing remained standing upright; it was a statue of an armored knight, positioned in an alcove beneath the pulpit.

"Who is this?" Flemming asked the old sexton. "Who is this figure that stands here so solemnly in marble, appearing to keep watch over the dead below?"

"I don't know," the old man replied, "but I heard my grandfather say it was the statue of a great warrior!"

"Now that's history for you!" the Baron declared. "That's what fame really amounts to! You get a marble statue erected in your honor, but then your name gets completely forgotten by the very sexton of your own parish, who can only recall that he once heard his grandfather mention you were some kind of great warrior!"

Flemming didn't respond, as his thoughts drifted to the days when a courageous reformer had thundered the first news of a revolutionary doctrine from that ancient pulpit, and the ceiling had resonated with the magnificent old hymns of Martin Luther.

When he shared his thoughts with the Baron, the only response he received was;

"After all, what's the point of all this preaching? Do you really think the fish that listened to St. Anthony's sermon were any better than those that didn't? I recommend you take a look at this saint's fish-sermon, as written down by Abraham à Santa Clara. You'll find it in your beloved Wonder-Horn."

The day at Langenschwalbach passed in this way, and the evening at the Allée-Saal was completely quiet, since no guests had yet arrived to occupy its rooms or sit beneath the trees in front of the entrance. By the following morning, even Flemming and the Baron had departed; the German's heart was pounding with eager longing to hold his sister in his arms, while his friend's heart didn't much care where he traveled, as long as he wasn't left too much by himself.

After a few hours of driving, they found themselves looking down from a hilltop directly onto the rooftops of Ems. The town lay there, nestled deep in the valley below them, as if some giant from Sirius, like the one described in Voltaire's tale of Micromegas, was holding it in the palm of his hand. Tall, sharp hills rose around them, casting their shadows into this picturesque valley, while the river Lahn wound along at their base. The travelers drove through the single main street, which consisted entirely of hotels and boarding houses. Sick visitors peered out from windows as they passed by. Others strolled slowly back and forth beneath the few bare trees that served as the public walkway, and a boy wearing a blue coat and red cap was herding three donkeys down the street. In essence, they had arrived at a fashionable spa town, one that had so far been touched by only a few scattered drops of the summer shower of visitors that typically arrives after the first warm days of the season.

When the Baron arrived at the London Hotel, he discovered not his sister waiting for him, but merely a letter from her explaining that she had changed her mind and traveled to the Baths of Franconia instead. This disappointment was something the Baron quietly accepted along with the letter, and he spoke no further about either matter. This was simply his nature; his approach to life's philosophy whether dealing with minor inconveniences or major events. That evening, they attended an aesthetic tea at the home of Frau Kranich, who was married to a wealthy banker from Frankfurt.

"I need to tell you about this Frau Kranich," the Baron said to Flemming as they walked. "She's a woman of talent and beauty, right in her prime. But unfortunately, she's extremely ambitious. Her obsession is making a name for herself in high society, and to achieve this goal she married a wealthy Frankfurt banker old enough to be her father, if not her grandfather, probably hoping he would die soon—because if any woman ever wanted to become a widow, it's her. But the old man is resilient and refuses to die. What's more, he's deaf, irritable, and stingy, and spends half his time bedridden. Despite her flaws, his wife is a model of virtue. She cares for the old gentleman as if he were a child. And to make matters worse, he despises society and won't allow his wife to entertain guests or go out socially."

"How can she possibly host evening parties then?" asked Flemming.

"I was just about to tell you," the Baron went on. "The cheerful lady has no desire for long evenings with the old gentleman in the back room—for being chained like a prisoner under Mezentius, face to face with a corpse. So she puts him to bed first, and—"

"Gives him opium."

"Yes, I imagine so; and then she throws herself a party without him knowing anything about it. This pattern of deception is truly despicable in itself, and must be especially painful for her, since she isn't a vulgar or immoral woman; but rather one of those who, lacking the strength to complete the sacrifice they had the courage to begin, find themselves trapped in a life of duplicity and lies."

They had now arrived at the house and were led into a brightly lit room full of guests. The hostess approached to greet them, wearing white and gliding across the room like a swan. After the usual greetings had been exchanged and Flemming had been properly introduced, the Baron spoke with a hint of mischief in his voice;

"And, my dear Mrs. Kranich, how is your good husband tonight?"

This question was about as subtle as a cannonball. But the lady responded with genuine innocence, completely unfazed by it.

"Same as always, my dear Baron. It's amazing how he keeps going. But let's not discuss these matters right now. I need to introduce your friend to his fellow countryman, the Grand Duke of Mississippi, who's equally notable for his wealth, his humility, and the remarkable simplicity of his behavior. He only drives six horses. Furthermore, he's recognized as a man of scholarship and devotion—he has his own private chapel and personal clergyman, who consistently preaches against the emptiness of material wealth. He also employs a private secretary whose only job is to smoke for him, so he can enjoy the fragrance of Spanish cigars without the effort of actually smoking."

"Definitely a man of genius!"

Here Flemming met his distinguished fellow countryman, a man who appeared to be made mostly of fabric, given the impressive show he put on with his collar, shirt front, and cuffs.

"Tell me, Mr. Flemming, what do you think of that Rembrandt?" he said, pointing to a painting on the wall. "Magnificent piece! The nobility of feeling and brilliance of light and shadow are absolutely first-rate. Just look at how fluid the water appears, and how silvery those clouds seem! Such mastery! There's a boldness of technique in that painting, Sir, that takes a trained eye to truly understand."

"Yes, absolutely—a copy!"

And that's where their conversation came to an end; at that very moment, the little Moldavian Prince Jerkin pushed his way through the crowd, carrying his snuff-box in his hand as always, and rushed over to Flemming, whom he had met in Heidelberg. He was anxious to show everyone that he could speak English, and in his eagerness he started off by making an error.

"Goodbye! Goodbye! Mr. Flemming!" he said, instead of good evening. "I am delighted to see you in Ems. Nice place—everything here is absolutely wonderful. I drink my water and feel great! Don't you think Mrs. Kranich has very beautiful skin?"

He was referring to skin. Flemming burst out laughing, but the Prince didn't notice because at that very moment he was shoved aside in the rush of a gallopade, and Flemming never saw his face again. At the same time, the Baron introduced a friend of his who also spoke English and said;

"You'll have dinner with me tonight. I have some Rhine wine that will tempt you."

Soon after, the Baron stood with a passionate, romantic woman leaning on his arm, examining a copy of Raphael's Fornarina.

"Oh! I wish I had been the Fornarina," sighed the passionate, romantic lady.

"Then, my dear Madam," the Baron replied, "I wish I had been Raphael."

A very tall man with fiery red hair and elaborate whiskers thought the same thing to himself as he waltzed around and around in one place, wearing the most unusual waistcoat. He looked like a blazing beacon light, warning people about the dangerous rocks where the winds of vanity would crash their ships. Eventually, his dancing partner grew tired of all the spinning and collapsed onto a sofa, just like a child's spinning top when it wobbles and topples over.

"You don't like the waltz?" asked an elderly French gentleman, noticing the expression on Flemming's face.

"Oh yes; among the ballet dancers at the Opera. But I admit, it sometimes makes me shudder to see a young libertine wrap his arms around the waist of a pure and innocent girl. What would you say if you saw him sitting on a sofa with his arms around your wife?"

"Just educational prejudice," the French gentleman responded. "I'm familiar with that situation. I've read all about it in the Bibliothèque de Romans Choisis!"

And the dance continued joyfully; bright eyes and flushed cheeks were abundant among the dancers;

"And they turned red, and grew warm,"

"And rested, breathing heavily, arm in arm,"

and the Strauss waltzes sounded pleasant to Flemming's ears, who, although he never danced, still thought to music like Henry of Ofterdingen in Novalis's romance. The spinning waltz got his imagination turning. And so the moments passed by, and Time's footsteps couldn't be heard over the sound of music and voices.

But suddenly this cheerful scene was interrupted. The door swung open wide, and the short figure of a gray-haired old man appeared, his face flushed and his eyes wild. He was only half-dressed, holding a silver candlestick with no candle lit. A sheet was wrapped around his head like a turban, and he stumbled forward with a vacant, confused expression, crying out;

"I am Muhammad, the king of the Jews!"

At that very moment he collapsed unconscious and was carried out of the room by the servants. Flemming looked at the hostess, and she was deathly pale. For a moment everything was chaos, and the dancing and music came to a halt. The effect on the guests was both ridiculous and terrifying. They attempted unsuccessfully to recover their composure. The entire gathering was like a corpse from which the soul had fled. Before long all the guests had scattered, leaving the lady of the house alone with her dim, dying lamps and even more sorrowful thoughts.

"Really," Flemming said to the Baron as they made their way home, "this doesn't feel like reality at all; it's like one of those stark contrasts you find in novels. Who can say, after experiencing this, that there isn't more romance in real life than what we find written in books!"

"Not more romance," said the Baron, "but a different romance."

A scene even more tragic had unfolded that evening in Heidelberg. As the sun was setting, two women walked along the romantic forest path that led to the Angel's Meadow, a small green clearing on the ridge of one of the tall hills that gaze at their own reflections in the Neckar River and listen to the solemn bells of Kloster-Neuburg. The evening shadows stretched wide and long across the landscape, and the cuckoo began to call.

"Cuckoo! Cuckoo!" called out the older of the two figures, reciting an old German folk rhyme,

"Cuckoo! Cuckoo!"

Tell me the truth,

Tell me honestly and clearly,

"How long must I remain unmarried and suffer!"

It was the voice of an evil spirit speaking through Madeleine; and the pale, trembling figure walking beside her, listening to those words, was Emma of Ilmenau. A young man met them where the path curved into the dense forest; and they vanished among the dark branches. It was the Polish Count.

The forget-me-nots gazed upward toward the sky with their gentle blue petals, growing peacefully in the Angel's Meadow. The mountain of All-Saints stood serenely in its magnificent, sacred silence; the river flowed so far beneath that the sound of its rushing waters could not be heard; there was no whisper of the evening breeze through the foliage, no noise on the ground or in the atmosphere; and yet on that very night, a star tumbled down from the heavens!

Chapter X. The Parting.

It was now that time of year which an old English writer calls the delightful month of June, and at that moment of the day when the rising moon looks directly at the setting sun. The stars were still sparse in the sky. But after the day's heat, the cool air and twilight came down like a blessing upon the earth, accompanied by all those soft sounds that are the quiet companions of the night.

Flemming and the Baron had spent the afternoon at the Castle. They had wandered together once more, and for the final time, through the magnificent ruins. Tomorrow they would part ways, possibly forever. The Baron was heading to Berlin to meet his sister, while Flemming, driven forward by the restless spirit inside him, yearned once again for a change of scenery and was traveling to the Tyrol and Switzerland. Unfortunately, he never told the fleeting moment, "Stay, for you are beautiful!" but instead reached forward into the uncertain future, with unfulfilled longings and purposeless desires that never ceased.

As the day was ending, they settled onto the terrace of Elisabeth's Garden. The sun had disappeared behind the blue hills of Alsace, and purple mist descended over the Rhine valley like the cloak of a departing prophet ascending in his chariot of fire. Above the castle walls and garden trees, the large moon emerged; between the competing daylight and moonlight, no shadows existed yet. Eventually, though, the shadows appeared—transparent and delicate outlines that gradually took on deeper form. In the valley below, only the river shone like steel, and scattered lamps began to glow throughout the town. The leafy linden trees stood majestically in the nearby garden, their trunks shrouded in darkness while their tops gleamed bronze in the moonlight. In his alcove within the great round tower, draped with ivy like a magnificent ghost, stood the gray statue of Louis with his dignified beard, chain mail shirt, and flowing cloak; his gentle, noble face gazed out into the quiet night like that of a prophet reading the stars. Periodically, the summer night's breeze swept through the ruined castle and trees, creating sounds as if nature were sighing in her sleep; for a brief moment overhead, the broad leaves softly struck against each other like bronze cymbals with a gentle ringing, and then everything fell silent except for the sweet, passionate songs of nightingales, which sing nowhere on earth more beautifully than in the gardens of Heidelberg Castle.

The time, the setting, and the approaching farewell between the two young friends had filled their hearts with a pleasant yet bittersweet excitement. They had been talking about the magnificent ancient ruin, the eras during which it was constructed, and the changes brought by time and war that had torn down its walls, leaving it "empty, except for the wind that whistles through its cracks."

"How sorrowful and majestic is the face of that statue over there," said Flemming. "It reminds me of the old Danish hero Beowulf; for watchful and grieving, he sees in his son's chamber the wine-hall abandoned, the haunt of the wind, silent; the knight sleeps; the warrior lies in darkness; there is no sound of the harp, no joy in the homes, as there was before."

"Exactly as you say," the Baron replied, "but it often amazes me that, coming from that vibrant green world of yours across the ocean, you should feel such deep interest in these ancient things. Sometimes you seem to have absorbed their essence so completely that you actually live in those bygone eras. For my part, I don't understand what appeal there is in the pale and weathered face of the Past that could so captivate a young man's soul. It strikes me as being like falling in love with one's grandmother. Give me the Present—warm, radiant, throbbing with life. She is my lover, and the Future stands waiting like my bride-to-be, for whom, to be honest, I care very little right now. Really, my friend, I wish you would pay more attention to this philosophy of mine and not squander the precious hours of youth on useless regrets about the past and vague, unclear yearnings for the future. Youth comes only once in a lifetime."

"Therefore," said Flemming, "let us enjoy it in such a way that we remain young even when we are old. As for me, I become happier as I age. When I compare my feelings and pleasures now with what they were ten years ago, the comparison strongly favors the present. Much of life's fever and restlessness has passed. The world and I regard each other more peacefully. My mind has greater composure. It has benefited me to be somewhat dried by life's heat and soaked by its rain."

"Now you're talking like an old philosopher," the Baron

replied, laughing. "But you're fooling yourself. I've never known a more restless, feverish spirit than yours. Don't think you've gained control yet. You're just anchored here in a quiet eddy of the stream; you'll soon be swept away again by the powerful current and whirlwind of chance. Don't trust this temporary calm. I know you better than you know yourself. There's something Faust-like about you; you want to grasp both the highest and the deepest; and 'reel from desire to enjoyment, and in enjoyment languish for desire.' When a brief change of feeling comes over you, you think the change is permanent, and so you live in constant self-deception."

"I admit," Flemming said, "there might be some truth in what you're saying. There are moments when my soul feels restless, and a voice echoes inside me, like the trumpet of an archangel, and thoughts that were buried long ago rise from their graves. During these times, my favorite activities and interests no longer appeal to me. Nature's peaceful expression seems to be mocking me."

"There definitely are times," the Baron replied, "when Nature appears not to care about her cherished children. She remains so endlessly peaceful and composed, so thoroughly maternal and tranquil, and shows so little concern whether her child's heart is breaking or not, that sometimes I nearly lose my temper. She cares so little about that as well, that out of pure stubbornness, I find myself becoming cheerful again, and then she smiles."

"I think we have to admit, though," Flemming went on, "that all of this comes from our own flaws, not from hers. How beautiful this green world we live in truly is! Look over there, see how the moonlight blends with the mist! What a magnificent night this is! Every person really does have a Paradise surrounding them until they sin, and the angel of a guilty conscience banishes them from their Eden. And even then there are sacred moments when this angel sleeps, and we return, and with the innocent eyes of a child, gaze into our lost Paradise once more—into the wide gates and peaceful solitudes of Nature. I experience this frequently. We have much to appreciate in the calm and solitude of our own thoughts. Wild celebration and boisterous laughter don't suit my temperament. I cherish that peace of soul in which we sense the gift of being alive, and which is itself a prayer and an expression of gratitude. I notice, though, that as I get older, I find myself loving the countryside less and the city more."

"Yes," the Baron interrupted; "and soon you'll find yourself loving the city less and the countryside more. Just admit it—you have this vague longing for both places, and you prefer the town or the country depending on whatever mood strikes you. I believe a person must have an extremely calm and content nature to put up with country living for very long. What's more, they must be quite satisfied with their own unimportant existence, quite pleased with themselves, to constantly focus on their own thoughts and inner life. At the very least, city living makes someone more accepting and open-minded when judging other people. You're not constantly absorbed in examining yourself, which is really just a more refined form of self-importance."

During conversations like this, the hours slipped by effortlessly, until finally the Castle clock from the Giant's Tower chimed twelve, its sound echoing as if it came from medieval times. The city clocks responded one after another, like sentries calling from their bell towers. Then distant, muffled sounds drifted through the air. Unclear words appeared to stain the misty atmosphere, like ink bleeding on damp paper. These were the bells from Handschuhsheimer and other villages scattered across the wide Rhine valley and throughout the Odenwald hills—enigmatic sounds that seemed to belong to another realm entirely.

Below them, in the shadow of the hills, the valley stretched out like an endless, dark abyss; and overhead were the secluded stars that, like nuns, walked through the sacred corridors of heaven. The city slept in the valley beneath; everything was asleep and quiet, except for the clocks that had just chimed twelve, and the turning, golden weathervanes that swam in the moonlight like golden fish in a glass bowl. Once more the summer night's breeze swept through the ancient Castle, and through the trees, and the nightingales sang beneath the dark, shadowy leaves, and Flemming's heart was filled with emotion.

When he went back to his room, a deep sense of complete loneliness washed over him. The night before starting a journey is always a gloomy night; for, as Byron says,

"When we part ways with even the most disagreeable people"

"And places, you keep staring at the church steeple!"

And how much more so when the location and people are delightful; as was the situation with those that Flemming was now departing from. It's no surprise he felt sorrowful and unable to sleep. Ideas flowed in and out of his mind, along with cheerful and dark imaginings, plus dreams and visions, while lovely faces appeared behind his shut eyelids, then disappeared, returned once more, and left again. He listened to the clock chime from one hour to the next, thinking to himself, "Another hour has passed." Eventually the birds started their morning songs; and occasionally the rooster crowed. He got up and gazed out into the pale dawn; and spread before him was the city he would soon be leaving behind, completely white and ghostly, resembling a city that had risen from its tomb.

"Everything must change," he said to the Baron as he embraced him and grasped his hand. "Friends must be separated and carried away by the flow of events, seeing each other rarely, and perhaps never again. Forever and always we are swept away in the whirlpools of time and chance. Beyond that, some of us have constant restlessness in our minds, just as Wodenblock had in his wooden leg; and like him we keep moving without rest or sleep, barely having time to shake a friend's hand as we pass by; and eventually we are seen rushing through some far-off country, worn down to nothing but bones, completely unrecognized."

Book III.

Opening Quote

"Turn off the lights as well;"
The moon gives me too much light to discover my fears;
And those devotions I must now fulfill,
Are written in my heart, not in your book;
"And I shall read them there without a candle."

Chapter I. Summer-Time.

They were right—those old German Minnesingers—to sing about the delightful summertime! What a season it is! How brilliantly June shines in the calendar! All the windows stand wide open, with only the Venetian blinds drawn shut. Here and there, a long ray of sunlight pours in through a gap. We can hear the gentle sound of wind moving through the trees, and as it grows stronger and picks up, distant doors slam shut with a sharp noise. The trees are thick with foliage, and the gardens overflow with flowers, both red and white. The entire air is filled with fragrance and sunlight. Birds are singing. The rooster struts around and crows proudly. Insects chirp in the grass. Yellow buttercups dot the green lawn like golden buttons, while the red clover blossoms sparkle like rubies. The elm trees extend their long, drooping branches nearly to the earth. White clouds drift overhead, and wisps of vapor streak the blue sky with silver lines. The white village shimmers in the distance against the dark hills. The river meanders through the meadow—carefree and lazy. It appears to cherish the countryside and feels no urgency to reach the ocean. Only the bee remains busy—the heated and irritable bee. Everything else is at leisure; he never rests and grows annoyed that anyone else should.

People drive out from the city to breathe fresh air and find happiness. Most of them carry flowers in their hands; bunches of apple blossoms, and even more often, lilacs. You residents of the crowded city, how delightful it must be for you to escape from the sweltering streets to the open fields, sweet with the scent of clover blossoms! How refreshing the cool, breezy country air, touched with the salt from the meadows! How wonderful, above all, the flowers, the countless, beautiful flowers!

Night has fallen. The red moon rises through the trees, and the stars are barely visible. In the deep shadows of darkness, coolness and dew settle down. I sit by the open window to take it all in, hearing only the voice of the summer wind. Like dark ships, the shadows of the large trees sit anchored on the rolling sea of grass. I can't see the red and blue flowers, but I know they're there. Far off in the meadow, the silver Charles River gleams. The sound of horses' hooves echoes from the wooden bridge. Then everything becomes quiet, except for the steady wind of the summer night. Sometimes I can't tell whether it's the wind or the sound of the nearby sea. The village clock chimes, and I feel that I'm not alone.

How different it is in the city! It's late, and the crowds have disappeared. You walk out onto the balcony and rest in the very heart of the cool, dew-filled night, as though you've wrapped her garments around yourself. The entire starry sky stretches out above you. Below lies the public walkway with its trees, like a bottomless, dark abyss, into whose quiet darkness the soul dives and drifts away, holding some cherished soul in its arms. The streetlights continue to burn up and down the long street. People pass by, casting strange shadows that are sometimes shortened and sometimes stretching away into the darkness before disappearing, while a new shadow appears behind the person walking and seems to overtake them on the sidewalk. The iron park gates close with a clanging sound. There are footsteps and loud voices—a commotion—a drunken fight—a fire alarm—then quiet returns. And now finally the city sleeps, and we can see the night. The late moon peers over the rooftops and finds no one to greet her. The moonlight is fragmented. It rests here and there in the squares and at the mouths of streets—sharp-edged, like chunks of white marble.

Under such a green, triumphant archway, dear Reader, surrounded by the fragrance of flowers and the melody of birds, you will move forward into this magical realm, as if passing through the Ivory Gate of dreams! And as an introduction and grand procession, one beautiful human voice, whose identity I cannot determine, but emerging from the heart of the Alps, performs this magnificent song, which the mountain echoes carry into the distance.

"Come, golden Evening! In the west"
Enthrone the storm-dispelling sun,
And let the triple rainbow rest
Over all the mountain tops—it is done;
The storm ends; fearless and radiant,
The rainbow stretches from one hill to another;
The sun descends; night advances;
Mont Blanc is still beautiful!
"There take your stand, my spirit; spread"
The world of shadows beneath your feet;
And notice how peacefully above,
The stars, like saints in glory, meet.
While hidden in magnificent solitude,
I find myself reflecting on Nature's grave,
And listen to the footsteps of Time as it passes by
Step through the silent darkness.
"All in a moment, crash on crash,"

From one cliff edge to another,
An avalanche's debris crashes down
Down to the deepest depths below,
Invisible; the ear alone
Chases the commotion until it fades away;
Echo to Echo, groan for groan,
From deep to deep, replies.
"Once again, silence seals the darkness,"
Darkness so thick you could almost touch it—but soon
The silver-clouded east reveals
The ghostly apparition of the moon at midnight;
In half-eclipse she raises her horn,
Yet, over the host of heaven supreme,
Brings the faint semblance of a morning,
With her awakening light.
"Ah! at her touch, these Alpine heights"
Illusions and false appearances emerge;
With darker shadows and more terrifying lights,
Appearing as she ascends the celestial sphere;
A crowd of pale ghosts!
I hold my breath in cold anticipation,
They appear incredibly delicate,
Lest they should vanish hence.
"I can breathe again, I breathe freely;"
You, Lake Geneva, once more I follow,
Like Diana's crescent moon far below,
As beautiful as Diana's face:
Pride of the land that gave me birth!
All that your waves reflect, I love,
Where heaven itself is brought down to earth,
Appears more beautiful than what lies above.
"Safe on your shores once more I wander;"
The spell of poetry has ended,

And here I am at the break of day,
Gazing on mountains as before,
Where all the unusual changes were brought about,
Were magical creations of my own imagination;
For, in that magical realm of imagination,
"Whatever I seek, I find."

Chapter II. Foot-Travelling.

Tell me, my soul, why are you restless? Why do you look forward to the future with such intense desire? The present is yours—and the past—and the future will be! If only you would look forward to the great hereafter with half the longing with which you yearn for an earthly future—which a few days at most will bring you! Look toward the meeting of the dead as you would toward the meeting of those who are absent! You glorious spirit-land! Oh, if only I could see you as you truly are—the realm of life, and light, and love, and the dwelling place of those beloved ones, whose existence has flowed onward like a silver-clear stream into the solemn-sounding depths, into the ocean of Eternity.

These were the thoughts flowing through Flemming's mind as he rested in complete solitude and stillness on the curved peak of one of the Furca Pass mountains, gazing upward with tears streaming down his face and passionate yearning filling his heart toward the blue expanse of sky above and the glaciers and snow-capped peaks surrounding him. Rising highest and most brilliant of all stood the Jungfrau peak, appearing close despite its distant location in the heart of the Lauterbrunnen Valley. There it towered, sacred and lofty and pristine, heaven's bride draped entirely in white, lifting the observer's thoughts toward the divine. Little did he realize then, as he stared at it with longing and joy, how quickly a presence would emerge within his own spirit, equally sacred, lofty, and pristine, and similarly directing his gaze heavenward.

The traveler lay there on the mountain peak, resting his tired body on the short, brown grass that looked more like moss than actual grass. He had sent his guide ahead so he could be alone. His spirit was filled with a wild and painful joy. The mountain air stirred him up; the mountain wilderness both attracted and drove him crazy. Every summit, every sharp, jagged ice formation, seemed to cut right through him. The silence was both terrible and magnificent. It was like the silence in a dying person's soul when they can no longer hear the sounds of the world. He felt as though he was taking off his earthly clothes. Heaven was close to him; but between him and heaven, every wrong thing he had ever done rose up enormous, like those mountain peaks, and breathed freezing air on him. Oh, don't let the suffering soul dare to look Nature in the face when she sits in royal splendor high up in the loneliness of the mountains; because her face is cold and harsh, and she doesn't look with compassion on her weak and mistaken child. It is the face of an accusing archangel who calls us to be judged. In the valley she wears the face of a Virgin Mother, looking at us with tearful eyes and an expression of pity and love!

But yesterday Flemming had traveled up the valley of the Saint Gothard Pass, through Amsteg, where the Kerstelenbach comes rushing down the Maderaner Valley from its snowy heights above. The road climbs steeply, winding along zigzag terraces. The mountainsides rise as barren cliffs, and from their cloud-covered peaks, silent beneath the thundering of the great torrent below, streams of snow-white foam cascade from rock to rock, like mountain chamois leaping. As you move forward, the landscape becomes wilder and more desolate. There isn't a single tree visible—not one human dwelling. Dark clouds, black as midnight, hang over you from the ravines above, while the mountain torrent below appears as nothing but a sheet of foam, sending up a constant roar. A sharp turn in the road suddenly reveals a towering bridge, spanning from cliff to cliff in a single leap. A terrifying waterfall howls beneath it like an evil spirit, filling the air with mist, while the mountain wind claps its hands and shrieks through the narrow pass, "Ha! ha!"—This is the Devil's Bridge. It carries the traveler across the frightening chasm and through a mountain tunnel into the wide, green, peaceful meadow of Andermath.

Even the bright morning that came after this dark day had not driven away the bleak feeling from Flemming's soul. His agitation grew as he wandered deeper and deeper into the mountains; and now, as he lay completely alone on top of the sunlit hill, surrounded only by glaciers and snow-covered peaks, his soul, as I have mentioned, was overwhelmed with an intense and agonizing joy.

A human voice interrupted his daydreaming. He looked up and saw not far from him the strong, muscular figure of a mountain shepherd approaching the place where he was lying. The man was young, dressed in simple country clothes, and carried a long walking stick in his hand. When Flemming stood up, the shepherd stopped and stared at him, as if he cherished seeing another human face, even that of a stranger, and yearned to hear a human voice, even if it spoke in a language he didn't understand. He responded to Flemming's greeting in the rough dialect of the mountains, and when asked questions, he said;

"I, along with two other men, am responsible for looking after two hundred cattle on these mountains. We stay here day and night throughout the two summer months, and for this work we each receive a Napoleon."

Flemming gave him half of his summer earnings. He was happy to perform a good deed in secret, and yet so close to heaven. The man accepted it as though it were rightfully his, like a toll collector; and shortly afterward left, leaving the traveler by himself. And the traveler continued his journey down the mountain, like someone who had lost his mind. He paused only to pick one brilliant blue flower, which bloomed completely alone in the enormous wilderness, and gazed up at him, as if to say; "O take me with you! don't leave me here all by myself!"

Soon he reached the magnificent Rhone glacier; a frozen waterfall, more than two thousand feet in height, and many miles wide at its base. It fills the entire valley between two mountains, extending back to their peaks. At the base it is curved, like a dome; and above, jagged and rough, and looks like a mass of enormous crystals, of a pale emerald color, mixed with white. A snowy layer covers its surface; but at every crack and opening the pale green ice gleams clearly in the sun. Its shape is that of a glove, lying with the palm facing down, and the fingers bent and pressed close together. It is a gauntlet of ice, which, centuries ago, Winter, the King of these mountains, threw down in challenge to the Sun; and year after year the Sun struggles in vain to lift it from the ground on the tip of his shining spear. A feeling of wonder and delight came over Flemming's soul when he saw it, and he shouted and cried out loud;

"How wonderful! How glorious!"

After spending several hours in the cold, barren valley, he climbed the steep Mayen-Wand on the Grimsel during the afternoon, passed the Lake of the Dead with its pitch-black waters, and through the melting snow and across slippery stepping-stones in the beds of countless shallow streams, he descended to the Grimsel Hospital, where he spent the night and considered it the most isolated and desolate place where anyone had ever slept.

The next morning, he woke up at dawn; and the rising sun found him already standing on the rustic bridge that hangs over the edge of the Falls of the Aar at Handeck, where the river plunges down a cliff into a narrow and terrifying abyss, enclosed by vertical rock walls. The beautiful Aerlenbach flows into it at a right angle; and halfway down, the two waterfalls merge into one. He continued his journey down the Hasli Valley into the Bernese

Oberland, restless and impatient for reasons he couldn't understand, rarely stopping, and never for long, then rushing forward again, like the rushing river whose path he followed, and in whose ice-cold waters he repeatedly bathed his wrists to cool the fever in his blood; for the midday sun was blazing hot.

His heart expanded in the widening valley, which became broader and more verdant with each step. The sight of human faces and homes comforted him; and through the summer grain fields, in the wide meadows of Imgrund, he walked with a heart that no longer ached, but only trembled, like our eyelids after we finish crying. As he climbed the hill on the opposite side, which borders this romantic valley, and, like a heavy yoke, rubs against the neck of the Aar, he accepted the old tradition that claims the valley was once a lake. From the hilltop he gazed southward upon a magnificent landscape of gardens, grain fields, woodlands, and meadows, and the ancient castle of Resti, overlooking Meyringen. And now all around him were birds singing, and welcome shadows from the leafy trees; and cascading waterfalls tumbling from the wooded cliffs, visible only but silent, the fluted columns dissolving into mist, and decorated with frequent spires and ornaments of foam, resembling the towers of an upside-down Gothic church. There, in one white sheet of foam, the Riechenbach cascades down into its deep basin, where the sun never penetrates. Face to face it watches the Alpbach falling from the hill across the way, "like downward-flowing smoke." When Flemming observed the countless streams sliding down the mountainside, and leaping with pure life and joy, he wished he could embrace them in his arms and become their companion, and celebrate with them in their freedom and happiness. Yet he was tired from the day's travel, and entered the village of Meyringen, nestled among cherry trees that were then heavy with fruit, more like a weary traveler than an inspired poet. As he climbed the tavern steps he said to himself, echoing the Italian Aretino: "He who has never been to a tavern knows not what paradise it represents. O sacred tavern! O wondrous tavern! sacred, because no gnawing worries exist there, nor exhaustion, nor suffering; and wondrous, because of the spits that turn by themselves round and round! Truly all courtesy and good manners originate from taverns, so full of bows, and Signor, sì! and Signor, nò!"

But even in the tavern he couldn't rest for long. That same evening at sunset he was floating on Lake Brienz in an open boat, positioned close beneath the Giessbach waterfall, listening to the peasants sing the Ranz des Vaches. He spent that night at the opposite end of the lake, in a large house that, like Saint Peter's at Joppa, stood beside the water. The following day he spent writing letters, reflecting in this green sanctuary, and paddling around the lake once more; and in the evening he traveled across the beautiful meadows to Interlaken, where many events occurred that kept him there for an extended time.

Chapter III. Interlachen.

Interlachen! How peacefully you rest by the edge of the swift-flowing Aar, nestled in the broad embrace of those romantic meadows, all sheltered beneath the spreading branches of enormous trees! Only the round towers of your ancient monastery rise above their peaks; the round towers themselves appear like a child's toys beneath the great church spires of the mountains. Right next to you lie lakes, connected by the flowing ribbon of the river. Before you stretches the magnificent valley of Lauterbrunn, where the cloud-crowned Monk and pale Virgin stand like Saint Francis and his Bride of Snow; and all around you spread fields, orchards, and green villages, from which church bells call to one another in the evening! The evening sun was setting when I first saw you! The sun of life will set before I forget you! Surely it was a scene like this that stirred the soul of the Swiss poet in his Song of the Bell!

"Bell! You ring out cheerfully,
When the wedding party
To the church he hurries!
Bell! You ring with solemn gravity,
When, on Sabbath morning,
Fields lie deserted!
"Bell! You ring out cheerfully;"
Do you count at evening,
Bedtime is approaching!
Bell! You sound mournfully;
Tell me about the bitter
Parting has passed!
"Tell me! How can you mourn?"
How can you rejoice?
Art is nothing but dull metal!
And yet all our sorrows,
And all our celebrations,
You feel them all!
"God has many wonders,"
Which we cannot understand,
Placed within your form!
When the heart is sinking,
You alone can raise it,
"Trembling in the storm!"

Paul Flemming got off at one of the main hotels. The owner came out to greet him. He had large eyes and wore a green coat, and he reminded Flemming of the innkeeper described in the Golden Ass, who had been transformed by magic into a frog and croaked to his guests from the dregs of a wine barrel. His establishment, he explained, was completely booked, as was every lodging in Interlachen; however, if the gentleman would step into the sitting room, he would arrange to find him a room somewhere in the area.

On the couch sat a man, reading; a heavyset man of about forty-five, plump, rosy-cheeked, and with a head that, being somewhat bald on top, resembled a crow's nest with a single egg in it. A cheerful face looked up from the book as Flemming walked in; and a warm voice called out;

"Ha! ha! Mr. Flemming! Is it really you, or am I seeing a ghost! I told you we would meet again! even though you wanted to say a permanent goodbye to your traveling companion."

Speaking these words, the robust gentleman stood up and shook Flemming's hand with great enthusiasm. Flemming returned the handshake just as warmly, recognizing in this rosy-cheeked figure a former travel companion, Mr. Berkley, whom he had parted ways with a week or two earlier while the man was struggling up the Righi mountain. Mr. Berkley was a wealthy Englishman; a cheerful, compassionate old bachelor who was equally notable for his practical wisdom and his peculiar habits. In other words, the foundation of his personality was solid, reliable common sense that had been refined and polished through education; but his strange and playful imagination used this steady base as a stage on which to perform her unusual antics. His greatest obsession was taking cold baths; he typically ate his breakfast while sitting in a tub of cold water and reading a newspaper. He would kiss every child he encountered; and to every elderly man he passed, he would say "God bless you!" with such genuine tone and facial expression that no one could question his authenticity. He brought to mind Roger Bontemps, or the Little Man in Gray; though with certain distinctions.

"The last time I had the pleasure of seeing you, Mr. Berkley," Flemming said, "was at Goldau, right as you were heading up the Rigi. I hope you enjoyed a beautiful sunrise from the mountaintop."

"No, sir, I wasn't!" Mr. Berkley replied. "It's all nonsense! Complete nonsense! They made such a fuss about their sunrise that I decided I wouldn't bother seeing it. So I stayed comfortable in bed and just peeked through the window curtain. That was plenty. Right above the house, on top of the hill, stood about fifty half-dressed, romantic people shivering in the wet grass, and a short distance from them, some poor soul was blowing a long wooden horn. That's your Righi sunrise, is it? I said to myself, and went back to sleep. The best thing I saw at the Culm was the notice on the bedroom doors warning that if the ladies used the quilts and blankets as shawls when they went out to see the sunrise, they'd have to pay for the laundry. Take my word for it, the Righi is complete nonsense!"

"Where have you been since then?"

"At Zurich and Schaffhausen. If you travel to Zurich, be careful about staying at the Raven. They will swindle you. They swindled me; but I got my payback, because when we arrived at Schaffhausen, I wrote in the Traveller's Book;"

Beware of the Raven of Zurich!

It's a bird that brings bad luck;

With a loud and dirty nest,

And a very, very long bill.

"If you go to the Golden Falcon, you'll find it there. I wrote those lines!"

"Bitter as Juvenal!" Flemming exclaimed.

"Not at all bitter," said Mr. Berkley. "Everything I've said is true. Go to the Raven and see for yourself. But this Interlaken! This Interlaken! It's the most beautiful place on earth," he went on, extending both arms as though he wanted to embrace what he loved so dearly. "There—just look out there!"

Here he gestured toward the window. Flemming looked out and saw a scene of extraordinary beauty. The plain was already covered by the brown shadows of summer twilight. From the cottage rooftops in Unterseen, thin columns of smoke rose here and there above the treetops and blended with the evening shadows. The Valley of Lauterbrunnen was filled with a blue mist. High above, in the clear, cloudless sky, the white peak of the Jungfrau glowed pink from the last kiss of the setting sun. It was a magnificent transformation of nature! And when the village bells started to ring, and a single voice in the far distance could be heard yodeling a ballad, it seemed to break rather than enhance the magic of a scene where silence was more beautiful than any sound.

For a long time they stared at the twilight landscape without speaking. Eventually people entered the parlor, removing their shawls and hats, and exchanged a few words with Berkley. To Flemming, all these visitors were strangers. For him, they were simply Mr. Brown and Mrs. Johnson, nothing more. The conversation focused on the day's various outings. Some had visited the Staubbach, others had gone to Grindelwald, still others to Lake Thun, and no one had ever before felt half the joy they had experienced that day. And so they sat in the fading light, as people enjoy doing at the end of a summer day. The lamps hadn't been lit yet, and you couldn't make out faces clearly, only voices and shadowy figures.

A woman dressed in black soon entered the room and took a seat by the window. She listened to the conversation more than she participated in it, but the few words she spoke came in a voice so melodious and soulful that it stirred Flemming's spirit like a heavenly whisper.

O, how amazing the human voice is! It truly serves as the soul's instrument! Human intelligence sits clearly visible on the forehead and in the eyes; and the human heart shows itself on the face. But the soul reveals itself only through the voice; just as God revealed himself to the ancient prophet in the quiet, gentle voice; and in a voice from the burning bush. The human soul can be heard, not seen. Only a sound reveals the flow of the eternal fountain, which remains invisible to humanity!

Flemming would have gladly sat and listened for hours to the sound of that mysterious voice. Deep down, he felt certain that whoever it belonged to must be beautiful. His imagination filled in the dim outline that his eyes could barely make out in the fading twilight, and in his mind, the figure already appeared like Raphael's stunning Madonna in the Dresden gallery. He had never been more wrong in his entire life. The voice did indeed belong to a beautiful person, that much was true; but her beauty was unlike that of any Madonna that Raphael had ever painted, as he would have discovered if he had waited until the lamps were lit. However, while he was lost in his daydream and mental portrait-painting, the landlord entered and informed him that he had located a room, which he asked him to come and examine.

Flemming said goodbye and left. Berkley went with him, saying he wanted to see what kind of place his young friend would be sleeping in.

"The room isn't what I'd prefer," said the innkeeper as he guided them across the street. "It's located in the old monastery. But tomorrow or the day after, you can certainly get a room at the main building."

The monastery's name captured Flemming's imagination in a delightful way. He was enough of a night owl to appreciate ruins and ancient chambers where nuns or monks had once slept. And he said to Berkley;

"So, you see, my home is going to be in a monastery. It already reminds me of a bird's nest I once saw on an old tower of Heidelberg castle, built in the jaws of a lion that used to serve as a water spout. But please tell me, who was that young woman with the gentle voice?"

"What young lady with the soft voice?"

"The young woman in black, who sat by the window."

"Oh, she's the daughter of an English officer who died recently in Naples. She's spending the summer here with her mother to recover her health."

"What is her name?"

"Ashburton."

"Is she beautiful?"

"Not at all; but extremely intelligent. A brilliant woman, I would say."

And now they had arrived at the monastery walls, passing through an arched entrance and directly beneath the round towers that Flemming had spotted earlier, rising with their cone-shaped roofs above the trees like tall candles topped with snuffers.

"It's not as bad as it appears," said the landlord, knocking on a small door in the main building. "The Bailiff lives in one section of it."

A servant girl holding a candle opened the door and led Flemming and Berkley to the room that had been reserved for them. The room was spacious and located on the ground floor, with pine wood paneling that remained unpainted. Three tall, narrow windows with lead frames and small glass panes faced south, offering a view toward the Lauterbrunnen valley and the surrounding mountains. A large square bed with a canopy and checkered curtains occupied one corner of the room. In another corner stood an enormous tiled stove decorated with painted designs that stretched nearly to the ceiling. The room's furnishings were completed by an old sofa, several high-backed antique chairs, and a table.

Flemming settled into his monk-like cell and sleeping quarters. He requested tea and started to feel comfortable in his new surroundings. Berkley spent the evening with him. When it was time to leave, he said;

"Good night! I leave you in the care of the Virgin and all the Saints. If the ghost of some old monk returns looking for his prayer book, give him my regards. If I were a younger man, you would definitely see a ghost. Good night!"

When he left, Flemming opened the window lattice. The moon had come up and cast silver light on the dark silhouettes of the nearby hills, while in the distance, the snow-covered peaks of the Jungfrau and the Silver-Horn gleamed like white clouds against the sky. Directly below the windows lay a flower garden, and the summer night air drifted up to him carrying the fresh scent of dew. The place felt wonderfully secluded and peaceful. He felt grateful for the fortunate chance that had brought him to such comfortable lodging, and that night he fell asleep thinking about the nuns who had once slept in these same quiet rooms. Yet neither veiled nun nor hooded monk visited his dreams, nor did he see Mary Ashburton's face or hear her voice.

Chapter IV. The Evening and The Morning Star.

Old Froissart tells us in his Chronicles that when King Edward saw the Countess of Salisbury at her castle gate, he believed he had never before encountered such a noble or beautiful lady; he was struck to his very core with a spark of pure love that lasted long afterward; he considered no woman in the world more worthy of being loved than she was. Paul Flemming felt exactly the same way when he saw the English lady in the beautiful light of a summer morning. I won't hide the truth. She is my heroine, and I intend to portray her with complete honesty and beauty, so that everyone will fall in love with her, and I most of all.

Mary Ashburton was twenty years old. Like the beautiful maiden Amoret, she was blossoming into womanhood. Those who claimed she wasn't beautiful were mistaken; and yet

"she was not beautiful,"

Nor beautiful—those words don't capture her essence.

But oh, her appearance had something extraordinary about it, "That needs a name!"

Her face held a wonderful fascination. It was such a calm, quiet face, with the light of the rising soul shining so peacefully through it. At times it wore an expression of seriousness—of sorrow even; and then it seemed to make the very air bright with what the Italian poets so beautifully call the lampeggiar dell' angelico riso—the lightning of the angelic smile.

And oh, those eyes—those profound, indescribable eyes, with drooping eyelids heavy with dreams and drowsiness, and within them a cold, living light, like that found in mountain lakes at dusk, or in the river of Paradise, flowing eternally,

"with a brown, brown current"

Under the eternal shade that never

"Ray of the sun lets in, nor of the moon."

I don't like eyes that twinkle like stars. The only beautiful ones are those that, like planets, have a steady, gentle glow—they're luminous without sparkling. Greek poets described the eyes of the Immortals this way. But I'm getting carried away.

The woman's appearance was remarkable. Each movement, each pose displayed grace combined with dignity, as though her inner spirit guided every gesture. In ancient poetic tradition, angels possessed such forms; it seemed as if her very soul had taken shape in the air around her. And what an extraordinary soul she possessed! Like a sacred sanctuary devoted to Heaven, similar to Rome's Pantheon, illuminated solely from above. The earthly desires that once took the form of pagan deities had vanished, replaced instead by the gentle and contemplative faces of Christ, the Virgin Mary, and the Saints. Therefore, nothing within her created discord; rather, a complete harmony existed between her physical form, her countenance, and her spirit—in essence, her entire being. Anyone who possessed a soul capable of understanding hers would inevitably fall in love with her, and once having loved her, could never love another woman again.

No wonder, then, that Flemming felt his heart drawn toward her as she passed him during her morning walk, while he sat alone beneath the large walnut trees near the cloister, contemplating Heaven but not thinking of her. She, too, was by herself. Her cheek was no longer pale but radiant and bright, filled with the energy of the summer air. Flemming watched her until she vanished, like a vision from his dreams, disappearing to who knows where. He wasn't yet in love, but he was very close to it; he gave thanks to God for creating such beautiful beings to walk upon the earth.

Last night he had heard a voice that spoke to his soul, and he could have simply continued on his journey without giving it another thought. But he would have heard that voice again later, every evening when he remembered this particular evening at Interlaken. Today he had seen the vision more clearly, and his restless soul had found peace. The place felt welcoming to him, and he couldn't bring himself to leave. He didn't question where this sense of calm came from. He simply felt it and found joy in that feeling, blessing the landscape and the summer morning as if they held some magical power.

"Have a pleasant morning dream," said a friendly voice, and at the same moment someone placed his hand on Flemming's shoulder. It was Berkley. He had approached without being seen or heard.

"I can tell by the smile on your face," he continued, "that this isn't some daytime nightmare."

"You're right," Flemming replied. "It was a pleasant dream, and you've chased it away."

"I'm happy to see that you've also driven away the dark thoughts that used to trouble you. I enjoy seeing people who are cheerful and happy. What's the point of surrendering to sadness in this beautiful world?"

"Ah! this beautiful world!" said Flemming, with a smile. "I really don't know what to make of it. Sometimes everything is pure joy and sunshine, and Heaven itself seems within reach. Then suddenly it shifts, becoming dark and sorrowful, with clouds blocking out the sky. Even in the lives of the most troubled among us, there are bright days like this when we feel we could embrace the entire world and kiss it. Then the gloomy hours arrive, when the fire won't burn in our fireplaces or in our hearts, and everything inside and outside becomes dreary, cold, and dark. Trust me, every heart carries its hidden sorrows that the world never sees, and often we label someone as cold when they're simply sad."

"And who says we don't?" Berkley cut in. "Come on, let's go get breakfast. The morning air has given me quite an appetite. I'm eager to say grace over a fresh egg and share a meal with my worst enemies—those city folks at the hotel. After breakfast, you need to give me your complete attention. I'm taking you to the Grindelwald!"

"Today, then, you're not having breakfast like Diogenes, but you're willing to leave your tub."

"Yes, for the pleasure of your company. I'll also blow out the light in my lantern, since I've found you."

"Thank you."

The breakfast went by without anything unusual happening. Flemming kept watching as each guest entered, but she didn't come—the guest he most wanted to see.

"And now for the Grindelwald!" said Berkley.

"Why are you in such a hurry? We have the entire day ahead of us. There's plenty of time."

"Not a moment to lose, I assure you. The carriage is at the door."

They drove up the Lauterbrunnen valley and turned east into the mountains around Grindelwald. They spent the day there, chilled to the bone by the freezing air that swept down from the Great Glacier, whose surface was covered with ice pyramids and blocks that looked like gravestones in a cemetery. It was an exhausting day for Flemming. He longed to be back in Interlaken and felt relieved when, as evening approached, he could see the cone-shaped towers of the monastery rising above the walnut trees once again.

That evening is marked in red letters in his personal history. It gave him another revelation of the beauty and excellence of the female character and intellect; not entirely new to him, yet now renewed and strengthened. It was from the lips of Mary Ashburton that the revelation came. Her figure rose, like a shimmering evening star, in the sky of his soul. He talked with her; and with her alone; and didn't know when to leave. All others were to him as if they weren't there. He saw their shapes, but saw them as the forms of lifeless objects. Finally her mother arrived; and Flemming saw in her just another Mary Ashburton, with beauty more mature;--the same forehead and eyes, the same majestic figure; and, as yet, no sign of age. He looked upon her with a feeling of delight, not unmixed with sacred reverence. She was to him the rich and glowing Evening, from whose heart the shimmering star was born.

Berkley didn't actively participate in the conversation, but he did something far more useful—he organized a carriage ride for the following day with the Ashburtons and naturally invited Flemming, who returned home that evening feeling elated and curious about a fashionably dressed man who stood at the hotel entrance and spoke to his companion as Flemming walked by.

"What do you call this place? I've been here for two hours already, and I find it incredibly boring!"

Chapter V. A Rainy Day.

When Flemming woke up the next morning, he saw the sky was dark and threatening. A curtain of mist hung from the mountain peaks, its heavy layers swaying back and forth in the valley below. Gentle summer rain was falling across the entire landscape. No admiring eyes would gaze up at the Staubbach that day.

A rainy day in Switzerland brings many activities to an abrupt halt. The coachman might drive to the tavern and then return to the stable, but no further. The sun-weathered guide can sit at the pub entrance if he wishes, and the boatman may whistle and curse at the clouds to his heart's content, but despite all this, no one ventures outside; no traveler sets out if he has the option to wait. The rainy day provides him with time for contemplation. He now has the opportunity to examine his experiences and settle his thoughts about the mountains. He also recalls that he has friends back home and catches up on his journal, which he has neglected for a week or longer, and letters that have been ignored even more, or he completes the rough pencil sketch he started yesterday outdoors. Overall, he doesn't mind that it's raining, even though he feels disappointed.

Flemming felt both sorry and disappointed, but this didn't stop him from visiting the Ashburtons at the scheduled time. When he arrived, he discovered them in the parlor. The mother was reading, while her daughter was working on touching up a sketch of Lake Thun. Following the customary greetings, Flemming took a seat close to the daughter and spoke;

"I don't think we'll see the Staubbach waterfall today; we'll only have this Giessbach falling from the clouds."

"Nothing more, I suppose. So we must be content to stay indoors and listen to the sound of the rain dripping from the eaves. It gives me time to finish some of these rough sketches."

"Drawing is such an enjoyable hobby," Flemming remarked, "and I can see you're quite talented at it. I'm impressed that you can actually draw a straight line. I've never looked through a woman's sketchbook before where all the towers didn't look like the Leaning Tower of Pisa. I always worry about the tiny figures standing beneath them."

"How ridiculous!" Mary Ashburton exclaimed, her smile cutting through the hazy fog of Flemming's mind like a ray of sunshine. "As for me, I do much better with straight lines than with any other kind. I've been spending the last half hour trying to make this water wheel circular, and it's never going to be round."

"Then let it stay as it is. It looks remarkably picturesque, and could be considered a new invention."

The woman kept drawing, while Flemming continued to stare at her beautiful face, frequently reciting to himself those lines from Marlowe's Faust;

"O thou art fairer than the evening air,

"Clothed in the beauty of a thousand stars!"

He definitely would have given himself away under Mrs. Ashburton's watchful maternal gaze, if she hadn't been completely engrossed in the ridiculous plot of a trendy novel. Before long, the beautiful artist had stopped drawing for a moment, and Flemming had picked up her sketchbook and was flipping through it from the start with growing pleasure, though he only dared express half of what he felt, even as he shared some observations and enthusiastic praise with her.

"This is truly a very beautiful sketch of Murten and the battlefield! How peacefully the landscape rests there by the lake, after the battle! Have you ever read the ballad by Veit Weber, the shoemaker, about this subject? He says the defeated Burgundians leaped into the lake, and the Swiss soldiers shot them down like wild ducks among the reeds. He fought in the battle and wrote the ballad afterwards;--

He had personally drawn his sword,
He who wrote this rhyme;
Until evening he mowed with the sword,
And sang the song at night."

"You need to give me the complete ballad," Miss Ashburton said; "it will help illustrate the sketch."

"And here's the sketch that goes with the ballad. Now we're suddenly racing down the Alps into Italy, and we're actually in Rome, unless I'm wrong. This must be a portrait of Homer, right?"

"Yes," the lady replied with some enthusiasm. "Don't you remember the marble bust in Rome? When I first saw that bust, it filled me with complete awe. That's not the face of a man, but of a god!"

"And you've done it no injustice in your copy," said Flemming, catching fresh enthusiasm from hers. "What classic grace the headband shows as it passes around that majestic forehead, holding back his flowing hair that blends with his beard! The face, too, is calm, majestic, godlike! Even the fixed and unseeing eyes don't spoil the image of the prophet! Those were the unseeing eyes of the blind old man of Chios. They seem to gaze with sorrowful dignity into the mysterious future; and the marble lips appear to recite that prophetic passage from the Hymn to Apollo; 'Let me also hope to be remembered in ages to come. And when anyone, born of human tribes, comes here as a weary traveler and asks who is the sweetest of the Singing Men who come to your feasts, and whom you most enjoy hearing, answer for me. It is the Blind Man who lives in Chios; his songs surpass all that could ever be sung!' But do you truly believe this is a portrait of Homer?"

"Absolutely not! It's nothing more than an artist's imagination. This is how Homer came to him in his dreams of the ancient world. Everyone, as you know, creates mental pictures of people and things they've never actually seen; and the artist brings them to life in marble or on canvas."

"And what picture do you have in your mind? Is it like this?"

"No; not completely. I've formed my impressions from a different source. Whenever I think of Homer, which isn't often, he appears before me, dignified and peaceful, just as the great Italian envisioned him; his expression neither sad nor happy, accompanied by other poets, and carrying a sword in his right hand!"

"That's an even more refined idea than this one," Flemming said. "I can tell from what you're saying, as well as from this book, that you have a genuine appreciation for art and truly understand what it represents. You've caught beautiful glimpses into that magical realm."

"I believe," the lady replied humbly, "that I'm not completely lacking in this sentiment. I certainly feel as deep and intense a love for Art as I do for Nature."

"But doesn't it often bother you to hear people talk about Art and Nature as if they're opposing and conflicting forces? Nothing could be further from the truth. Nature reveals God to us; Art reveals humanity to us. That's really all Art means. Art is Power. That's what the word originally meant. It's the creative force through which the human soul expresses itself, using some external form or visible sign. Just as we can always hear God's voice, walking in the garden in the cool evening air, or beneath the starlight, where, to quote one of this poet's lines, 'high prospects and the brows of all steep hills and pinnacles thrust up themselves for shows'—in the same way, under the twilight and starlight of bygone eras, we hear humanity's voice, walking among the works of human hands, with city walls and towers and church spires thrusting themselves up for display."

The woman smiled at his enthusiasm, and he went on:

This, however, is just a comparison; Art and Nature are more closely connected than mere comparisons can show. Art reveals humanity; and not only that, but it also reveals Nature speaking through human beings. Art already exists within Nature, and Nature is recreated through Art. Just as water vapor rises from the ocean, drifts toward land and falls as rain, then flows back to the ocean through rivers, so thoughts and images of things shower down upon the human soul, then flow out again as living streams of Art, and return to the great ocean that is Nature. Art and Nature are not in conflict, then, but always work together in harmony within each other.

Enthusiasm creates more enthusiasm. Flemming spoke with such clear interest in the topic that Miss Ashburton couldn't help but show some interest in what he was saying; and, encouraged by this response, he continued;

In this amazing world where we live, which is the World of Nature, humanity has created another world that is almost equally amazing, which is the World of Art. And it exists wrapped up and surrounded by the other,

'And the clear region where it was born,
Round in itself incloses.

Taking this perspective on art, I believe we can more easily grasp the artist's skill and understand what sets him apart from the simple amateur. What we consider miracles and marvels of art are not miraculous to the person who brought them into being. These works emerged from the natural stirrings of his own magnificent soul. Sculptures, paintings, churches, and poems are merely reflections of himself—reflections captured in marble, pigments, stone, and language. He perceives and appreciates their beauty, yet he conceived these ideas and brought forth these creations as effortlessly as lesser minds produce inferior thoughts and works. Perhaps even more effortlessly. Hazy visions and forms of beauty drifting through the consciousness, the outlines of things still uncertain or poorly formed, becoming flawless only when expressed through art—this Possible Intellect, as the Scholastic Philosophers called it—the artist possesses in common with all of us. Those who appreciate art are numerous. However, the Active Intellect, the force of creation—the ability to transform these forms and visions into art, to give substance to the undefined and make it complete, belongs to him alone. He shares this gift with very few. He does not understand where this ability comes from or how it works. He knows only that it exists; that God has granted him this power, which has been withheld from others.

"I should have realized you were from Germany," the woman said with a smile, "even if you hadn't mentioned it. You're clearly passionate about the Germans. As for me, I can't stand their rough language."

"You'd enjoy it more if you understood it better," Flemming replied. "It doesn't sound harsh to me at all; instead, it feels like home—warm, genuine, and deeply emotional, like the sound of cheerful voices gathered around a fireplace on a winter evening, when the wind howls outside and the fire pops, crackles, and sparks. I truly do love the Germans; the men are so robust and sincere, and the young women so gentle and faithful!"

"I always picture men smoking pipes and drinking beer, while women are busy with their knitting."

"Oh, those are English prejudices," exclaimed Flemming. "Nothing can be more--"

"And their literature itself appears to my mind in the same way."

"I can see you've only read English reviews and criticisms, and you have this notion that all German books somehow smell like grocery stores—of brown paper wrapping filled with greasy pastries and bacon slices, and of food frying in stuffy back rooms. This prejudice is keeping you locked out of a magnificent world of poetry, romance, and dreams!"

Mary Ashburton smiled, and Flemming kept flipping through the pages of the sketchbook, making the occasional comment or clever remark. Eventually he reached a page that had something written on it in pencil. People with vivid imaginations are usually curious, and they're always curious when they're a little bit in love.

"Here's a pencil sketch," he said, with a pleading look, "that I would really like to examine along with the others."

"You're welcome to do that if you'd like, but you'll discover it's the weakest drawing in the entire book. I was attempting one day to capture what an artist's life in Rome looked like in my mind's eye, and this is what came of it. Maybe it will bring back some fond memories for you."

Flemming didn't wait any longer; he read with the eyes of a lover, not a critic, the following description, which filled him with a fresh enthusiasm for Art, and for Mary Ashburton.

I often think with joy about the life of a young artist in Rome. A foreigner from the cold and dreary North, he has traveled across the Alps and journeyed to the Eternal City with the dedication of a pilgrim. He might live on the Pincian Hill, where nearly every house is home to artists from other countries. The very room where he stays has housed them since ancient times. Their names cover the walls completely, and perhaps some additional trace of them remains in a crude drawing on the window shutter, along with an inscription and a date. In his mind, these things make the place sacred. Even these names, though he doesn't know them, still carry meaning for him.

In that warm climate, he wakes with the sunrise. The night mists are already drifting away across the Campagna toward the sea. Looking out from his window, above and beyond their white layers, he can make out the shimmering blue waters at Ostia. The sun climbs over Soracte—over his own cherished mountain, though it's no longer a place of worship as it once was. In front of him, the ancient house where Raphael once lived casts its long, dark shadow down into the center of modern Rome. The city remains asleep and quiet. But above its shadowy rooftops, more than two hundred church spires catch the morning light on their golden weather vanes. Soon the bells start to ring, and as the artist

138

listens to their melodious sounds, he realizes that in each of those churches, above the main altar, hangs a painting created by some master artist, whose beauty stands between him and heaven, leaving him unable to pray but only to marvel in wonder.

Among these works of art he spends his days, but most often in St. Peter's and the Vatican. Up the enormous marble staircase, through the Corridor Chiaramonti, through entrance halls, galleries, and rooms, he moves as if in a dream. Everything is filled with busts and statues, or decorated with bold frescoes. What magnificent forms of strength and beauty! What glorious creations of the human mind! And in that final chamber, standing alone on his pedestal, the Apollo discovered at Actium—in such a majestic pose, with such a noble expression, lifelike, godlike!

"Or perhaps he enters the painters' studios; but ventures no farther than the second room. For in the center of that chamber stands a magnificent painting on its massive easel, appearing unfinished, though more than three centuries ago the master artist brought it to completion, then set down his brush forever, leaving this final gift to humanity. It is Raphael's Transfiguration of Christ. A child gazes at the stars with no greater awe than this artist feels while studying this masterpiece. He understands how many years of dedicated study are captured in that work. He knows the challenging journey toward artistic excellence, having himself begun those initial steps.--In this way he remembers the moment when that vast canvas was first mounted on its frame, and Raphael stood before it, applying the initial colors, watching each figure gradually come to life, and 'gazed upon his creation with satisfaction, pleased that it had turned out so magnificently.' He also remembers the moment when, with the work complete, the brush fell from the master's failing hand, and his eyes closed to witness a more magnificent transfiguration, and finally the deceased Raphael rested in his own workshop, before this extraordinary painting, more magnificent than any military victor beneath the flags and heraldic displays of his funeral!"

"Do you think that such sights and thoughts as these don't stir the heart of a young man and an artist! And when he steps out into the open air, the sun is setting, and the gray ruins of an ancient world welcome him. From the Palace of the Caesars he gazes down into the Forum, or toward the Colosseum; or looking westward sees the final sunlight hit the bronze Archangel that stands upon the Tomb of Adrian. He walks through a world of Art in ruins. The very street lamps that light his way home burn before some painted or carved image of the Madonna! What surprise is it, if dreams come to him in his sleep—indeed, if his entire life seems like a dream to him! What surprise, if, with a passionate heart and swift hand, he tries to recreate those dreams in marble or on canvas."

Foolish Paul Flemming! He both admired and praised this little sketch, yet was too blind to see that it was written from the heart, not from the imagination! Foolish Paul Flemming! He thought that a girl of twenty could write this way without a reason! Right after this came another pencil sketch, which he also read with the lady's permission. It was this.

"The entire period of the Middle Ages feels very strange to me. Sometimes I can't convince myself that the things history tells us actually happened; that such an unusual world was part of our world—that such an extraordinary life was part of the life that seems so emotionless and ordinary to those of us living it today. Only when I stand among ruined castles that gaze at me so sadly, and look at the heavy armor of ancient knights hanging on the wooden panels of Gothic rooms; or when I walk through the corridors of some dim cathedral, whose walls tell stories of ancient times, and whose very bells have been blessed, and see the carved wooden seats in the choir, where countless generations of monks have sat and sung, and the graves where they now rest in silence, never to wake again for their midnight prayers—only at such moments does the history of the Middle Ages become real to me, rather than just a passage from a romance novel."

Similarly, the illuminated manuscripts from those eras possess this same ability to transform the dead past into a living present in my thoughts. What fascinating figures are displayed on the creaking parchment, making its yellowed pages come alive with vibrant colors! You feel as though you've stumbled upon them unexpectedly. Their faces show expressions of amazement. They all appear to have just been awakened from their slumber by the noise you created when you unfastened the bronze clasps and opened the intricately carved oak covers that swing on hinges like the massive gates of a city. Some dedicated monk devoted his entire long life to constructing that city. What extraordinary inhabitants he filled it with! Adam and Eve standing beneath a tree, she holding the apple in her hand; the patriarch Abraham with a tree sprouting from his body and his descendants perched like owls upon its branches; ladies with flowing golden hair; knights in armor wearing the most elaborate, long-pointed shoes; tournaments and contests; and Minnesingers and lovers whose heads reach up to the towers where their ladies are seated; and everything so angular, so uncomplicated, so innocent—all posed in such straightforward positions, with such large eyes, and extending such long, thin fingers! These elements are typical of the Middle Ages and convince me of the authenticity of history.

At that moment Berkley walked in, carrying a Swiss cottage he had just purchased as a gift for someone's child back in England, along with a walking stick topped with a chamois horn that he had bought for himself. This was the first time Flemming had felt disappointed to see the well-meaning man. His arrival disrupted the wonderful private conversation he was having with Mary Ashburton. He genuinely found Berkley tedious and was surprised he had never noticed this before. Mrs. Ashburton also had to set aside her book, and the conversation shifted to include everyone.

Remarkably, the Swiss dinner hour of one o'clock couldn't come quickly enough for Flemming. It didn't even strike him as early, since he would be sitting next to Mary Ashburton, and during dinner one could speak so much without others listening in.

—————

Chapter VI. After Dinner, And After the Manner of The Best Critics.

When the scholarly Thomas Diafoirus courted the beautiful Angélique, he pulled a medical thesis from his pocket and offered it to her as the first expression of his intellectual gifts; at the same time, he asked her, with her father's consent, to come watch the dissection of a woman on whom he would give a lecture. Paul Flemming did almost exactly the same thing, and so frequently that it had become second nature to him. He was constantly pulling from his pocket or his memory some fragment of verse or tale, and asking some lovely Angélique, whether with her father's approval or without it, to witness the dissection of an author about whom he planned to speak. He would soon demonstrate this tendency to Mary Ashburton.

"What books do we have here for afternoon reading?" Flemming asked, picking up a volume from the parlor table after they had returned from the dining room. "Oh, it's Uhland's Poems. Have you read anything by him? He and Tieck are the finest living poets in Germany. They compete for the crown of excellence. Let me give you a German lesson this afternoon, Miss Ashburton, so that no one can accuse you of 'neglecting the sweet benefit of time, to dress your years with angel-like perfection.' I've opened randomly to the ballad of the Black Knight. You can repeat the German after me, and I'll translate it for you. Pfingsten war, das Fest der Freude!"

"I could never force my reluctant lips to make such sounds. So I ask you not to confuse me with your German, but please read me the ballad in English."

"Well, then, listen. I will improvise a translation for your own particular benefit."

It was Pentecost, the Feast of Gladness,
When forests and meadows cast away all their sorrow.
Thus the King began to speak;
'So from the halls
Of the ancient Hofburg's walls,
A rich and abundant Spring will arrive.
"Drums and trumpets echo loudly,"
Wave the red banners with pride.
From the balcony, the King watched;
In the clash of spears,
Fell all the cavaliers,
Before the king's brave son.
"To the barrier of the fight,"
At last, a knight dressed in black came riding.
"Sir Knight! Tell me your name and coat of arms!"
"Should I speak it here,
You would be struck with terror;
"I am a Prince of great power!"
"When he rode into the tournament grounds,
The sky above darkened with gathering clouds.
And the castle began to rock.
At the first strike,
The young man fell from his horse's saddle.
Barely recovers from the shock.
"Pipe and viol call the dances,"
Torchlight flickers through the towering halls;
Waves a mighty shadow in.
With a gentle demeanor

Does ask for the maiden's hand,
Does the dance begin with her.
"Danced in black iron armor,"
Danced a measure weird and dark,
Coldly wrapped her arms and legs around.
From breast and hair
Down from her falls the fair
Flowers withered and fell to the ground.
"To the lavish feast came
Every Knight and every Dame.
Between son and daughter, completely distraught,
With a sorrowful heart
The ancient King reclined,
Looked at them quietly, lost in thought.
"Both children looked pale,"
But the guest picked up a drinking cup;
"Golden wine will make you whole!"
The children drank,
Offered many polite expressions of gratitude;
"Oh, that drink was very refreshing!"
"Each one embraces the father's chest,"
Son and daughter; and their faces
Colorless grow utterly.
Whichever way
The frightened father appears pale and gray.
He watches his children die.
"Woe! the blessed children both,
Take joy in your youth;
"Take me too, the heartbroken father!"
The Grim Guest spoke,
From his empty, echoing chest;
"I gather roses in the spring!"

"That really is a remarkable ballad!" said Miss Ashburton, "but it's rather too dark and eerie for this dreary afternoon."

"It starts joyfully with the Pentecost celebration and the red banners flying at the ancient castle. Then the contrast is skillfully handled. The Knight dressed in black armor, the sweeping entrance of the powerful shadow during the dance, and the falling of the withered flowers are all vividly brought to life in the reader's mind. Nevertheless, it tells its own tale and requires no further explanation. Here we have something in a different style, though still sorrowful. The Castle by the Sea. Should I read it?"

"Yes, if you like."

Flemming read;

"Have you seen that magnificent castle,
That Castle by the Sea?
Golden and red above it
The clouds drift beautifully.
"And gladly it would bend downward"
To the mirrored wave below;
And it eagerly wants to rise upward
In the evening's crimson glow.
"I have seen that castle well,
That Castle by the Sea,
And the moon above it standing,
And the mist rises solemnly.
"The winds and the waves of ocean,
Had they a merry chime?
Did you hear, from those high chambers,
The harp and the minstrel's rhyme?
"The winds and the waves of ocean,
They rested peacefully.
But I heard a sound of wailing carried on the strong wind,
And tears came to my eyes.
"And did you see on the towers"

The King and his royal bride?
And the wave of their crimson mantles?
And the golden crown of pride?
"Did they not lead forth in ecstasy"
A beautiful young woman there?
Radiant as the morning sun,
Beaming with golden hair?
"I clearly saw the ancient parents,
Without the crown of pride;
They were moving slowly, dressed in garments of grief,
No young woman stood beside them!
"How do you like that?"

"It is very graceful and pretty. But Uhland seems to leave a great deal to his reader's imagination. All his readers should be poets themselves, or they will hardly understand him. I admit, I barely understand the passage where he speaks of the castle bending downward to the reflected wave below, and then rising upward into the shining sky. I assume, however, he wants to express the brief illusion we feel when seeing a perfect reflection of an old tower in the sea, and we look at it as if it were not just a shadow in the water; and yet the real tower rises far above, and seems to drift in the crimson evening clouds. Is that what he means?"

"I would certainly think so. To me, it's all like a beautiful landscape of clouds—something I understand and feel deeply, yet I might struggle to put into words if I had to explain it."

"And why must we always provide explanations? Some emotions simply cannot be translated into words. No language has been created to express them. They shine upon us beautifully through the hazy dusk of imagination, yet when we draw them near and examine them under the harsh light of logic, they instantly lose their beauty; much like fireflies, which glow with such an ethereal radiance in the evening shadows, but when brought into a room lit by candles, reveal themselves to be merely insects, no different from countless others."

"Absolutely right. Sometimes we should simply allow ourselves to experience pure feeling. Here we have a beautiful piece that calms the soul like evening shadows falling gently, like the refreshing coolness of dusk after a sweltering day. I won't offer you my own plain translation, since I've stored in my mind another version that, while not word-for-word accurate, matches the original's beauty. Notice how elegantly it begins."

"Many years have passed and been buried in time,"
Since I crossed this turbulent sea;
And the evening, beautiful as always,
Shines on ruin, rock, and river.
"Then, in this same boat, beside,
Two old and trusted comrades sat together;
One with all the honesty of a father,
One with all the fire of youth.
"One worked on earth in silence,"
And he quietly searched for his grave;
But the younger, more radiant form
Died in battle and in storm!
"So, whenever I turn my eye
Looking back on the days that have passed,
Sad thoughts about friends come over me,--
Friends who completed their journey before me.
"Yet what connects us, friend to friend,
But can one soul truly merge with another?
Those hours from long ago were like the soul itself;
Let us walk in spirit once more!
"Take, O boatman, three times your fee;"
Take it—I give it willingly;
For, unseen by you,
"Two spirits have crossed paths with me!"

"Oh, that is beautiful—'beautiful exceedingly!' Who translated it?"

"I don't know. I wish I could figure him out. It's certainly done admirably; though in the rhythm of the original there's something like the rocking motion of a boat, which isn't preserved in the translation."

"And is Uhland always so calming and uplifting?"

"Yes, he usually gazes into the spiritual realm. I'm currently attempting to locate a short poem here about the Death of a Country Clergyman, in which he presents a lovely image. However, I can't find it right now. It doesn't matter. He portrays the soul of the kind elderly man coming back to earth on a brilliant summer morning, standing among the golden grain and the red and blue blossoms, and gently welcoming the harvesters just as he used to do. The concept is beautiful, isn't it?"

"Yes, very beautiful!"

"But there's nothing unhealthy or gloomy about Uhland's thinking. He's always refreshing and energizing, like a crisp morning breeze. In this way, he's completely different from writers like Salis and Matthisson."

"And who are they?"

Two melancholy gentlemen who saw life as nothing more than a gloomy swamp, walking along its edges with delicate handkerchiefs in their hands, weeping and sighing, and beckoning to Death to come and carry them across the dark waters. And now their souls dwell in the verdant meadows of German poetry, like two weeping willows drooping over a grave. To read their verses is like strolling through a village cemetery on a summer evening, reading the words carved on tombstones and remembering tender memories of those who have passed away; while overhead,

Listen! In the sacred grove of palm trees,
Where life flows freely like a stream,
Echoes, in the angels' psalms,

"Sister spirit! I greet you!"

"How beautifully those lines flow with such musical rhythm! Are they written by Matthisson?"

"Yes; and they truly flow with musical quality. I wish I had his poems with me here. I would love to read you his Elegy on the Ruins of an Ancient Castle. It's written in imitation of Gray's Elegy. Have you been to Baden-Baden?"

"Yes; last summer."

"And have not forgotten--"

"The old castle? Of course not. What a magnificent ruin it is!"

"That is the setting of Matthisson's poem, and it appears to have filled the melancholy poet with more inspiration than usual."

"I would really love to see the poem. I remember that old ruin with such wonderful fondness."

"I'm sorry I don't have a translation of it for you. Instead, I'll share a beautiful and melancholy poem by Salis. It's called the Song of the Silent Land."

"Into the Silent Land!"

Ah! Who will guide us there!

Clouds in the evening sky gather more darkly,

And broken shipwrecks lie scattered more densely along the shore.

Who guides us with a tender touch,

Thither, oh, thither.

Into the Silent Land?

"Into the Silent Land!"

To you, endless territories

Of all perfection! Gentle morning visions

Of beautiful souls! Eternity's own band!

Who stands firm in life's battle,

Shall bear Hope's tender blossoms

Into the Silent Land!

"O Land! O Land!"

For all the broken-hearted
The gentlest messenger assigned to us by our destiny,
Beckons, and stands with torch held upside down
To guide us with a tender touch
Into the land of the great departed,
Into the Silent Land!
"Isn't that a beautiful poem?"

Mary Ashburton didn't respond. She had turned away to conceal her tears. Flemming was surprised that Berkley could claim she wasn't beautiful. Yet he felt more pleased than insulted by the comment. In that moment, he realized how wonderful it would be to have someone who appeared beautiful to him alone, and yet to him would be more beautiful than anyone else in the world! How radiant the world seemed to him with that thought! It was like one of those paintings where all the light radiates from the Virgin's face. Oh, there is nothing more sacred in our lives than the first awareness of love—the first flutter of its delicate wings; the first gentle sound and breath of that wind which will soon sweep through the soul, either to purify or to destroy!

Old historical accounts tell us that the great Emperor Charlemagne used to stamp his royal decrees with the hilt of his sword. The even greater Emperor, Death, stamps his decrees with the blade itself; and they are both signed and carried out with a single stroke. That night, Flemming received a letter from Heidelberg informing him that Emma of Ilmenau had died. The fate of this unfortunate young woman deeply affected him, and he thought to himself;

"Father in Heaven! Why was this weak and troubled child's fate so difficult! What had she done to face such temptation in her vulnerability and be destroyed? Why did you allow her tender feelings to mislead her in this way?"

And through the silence of that terrifying midnight, the sound of an avalanche responded from the far-off mountains, and appeared to say;

"Peace! Peace! Why do you question God's providence!"

Chapter VII. Take Care!

The valley of Lauterbrunnen is beautiful with its green meadows and towering cliffs that hang overhead. The ruins of Unspunnen castle stand like an armed guard at the entrance to this magical land. The snow-covered mountains rise peacefully in the distance. More beautiful than the Rock of Balmarusa, that imposing cliff face gazes down at us; and from the highest point, the white banner of the Brook of Dust gleams and flutters in the bright sunlight!

It was a bright, beautiful morning following the night's rain. Every dewdrop and raindrop contained an entire heaven within it; and so did the heart of Paul Flemming, as he drove up the Valley of Lauterbrunnen with Mrs. Ashburton and her dark-eyed daughter—the Valley of Fountains-Only.

"How beautiful the Jungfrau looks this morning!" he exclaimed, looking at Mary Ashburton.

She believed he was referring to the mountain and agreed. However, he was also referring to her.

"And beyond that, the mountains," he went on, "the Monk and the Silver-horn, the Wetter-horn, the Schreck-horn, and the Schwarz-horn—all those magnificent messengers of Nature, whose sermons are avalanches! Have you ever seen anything more magnificent!"

"Oh yes. Mont Blanc is far more impressive when you see it from the hills across the way. That's where I was most deeply moved by the magnificence of Swiss scenery. It was a morning just like this one; and the clouds, drifting about on their enormous, shadowy wings, only made the scene more magnificent. Before me stretched the entire panorama of the Alps; pine forests standing dark and solemn at the base of the mountains; and halfway up, a veil of mist; above which rose the snowy peaks, and sharp spires of rock, which seemed to float in the air, like a fairy world. Then the glaciers stood on either side, winding down through the mountain valleys; and, high above everything, rose the white, dome-like summit of Mont Blanc. And again and again from the shroud of mist came the terrible sound of an avalanche, and a continuous roar, like the wind through a forest of pines, filled the air. It was the roar of the Arve and Aveiron, breaking from their icy sources. Then the mists began to clear away; and it seemed as if the whole sky were rolling together. It brought to my mind that sublime passage in the Apocalypse; 'I saw a great white throne; and him that sat thereon; before whose face the heavens and the earth fled away, and found no place!' Oh, I cannot believe that upon this earth there is a more magnificent scene."

"It must be truly magnificent," Flemming replied. "And those massive glaciers—enormous creatures with jagged peaks, slowly crawling down into the valley! People say they actually do move."

"Yes; thinking about this filled me with an odd sense of wonder and fear. These glaciers reminded me of the dragons from Northern legends that descend from the mountains and consume entire villages. There was once a small village in Chamonix that its residents completely abandoned because they were so frightened by the approaching icy monster. But is it really possible that you've never visited Chamonix?"

"Never. The great marvel still remains unseen by me."

"Then why are you staying here for so long? If I were in your position, I wouldn't waste a single hour."

These words swept across the budding hopes in Flemming's soul like a cold wind blowing over spring flowers. He endured it as well as he could and shifted the conversation to another topic.

I won't attempt to describe the Valley of Lauterbrunnen or the beautiful day we spent there. I know that my kind reader possesses the wonderful gift of poetic imagination and can already picture how the mountains tower upward, how the waterfalls cascade down, and how the lovely valley stretches between them. You can envision how the shepherd plays his horn along the dusty road, and how travelers arrive and depart in horse-drawn carriages, like characters in a Punch and Judy puppet show. You already understand how romantic women sketch picturesque landscapes while charming gentlemen collect beautiful flowers, and how cold food tastes delicious in the shade of trees, and how quickly time passes when we're in love with our beloved close by. However, I must share one small incident, in case your imagination might not conjure it on its own.

Flemming was still sitting with the ladies on the green slope near the Staubbach, or Brook of Dust, when a young man dressed in green came down the valley. He was a German student with blonde curls hanging over his shoulders and a guitar in his hand. His walk was confident and energetic, and his face showed the happy expression of youth and good health. He approached the group with a polite greeting and, following the custom of traveling students, asked for charity with the self-assured manner of someone who rarely faced rejection. He wasn't turned away this time either. Being around those we love makes us kind and generous. Flemming gave him a gold coin, and after a brief conversation, the student sat down at a short distance on the grass and began to play and sing. Amazing and numerous were the beautiful harmonies and sorrowful sounds that came from that small instrument when touched by the student's skilled hands. Every emotion of the human heart seemed to find expression there and awaken a similar feeling in the hearts of those listening to him. He sang beautiful German songs filled with yearning and pleasant melancholy, hope and fear, passionate longing, and heartbreaking sorrow that brought tears to Mary Ashburton's eyes, even though she couldn't understand the words he was singing. Then his face lit up with triumph, and he struck the strings like a drum and sang;

"Oh, how loudly the drum beats!"
Close beside me in the fight,
My dying brother says, Good Night!
And the terrible roar of the cannon
Screams the loud halloo of Death!
And the drum,
And the drum,
"Beats so loud!"

Many people praised the young musician when he finished playing, and as he stood up to leave, they kept asking him to perform one more song. So he played an energetic introduction, looked directly at Flemming, and sang this short song with a cheerful smile, still singing in German.

"I know a beautiful young woman,"
Take care!
She can be both deceitful and friendly at the same time.
Beware! Beware!
Trust her not,
She is deceiving you!
"She has two eyes, so soft and brown,"
Take care!
She glances sideways and looks down,
Beware! Beware!
Trust her not,
She is deceiving you!
"And she has hair of a golden color,"
Take care!
And what she says, it is not true,
Beware! Beware!

Trust her not,
She is deceiving you!
"She has a bosom as white as snow,"
Take care!
She understands exactly how much is best to reveal.
Beware! Beware!
Trust her not,
She is deceiving you!
"She gives you a beautiful woven garland,"
Take care!
It's foolish for you to wear that cap.
Beware! Beware!
Trust her not,
"She is deceiving you!"

He sang the final stanza in a laughing, triumphant tone that rang out above the loud clanging of his guitar, like the mocking laughter of Till Eulenspiegel. Then he slung his guitar over his shoulder, removed his green cap, and bowed to the ladies in the manner of Gil Blas; he waved his hand in the air and walked briskly down the valley, singing "Adé! Adé! Adé!"

Chapter VIII. The Fountain of Oblivion.

The power of magic during medieval times brought forth monsters that relentlessly pursued the unfortunate magician wherever he went. Similarly, the power of Love throughout all eras brings forth angels that follow the joyful or sorrowful lover everywhere, even into their dreams. Paul Flemming now found himself haunted by such an angel, both in his waking hours and during sleep. He moved through life as if in a dream, barely aware of the people surrounding him. A beautiful face gazed at him from every page of each book he opened, and it was Mary Ashburton's face! A gentle voice spoke to him in every sound that reached his ears, and it was Mary Ashburton's voice! Days and nights followed one another in their pleasant rhythm of light and darkness, yet for him the passage of time felt like nothing more than a dream. When he rose each morning, his thoughts turned only to her, wondering whether she had awakened yet; and when he retired each evening, he thought only of her, and how, like the Lady Christabel,

"She gently removed her clothes,"

"And lay down in her loveliness."

Throughout the entire day he remained with her, whether in actual presence or in daydreams that felt almost as vivid; for in every fevered vision during his waking moments, her beautiful figure moved like Beatrice's form through Dante's paradise; and as he rested during the summer afternoon, occasionally hearing the wind rustling through the trees and the sound of Sunday church bells rising toward heaven, sacred hopes and prayers rose with them from the depths of his soul, pleading that his love might not be unrequited! And whenever, in quiet solitude, he gazed into the silent, solitary face of Night, he remembered the passionate verses of Plato;--

"Do you look at the stars? If I were heaven,"

"With all the eyes of heaven, I would look down upon you!"

How beautiful it is to love! Even you, who sneer at this page and laugh with cold indifference or scorn when others are around you, you too must acknowledge its truth when you are alone; and confess that a foolish world tends to laugh in public at what it privately reveres as one of the highest impulses of our nature—namely, Love!

One by one, the people we love leave us behind. Yet our feelings for them remain, and like vines, they reach out with their broken, injured tendrils searching for something to hold onto. The wounded heart needs healing balm, and there is nothing that can provide this except the love of another person—nothing but the affection of a human heart! In this way, Flemming's damaged and broken feelings began to lift themselves up from the ground and wrap around this new person. Days and weeks went by, and like the Student Crisostomo, he stopped loving because he started to worship her. Mixed with this worship was a prayer that in those quiet moments when the world is silent, and the voices of praise are hushed, and contemplation comes like dusk, and the young woman, lost in her daydreams, counted how many friends she had, some voice in the holy silence of her thoughts might speak his name! And was this really happening? Did any voice in the holy silence of her thoughts speak his name?—We will find out soon.

They were sitting together one morning on the green, flowering meadow beneath the ruins of Burg Unspunnen. She was drawing the ruins. All the birds were singing, as though there were no broken hearts, no wrongdoing or sadness in the world. The clear air was so still that the shadows of the trees appeared etched onto the grass. The faraway snow-covered peaks gleamed in the sunlight, and nothing looked threatening except the square tower of the ancient ruin looming above them.

"What a shame," said the woman, pausing to rest her tired fingers. "What a shame that there's no ancient legend tied to these ruins."

"I'll make you one, if you'd like," said Flemming.

"Can you create new traditions?"

"Oh yes; I created three just the other day for the Rhine, and one very old one for the Black Forest. A lady with wild, tangled hair; a robber wearing a terrible slouched hat; and a night storm among the howling pines."

"Delightful! Do make one for me."

"With the greatest pleasure. Where would you like the scene to take place? Here, or in the Black Forest?"

"In the Black Forest, by all means? Begin."

"First, promise me you won't interrupt. If you break these delicate threads of thought, they'll drift away like spider silk on the breeze, and I'll never be able to get them back."

"I promise."

"Listen, then, to the Tradition of 'The Fountain of Oblivion.'"

"Begin."

Flemming was lying back on the flower-covered grass at the woman's feet, gazing up with distant eyes into her lovely face, and then up into the leaves of the linden trees above.

"Gentle Lady! Do you remember the linden trees of Bülach, those tall and majestic trees, with soft down covering their gleaming leaves and rustic benches beneath their overhanging branches! A leafy shelter, perfect to be the dwelling of an elf or fairy, where I first declared my love to you, you cold and stately Hermione! A little peasant girl stood nearby, and listened the entire time, with eyes full of wonder and delight, and an unconscious smile, to hear the stranger continue speaking in tones deep yet gentle—no one else was with us in that moment, except God and that peasant child!"

"Why, it's written in rhyme!"

"No, no! The rhyme exists only in your imagination. You promised you wouldn't interrupt me, and you've already broken the delicate threads of the sweetest dream that any poet's mind has ever created."

"It certainly did rhyme!"

This was the daydream of the student Hieronymus, as he sat at midnight in his room, with his hands clasped together, resting on an open book that he should have been reading. His pale face was lifted upward, and his pupils were wide as if the spiritual realm had opened before him, and some beautiful vision was standing there, pulling the student's soul through his eyes up into Heaven, just as the evening sun through breaking summer clouds seems to draw the earth's vapors into itself. Oh, what a sweet vision it was!

I can see it before me now!

Near the student stood an ancient bronze lamp, decorated with mysterious figures carved into its surface. This was a magical lamp that had once belonged to the Arabian astrologer El Geber in Spain. Its light shone as beautifully as starlight, and night after night, as the solitary scholar sat alone reading in his high tower, the lamp's glow pierced through the fog, darkness, and falling rain, streaming out into the night where many sleepless eyes could see it. For the poor Student Hieronymus, this was a miraculous Aladdin's Lamp, because within its flame a divine presence revealed herself to him and displayed wondrous treasures. Each time he opened a heavy, ancient book, it felt as though an angel was opening the gates of Paradise before him, and he had already become known throughout the city as Hieronymus the Learned.

"But, alas! he could no longer read. The spell was broken. Hour after hour he sat with his hands clasped in front of him, his bright eyes staring into emptiness. What could so deeply trouble the studies of this sorrowful young man? Lady, he was in love! Have you ever been in love? He had seen the face of the beautiful Hermione; and just as when we carelessly look at the sun, our dazzled eyes, even when closed, still see it; so he saw by day and by night the glowing image of her upon whom he had too recklessly gazed. Alas! he was miserable; for the proud Hermione scorned the love of a poor student, whose only treasure was a magic lamp. In marble halls, and among the cheerful crowd that adored her, she had nearly forgotten that such a person existed as the Student Hieronymus. The devotion of his heart had been to her merely like the fragrance of a wildflower, which she had carelessly crushed beneath her foot while walking by. But he had lost everything; for he had lost the peace of his mind; and his troubled soul reflected only shattered and twisted images of reality. The world mocked the poor student, who, in his torn and worn cassock, dared to raise his eyes to the Lady Hermione; while he sat alone, in his empty chamber, and endured in silence. He recalled many things, which he wished he could forget; but which, if he had forgotten them, he would want to remember again. Such were the linden trees of Bülach, under whose delightful shade he had declared his love to Hermione. This was the scene which he most wanted to forget, yet most loved to remember; and of this he was now dreaming, with his hands clasped upon his book, and that kind of melody in his thoughts, which you, Lady, mistook for verse.

Suddenly the cathedral clock struck twelve with a melancholy clang. It awakened the Student Hieronymus from his reverie; the sound echoed in his ears, like the iron hooves of Time's galloping horses. The magical hour had arrived, when the spirit of the lamp most eagerly revealed herself to her devoted follower. The bronze figures appeared to come alive; a white mist rose from the flame and spread throughout the room, whose four walls expanded into magnificent cloudy vistas; a scent, like that of wildflowers, filled the air; and a dreamlike melody, resembling distant, sweet-sounding bells, announced the arrival of the midnight spirit. Through his flowing tears the heartbroken Student saw her once again descending a mountain pass in the snowy cloud-covered peaks, as, at dusk, the dewy evening star emerges from the heart of the fog, and takes its place in the heavens. As she drew near, his soul became more peaceful; for her presence was, to his fevered heart, like a tropical night—beautiful and calming and refreshing. Finally she stood before him revealed in all her splendor; and he understood the visible language of her gentle but wordless lips; which seemed to say: 'What does the Student Hieronymus desire tonight?' 'Peace!' he replied, lifting his joined hands, and smiling through his tears. 'The Student Hieronymus begs for peace!' 'Then go,' said the spirit, 'go to the Fountain of Oblivion in the deepest wilderness of the Black Forest, and throw this scroll into its waters; and you shall find peace once more.' Hieronymus opened his arms to embrace the spirit, for her face took on the features of

Hermione; but she disappeared; the music stopped; the splendid cloudscape collapsed and crumbled away; and the student was alone within the four bare walls of his room. As he lowered his head, his gaze fell upon a parchment scroll, which was lying next to the lamp. Upon it was written only the name of Hermione!

The next morning Hieronymus tucked the scroll into his shirt and set off to find the Fountain of Oblivion. After several days of travel, he reached the edge of the Black Forest. He stepped into that shadowy realm with a sense of fear, walking beneath gloomy pines and cedars whose branches spread wide and intertwined. As these trees swayed back and forth, they filled the air with somber twilight and mournful sounds. The deeper he ventured into the forest, the more the drooping moss hung like drapes from the overhead branches, gradually blocking out the heavenly light. He realized the Fountain of Oblivion was close by. Already he could hear the sound of cascading water mixing with the rumbling of the pine trees above. Soon he reached a river that flowed with dignified grandeur through the forest, tumbling with a heavy, metallic crash into a still and lifeless lake. Above this lake, the forest branches came together and intertwined, creating endless darkness. This was the Fountain of Oblivion.

At the edge of the water, the student stopped and stared into the dark depths with an unwavering gaze. The waters were crystal clear, darkened only by shadows. As he looked deeper, he saw far below in the silent depths faint and unclear outlines, swaying back and forth like the folds of a white dress in the twilight. Then clearer and more lasting shapes emerged—shapes his mind recognized yet had forgotten and now remembered again, like pieces of a dream. Finally, far, far beneath him, he saw the great city of the Past, with quiet marble streets, walls covered in moss, and spires rising with a wave-like, flickering movement. Among the crowds filling those streets, he saw faces that had once been familiar and precious to him, and he heard sad, sweet voices singing, "Don't forget us!

Don't forget us!" Then came the distant, mournful sound of funeral bells tolling below in the city of the Past. But in the gardens of that city, children were playing, and among them was one who had his features as they had been in childhood. The boy was leading a little girl by the hand, often caressing her and decorating her with flowers. Then, like a dream, the scene shifted, and the boy had grown older and stood alone, gazing into the sky. As he looked up, his face changed again, and Hieronymus saw him as if it were his own reflection in the clear water. Before him stood a beautiful maiden whose face resembled Hermione's, and he worried that the scroll might have fallen into the water as he leaned over it. Startling as if from a dream, he reached into his chest and breathed with relief when he found the scroll still there. He pulled it out and read the blessed name of Hermione, and the city beneath him disappeared, and the air became fragrant like the scent of May flowers, and light streamed through the shadowy forest and shone upon the lake. The Student Hieronymus pressed the dear name to his lips and cried out with tears streaming down his face, "Despise me as you wish, still, still I will love you; and your name shall brighten the darkness of my life and make the waters of Oblivion smile!" And the name was no longer Hermione, but had changed to Mary; and the Student Hieronymus—is lying at your feet! Oh, gentle Lady!

"I did hear you speak
Far above singing; after you had left
I became familiar with my heart, and explored
"What stirred it so! Alas! I found it love."

———————

Chapter IX. A Talk on The Stairs.

No! I won't describe that scene, or how pale the dignified lady sat at the edge of the green, sunlit meadow! Some women's hearts flutter like leaves with every whisper of love that touches them, then grow quiet once more. Others, like the ocean, are stirred only by storm winds and aren't easily calmed. Mary Ashburton's proud heart was just like that. It had stayed unmoved by this stranger's presence, and the sound of his footsteps and voice stirred no feeling within her. He had fooled himself! They walked home in silence through the green meadow. Even the sunshine felt melancholy, and the rising wind through the old ruins above them sounded like hollow laughter in his ears!

Flemming walked directly to his room. Along the way, he passed the walnut trees where he had first glimpsed Mary Ashburton's face. Without thinking, he shut his eyes. Tears filled them completely. Oh, there are spots in this beautiful world that we never want to see again, no matter how precious they might be to us! The towers of the ancient Franciscan monastery had never appeared so dark and foreboding as they did at that moment, even though the brilliant summer sunlight was streaming down on them.

In his room he found Berkley. He was looking out of the window, whistling.

"Tonight I'm leaving Interlaken for good," Flemming said quite suddenly. Berkley stared at him.

"Absolutely! Please tell me what's wrong? You look as white as a sheet!"

"And I have every reason to look pale," Flemming replied with bitterness. "Hoffmann writes in one of his notebooks that on March eleventh, at exactly half past eight o'clock, he was a fool. That's exactly what I was this morning at half past ten o'clock, and what I am now, and what I suppose I always will be."

He attempted to laugh, but couldn't manage it. He then told Berkley the entire story from start to finish.

"This is a terrible situation!" Berkley exclaimed when he had finished. "How strange! Yet I've long stopped being surprised by women's unpredictable behavior. Didn't Pan win over the pure Diana? Didn't Titania fall in love with Nick Bottom and his donkey's head? Do you think young women's hearts are no longer affected by the magic of love? Trust me, she's in love with someone else. There has to be some explanation for this. No; women never need explanations, except their own desires. But don't worry about it. Stay strong. Worry never helped anyone. After all,--what is she? Who is she? Just a--"

"Quiet! Quiet," Flemming cried out, extremely agitated. "Don't say another word, I beg you. Don't try to comfort me by putting her down. She's still very precious to me; a beautiful, noble woman with high principles."

"Yes," Berkley replied; "that's how it is with all of you young men. You see a beautiful face, or something else, you don't know what, and flickering reason says goodnight; goodbye to common sense. The imagination clothes the beloved with a thousand extraordinary charms; dresses her in all the purple and fine linen, all the rich clothing and adornments, of human nature. I did the same thing when I was young. I was once as desperately in love as you are now; and went through all the

'Delicious deaths, soft exhalations

Of the soul; precious and sacred dissolutions,

A thousand unknown rituals

Of joys, and refined delights.

I fell deeply in love and was turned away. "You're infatuated with certain qualities," the woman told me. "To hell with your qualities, Madam," I replied; "I don't know anything about qualities." "Sir," she responded with composure, "you've been drinking." And so we went our separate ways. She later married someone else, who presumably understood something about qualities. I've encountered her just once since then, and only once. She was carrying a baby dressed in yellow. I can't stand babies dressed in yellow. How relieved I am that she didn't marry me. Someday, you'll be grateful that you were rejected. Trust me on this.

"All that doesn't stop my situation from being a very sad one!" said Flemming sadly.

"Oh, don't worry about fate," Berkley said with a laugh, "as long as you don't end up like Lot's wife. If the cucumber tastes bitter, throw it away, as the philosopher Marcus Aurelius says in his Meditations. Forget about her, and everything will be as if you never knew her."

"I will never forget her," Flemming responded, speaking with considerable gravity. "It's not my pride that has been hurt, but my heart, and this injury runs too deep to ever fully mend. I will carry this pain with me for the rest of my life. I no longer wish to participate in society, but instead will live only within the realm of my own mind. All profound and extraordinary experiences, whether they bring happiness or grief, elevate us beyond this earthly existence; and we would be wise to maintain this higher perspective at all times. Until now, I have failed to do this. But from this moment forward, I will not come back down; I will remain separate and above the world, accompanied by my sorrowful, yet sacred thoughts."

"Wow! You should get out into society; the excitement and activity will cure you within a week. If you meet a woman who really appeals to you and you want to marry her, but she won't consider such a terrible idea, I can only see one solution: find someone else who appeals to you even more and who will be open to it."

"No, my friend; you don't understand who I am," Flemming said, shaking his head. "I love this woman with deep and lasting devotion. I will never stop loving her. This might be insanity on my part, but that's how it is. What a tragedy! Long ago, Paracelsus wasted his life trying to discover the elixir of life, which turned out to be nothing more than alcohol in the end. Instead of achieving immortality on earth, he died drunk on a tavern floor. The same thing happens to many of us. We waste our best years extracting the most beautiful moments of life into love potions that don't make us immortal after all—they just make us drunk. By Heaven! We're all completely insane."

"But are you absolutely certain the situation is completely hopeless?"

"Completely! Absolutely!"

"And yet I can see you haven't given up all hope. You still tell yourself that the lady's heart might change. The great secret of happiness lies not in enjoying, but in giving up. But it's difficult, very difficult. Hope has as many lives as a cat or a king. I'm sure you've heard the old Italian proverb, 'The King never dies.' But perhaps you've never heard that at the court of Naples, where the dead body of a monarch lies in state, his dinner is brought up to him as usual, and the court physician tastes it to make sure it hasn't been poisoned, and then the servants carry it out again, saying 'The King does not dine today.' Hope in our souls is King; and we also say, 'The King never dies.' Even when in reality he lies dead within us, in a kind of solemn mockery we offer him his usual food, but are forced to say, 'The King does not dine today.' It must be a terrible day, indeed, when a king of Naples has no appetite for his dinner! but you yourself are proof that the King never dies. You are feeding your King, although you say he is dead."

"To show you that I don't want to hold onto false hope," Flemming replied, "I'll be leaving Interlachen tomorrow morning. I'm heading to the Tyrol."

"You're right," Berkley said. "Nothing helps with sorrow quite like moving fast through the open air. I'll come with you, though

I imagine your conversation won't be very diverse—nothing but Edward and Kunigunde."

"What do you mean by that?"

"Go to Berlin, and you'll find out. But joking aside, I'll do everything I can to cheer you up and help you forget the Dark Lady and this unfortunate incident."

"Accident!" Flemming exclaimed. "This isn't an accident at all, but God's Providence that brought us together to punish me for my sins."

"Oh, my friend," Berkley interrupted, "if you see God's hand so clearly in every single thing that happens in your life, you'll end up thinking you're some kind of apostle or special messenger. I don't see anything particularly unusual in what's happened to you."

"What! Not when our souls are so connected to each other! When we seemed so perfectly made to be together—to be one!"

"I've often noticed," Berkley replied coldly, "that people with similar souls rarely marry each other; almost as rarely as those who are related by blood. There does seem to be something like spiritual incest. So, passionate lover, don't try to convince yourself and your disdainful lady that you have kindred souls; but rather the opposite; that you are very different; and each lacking in those qualities that most define and distinguish the other. Believe me, your courtship will be more successful then. But good morning. I need to get ready for this unexpected trip."

The next morning, Flemming and Berkley set out for Innsbruck, much like Huon of Bordeaux and Scherasmin heading toward Babylon. Berkley had taken it upon himself to comfort his friend, a task he carried out like an old Spanish Matadora—a woman whose job was to care for the sick and press her elbow into the belly of the dying to ease their suffering.

Book IV.

Opening Quote

"Mortal, they softly say,
Peace to your heart!
We too, yes, are mortal,
Have been as you are;
Hope-lifted, doubt-depressed,
Seeing in part,
Tested, distressed, tempted,--
"Sustained—as you are."

———————

Chapter I. A Miserere.

In the Orlando Innamorato, Malagigi, the sorcerer, puts everyone to sleep by reading to them from a book. Some books possess this power naturally and require no sorcerer. Worried, dear reader, that mine might be one of these books, I have included these introductory chapters throughout, like choir stalls or mercy seats in a church, decorated with ornate canopies and carved poppy heads above them, where you can sit down and rest.

No—the comparison isn't a poor one. This book does bear some resemblance to a cathedral, built in the Romanesque style, complete with spires, flying buttresses, and rooftops,

"Decorated with gargoyles of greyhounds and many lions"

Made of fine gold, with various different dragons.

You step into its shade and coolness, escaping from the hot streets of life; a mysterious light flows through the painted glass of the golden windows, coloring the pointed arches and folded leaves of the window frames, and the cherubs and holy water fonts below. Here and there stands an image of the Virgin Mary; and other statues, "in various garments, called mourners, stand in enclosures built around the tomb"; and, above everything, rises the enormous dome of heaven, with its star-shaped moldings, and the blazing constellations, like the mosaics in the dome of St. Peter's. Haven't you heard funeral psalms from the chapel? Haven't you heard the sound of church bells, as I promised; mysterious sounds from the Past and Future, as from the bell towers outside the cathedral; just such a sorrowful, rich, liquid ringing of bells, as is sometimes heard at sea, from distant cities far below the horizon?

I don't know how this Romanesque style of architecture, which can be quite elaborate at times, might appeal to the critics. Perhaps they would prefer that I had left out some of my numerous decorative elements—my intricate patterns, roses, fantastical spouts, crucifixes, and Galilee towers. But would it still have been truly Romanesque then?

But perhaps, dear reader, you are one of those who think the days of romance are gone forever. Don't believe it! Oh, don't believe it! You have at this very moment in your heart as sweet a romance as was ever written. You are not less a woman because you do not sit high in a tower with a falcon on your wrist! You are not less a man because you wear no armor or chainmail, and do not go on horseback after foolish adventures! No, no! Everyone has a romance in their own heart. All that has blessed or inspired awe in the world lies there; and

"The oracle within him, that which lives,
He must call upon and examine—not lifeless books,
"Not ordinances, not moldy, decaying papers."

Eventually, everyone must write certain chapters of their personal story, whether through words or deeds. These chapters will reveal the truth, because Truth is a thought that has dressed itself in the right clothing of either words or actions. Meanwhile, Falsehood is a thought that disguises itself in words or actions that don't belong to it, appearing before the unseeing old world just as Jacob appeared before the patriarch Isaac, wearing the fine clothes of his brother Esau. And the world, like the patriarch, is frequently fooled; because although the voice sounds like Jacob's voice, the hands feel like Esau's hands, and the False steals the birthright and blessing away from the True. This is why the world so often raises its voice and cries.

That delightful and imaginative Chinese romance, the Shadow in the Water, concludes with the hero marrying both heroines. I hope my kind reader feels curious to discover how this earthly romance ends, and whether it contains any marriage whatsoever.

That is exactly what I'm thinking about right now, as I sit here by my comfortable bedroom window, enjoying the gentle breeze of a beautiful summer morning, watching the movements of the golden robin perched on its swaying nest at the very tip of a hanging branch on that elm tree over there. The wide meadows and the steel-blue river bring back memories of the meadows of Unterseen and the river Aar; and beyond them rise magnificent snow-white clouds, stacked up like the Alps. In this way, the spirits of Washington and William Tell seem to walk side by side through these heavenly fields; for it was here, in days long past, that our great Patriot lived; and those clouds look so much like the snowy Alps that they inevitably remind me of the Swiss. What noble examples of lofty purpose and unwavering determination! Don't they move like Hyperion across the heavens? Weren't they also children of Heaven and Earth?

Nothing could be more beautiful than these summer mornings, or the southern window where I sit and write in this old mansion that resembles an Italian villa. But oh, this exhaustion—this weariness—when everything around me is so bright! This morning I have an unusual craving for flowers; a desire to walk among the roses and carnations and breathe in their fragrance, as if it might restore me. I wish I knew the person who called flowers "the fugitive poetry of Nature." From this distance, from these academic shadows—from this leafy, blooming, and beautiful Cambridge, I reach out my hand to grasp his, as the hand of a poet! Yes, this morning I would rather walk with him among the cheerful flowers than sit here and write. I feel so tired!

Old men with their walking sticks, as the Spanish poet says, are always knocking at death's door. But I'm not old. The Spanish poet could have included young people too.—It doesn't matter! Be brave, and move forward! The Romance must be completed; and completed quickly.

Oh, you struggling writer! You need to dig much deeper into the human heart! Strike those chords—strike those profound chords with greater courage, or your words will fade away like whispers, and no one will hear them except yourself! And to encourage you in your lonely work, remember that an author's private studies are like the hidden foundations that support the bridge of his reputation, stretching across the dark waters of being forgotten. These foundations remain unseen, but without them, no lasting achievement can stand firm!

And now, Reader, since the sermon has ended, and we remain seated here in this Miserere, let us read aloud a page from the ancient parchment manuscript on the lectern in front of us; let us chant it through these shadowy aisles, like a Gregorian Chant, and awaken the slumbering congregation!

"I have read about the great river Euripus, which ebbs and flows seven times a day with such force that it carries ships with full sails directly against the wind. Seven times in an hour, hasty opinions ebb and flow in the torrent of reckless and troubling thoughts, carrying harsh criticism and malicious slander directly against the wind of wisdom and sound judgment."

In secula seculorum! Amen!

Chapter II. Curfew Bells.

Welcome, Disappointment! Your hand is cold and hard, but it is the hand of a friend! Your voice is stern and harsh, but it is the voice of a friend! Oh, there is something magnificent in quiet endurance, something magnificent in the determined, unwavering resolve to suffer without complaint, which makes disappointment often better than success!

Emperor Isaac Angelus made a treaty with Saladin and attempted to buy the Holy Sepulchre with gold. Richard the Lionheart rejected such an alliance and sought to reclaim it through battle. This is how weak minds make agreements with the passions they cannot conquer, and attempt to buy happiness at the cost of their principles. But the determined will of a strong person rejects such methods and fights nobly against their enemy to accomplish great things. Therefore, whoever you are that suffers, do not try to scatter your sorrow with the world's empty words, nor silence its voice with mindless celebration. It is a false peace that is bought through self-indulgence. Instead, take this sorrow into your heart and make it part of yourself, and it will strengthen you until you are powerful once more.

The shadows of the mind work just like the shadows of the body. In the morning of life, they all fall behind us; at midday, we step on them and crush them beneath our feet; and in the evening, they stretch out long, wide, and growing deeper in front of us. Aren't the sorrows of childhood just as dark as those we face in old age? Aren't the morning shadows of life just as deep and wide as those that come in the evening? Yes, they are; but morning shadows quickly disappear, while evening shadows reach forward into the night and blend with the approaching darkness. Man is conceived in joy and born in suffering; and these experiences foreshadow the ecstasy and struggle that will define his entire life from the very start. But human life on this beautiful earth consists mostly of small pains and small pleasures. The great wonder-flowers bloom only once in a person's lifetime.

A week had already passed since the events described in the last chapter. Paul Flemming continued on his path, a sorrowful man, "drinking the sweet bitterness of his grief." He didn't curse fate or blame Providence, but endured his pain in silence. It's a noble quality in a lover's nature that he thinks no ill of the one he loves. What he endured wasn't a sudden storm of emotion that passes quickly with great noise and leaves the heart clearer afterward; instead, a dark specter had emerged in the clear night, and like that of Adamastor, it blocked out the stars. Even when it disappeared for a while, the deep sound of the groaning ocean could still be heard from far away, echoing through many dark and solitary hours. And so he traveled onward, wrapped in hopeless darkness, paying little attention to everything around him. His mind was troubled. That one face was always in front of him; that one voice forever speaking;

"You are not the Magician."

It's truly painful to be misunderstood and undervalued by the people we love. However, we must learn to endure this in our lives without complaint, because it's a story that happens over and over again.

There are people in this world for whom local connections mean nothing. The spirit of a place doesn't speak to them. Even on battlefields, where this spirit's voice usually rings loudest, they hear only the sound of their own voices; they encounter there only their own dull and scholarly thoughts, just as the old grammarian Brunetto Latini met a poor student riding a bay mule on the plain of Roncesvalles. This hadn't always been true for Paul Flemming, but it had become so now. He felt no interest in the landscape surrounding him. He barely glanced at it. Even the treacherous mountain passes, where the sharp-eyed Tyrolean peasant had watched his enemy from his rocky perch, and the roaring, muddy torrent below, which had swallowed the bloody corpse that fell from the rocks like a crushed worm, stirred no strong feeling in his heart. Everything around him seemed dreamlike and unclear; everything within felt dim, as during a solar eclipse. Just as the moon, whether visible or hidden, controls the ocean's tides, so that lady's face, whether present or absent, controlled the tides of his soul; both day and night, both awake and asleep. In every pale face and dark eye he saw a likeness to her; and what the day refused him in reality, the night granted him in dreams.

"This is a strange, fantastic world," said Berkley, after a very long silence, during which the two travelers had been sitting each in his corner of the traveling carriage, wrapped in his own thoughts. "A very strange, fantastic world; where each person pursues his own golden bubble, and laughs at his neighbor for doing the same. I have been thinking how a moral scientist would classify our species. I think he would divide it, not as Lord Byron did, into two great classes, the bores and those who are bored, but into three, namely; Happy Men, Lucky Dogs, and Miserable Wretches. This is more true and philosophical, though perhaps not quite so comprehensive. He is the Happy Man, who, blessed with modest comfort, a wife and children,--sits enthroned in the hearts of his family, and knows no other ambition, than that of making those around him happy. But the Lucky Dog is he, who, free from all domestic cares, strolls up and down his room, in morning gown and slippers; drums on the window of a rainy day; and, as he stirs his evening fire, snaps his fingers at the world, and says, 'I have no wife nor children, good or bad, to provide for.' I had a friend, who is now no more. He was taken away in the bloom of life, by a very rapid--widow. He was by birth and by profession a dandy,--born with a monocle and a cane. King of the hill, he flapped his wings, and crowed among the feathered tribe. But alas! a fair, white hen has torn his crest out, and he shall crow no more. You will generally find him of a morning, sniffing around a meat cart, with domestic happiness written in every line of his face; and sometimes meet him in a side street at noon, hurrying homeward, with a beef steak on a wooden skewer, or a fresh fish, with a piece of tarred string run through its gills. In the evening he rocks the cradle, and gets up in the night when the child cries. Like a barbarian, of the Dark Ages, he consults his wife on all important matters, and looks upon her as a being of more than human goodness and wisdom. In short, the ladies all say he is a very domestic man, and makes a good husband; which, confidentially, is only a more polite way of saying he is hen-pecked. He is a Happy Man. I have another dear friend, who is a sixty-year-old bachelor. He has one of those well-oiled dispositions, which turn upon the hinges of the world without creaking. The prime of life is over with him; but his old age is sunny and cheerful; and a merry heart still nestles in his tottering frame, like a swallow that builds in a tumble-down chimney. He is a devoted admirer of ladies. The rustle of a silk gown is music to his ears, and his imagination is continually led astray by some will-o'-the-wisp in the shape of a lady's bodice. In his devotion to the fair sex,--the muslin, as he calls it,--he is the gentle flower of chivalry. It is amusing to see how quickly he picks up the scent of a lady's handkerchief. When once fairly in pursuit, there is no such thing as throwing him off the trail. His heart looks out through his eye; and his inward delight tingles down to the tail of his coat. He loves to bask in the sunshine of a smile; when he can breathe the sweet atmosphere of kid gloves and linen handkerchiefs, his soul is in its element; and his supreme delight is to pass the morning, to use his own quaint language, 'in making dodging calls, and wiggling round among the ladies!' He is a lucky dog!"

"And I suppose you'll use me as an example of the Miserable Wretches category," said Flemming, trying to go along with his friend's joke. "I'm certainly miserable enough. You can make me the stuffed bear—the representative specimen of this group."

"Absolutely not," Berkley responded; "you haven't fallen that far. Only someone who becomes enslaved by their own desires, or by the desires of others, is truly miserable. I have faith that you'll never find yourself in such a situation. Why do you look so pale and sickly, devoted lover? Do you recall Sir John Suckling's song?"

"Why do you look so pale and sickly, foolish lover;"
Why are you so pale?
Will, if looking good can't win her over,
Looking ill will prevail?
Why are you so pale?
"Why are you so quiet and silent, young sinner;
Please, why are you so silent?
Will, if speaking eloquently cannot win her over,
Saying nothing will do it?
Please, why are you so silent?
"Stop, stop, for shame! this cannot move,"
This cannot take her!
If she doesn't love on her own,
Nothing will make her!
"The devil take her!"
"How do you like that?"

"I'm telling you to stop, just stop this nonsense," Flemming replied. "Why are you quoting songs from that clever but immoral era? Don't you have any better comfort to give me? How many times do I have to tell you that I hold no grudge against the lady? I don't blame her for not loving me. I want her to be happy, even if it means sacrificing my own happiness."

"That's generous of you, and you deserve something better. But you speak so metaphorically about everything that a stranger would think you have no genuine emotions—and are only imagining yourself to be in love."

"The way people express their emotions varies from person to person. It's not always straightforward. Some people, when they become excited or emotional, naturally speak using metaphors and comparisons. This doesn't mean they feel any less deeply than others. We can see this clearly in our everyday ways of speaking. It all depends on the individual."

"Lord, have mercy!"

"Well, criticize my way of speaking as much as you want. What I'm demanding is that you don't speak badly of the lady. When have you ever heard me say a single word against her?"

"Oh! Now you're talking like Launce to his dog!"

Their conversation, which had started so cheerfully, was suddenly cut short by a loud crash of thunder that signaled an approaching storm. The afternoon was growing late, and the entire sky had turned black with low-hanging, drifting clouds. Even darker, the storm moved forward majestically from the southwest, accompanied by nearly continuous rumbles of distant thunder. The wind appeared to be attacking a fortress of clouds and advanced with swirling dust, the green flags of tree branches whipping through the air, heavy booming sounds, and occasional explosive bursts, like a gunpowder cart exploding. Mixed with these sounds came the ringing of church bells from a nearby village. All the bells were tolling mournfully to drive away lightning strikes. At the village entrance stood a large wooden crucifix, surrounded by a gathering of priests and villagers kneeling in the wet grass beside the road, their hands and eyes raised toward heaven, praying for rain. Their prayer was quickly granted.

The travelers continued their journey through the fierce wind and rain. They had departed from Landeck and hoped to arrive in Innsbruck before midnight. Darkness fell, and Flemming drifted off to sleep beneath the thunderous storm above, while below his feet the roaring Inn River rushed past—a mountain torrent leaping forward as wild and untamed as when it first emerged from its birthplace in the remote valleys of Engadin. It served as a fitting symbol of himself, racing through the night in this same manner. His sleep lasted a long time but was restless and interrupted, and eventually he woke up in fear because he heard a voice speak clearly in his ear, saying these words:

"They have brought the dead body."

They were driving past a cemetery at the edge of a town, and among the gravestones a faint lamp flickered before a statue of the Virgin Mary. The scene looked otherworldly and haunting. Flemming almost expected to witness the spirits of the dead gathering to enter the church and chant their midnight service. He tried to speak to Berkley, but got no response; his companion was sound asleep.

"Then it was only a dream," he said to himself; "yet how clear that voice sounded! Oh, if we possessed spiritual senses to see and hear things that are now invisible and silent to us, we would witness the entire atmosphere filled with the departing souls of that enormous crowd which dies every moment—we would see them rising like delicate mists toward heaven, and hear the thunderous blast of the archangel's trumpet echoing endlessly throughout the universe and announcing the terrible judgment day. Truly the soul does not depart alone on its final journey, but spirits of its own kind accompany it, when not ministering angels; and they travel in groups to that unknown realm! Neither in life nor in death do we stand alone."

He dozed off repeatedly throughout the journey, and eventually, well past midnight, arrived in Innsbruck in a drowsy, half-conscious state. His mind was flooded with hazy memories of the incredibly dreary nighttime trip—ascending steep hills and descending into pitch-black valleys, the brief clatter of wheels on the cobblestone streets as they passed through towns, followed by the deep, echoing rumble and pounding on the muddy ground. He remembered the complete darkness of the night, the thunder and lightning and downpour, the roaring of rushing water cascading through deep gorges alongside the road, and the wind howling through the mountain passes with a sound so loud and prolonged it resembled the unstoppable laughter of the gods.

The travelers didn't stay long in Innsbruck the next day. However, they made sure to visit Maximilian's tomb in the Franciscan Church of the Holy Cross, where they looked with considerable admiration at the twenty-eight enormous bronze statues of Godfrey of Bouillon, King Arthur, Ernest the Iron-man, Frederick of the Empty Pockets, and other kings and heroes that stand leaning on their swords between the church columns, as though they were guarding the tomb of the dead. These statues reminded Flemming of the bronze giants that strike the hours on the bell tower of San Basso in Venice, and of the flail-armed monsters that guarded the gateway of Angulaffer's castle in Oberon. After looking at these motionless guards for a while, they left and walked through the public gardens, with the jagged mountains rising directly above their heads, and tall, melancholy pine trees all around them, like Tyrolean peasants with shaggy hair; at their feet rushed the wild torrent of the Inn River, sweeping through the middle of the town with muddy waves. In the afternoon they continued their journey toward Salzburg through the magnificent mountain passes of Waidering and Unken.

Chapter III. Shadows On the Wall.

On the following morning Flemming woke up in a room at the Golden Ship inn in Salzburg, just as the clock in the cathedral across the street was striking ten. The window shutters were closed, and the room was almost completely dark. He was lying on his back with his hands folded across his chest, staring up at the white curtains above him. He imagined them to be the white marble canopy of a tomb, and himself the marble statue lying beneath it. When the clock finished striking, the twenty-eight massive bronze statues from the Church of Holy Rood in Innsbruck walked into the room and positioned themselves along the walls, which expanded into dimly lit aisles and archways. On the painted windows he saw Interlaken, with its Franciscan monastery and the Square Tower of the ruins. In a hanging ornament overhead stood the German student, appearing as Saint Vitus; and on a washbasin, or holy water font below, sat a cherub with the form and face of Berkley. Then the organ pipes began to sound, and he heard the voices of an unseen choir singing. And soon the gilded gates in the bronze screen before the altar opened, and a wedding procession passed through. The bride was dressed in medieval clothing and held a book in her hand with velvet covers and golden clasps. It was Mary Ashburton. She looked at him as she walked by. Her face was pale, and there were tears in her beautiful eyes. Then the gates closed again, and one of the wooden poppy-heads above a carved choir stall, shaped like an owl, flapped its broad wings and hooted, "To-whit! to-whoo!" Then the entire scene changed, and he imagined himself as a monk's head on a rain spout, and it was raining miserably, and Berkley was standing underneath with an umbrella, laughing!

In other words, Flemming was burning with fever and delirious. He stayed in this condition for a week. The first thing he became aware of was hearing the doctor speak to Berkley;

"The crisis has passed. I now believe he is out of danger."

He then drifted into a peaceful sleep; the raging fever had vanished like a furious, crimson cloud, and the cooling summer rain started to fall like gentle drops on the dry ground. Another week passed; and Flemming was now "sitting clothed, and in his right mind." Berkley had been reading aloud to him; and still gripped the book in his hand, with his index finger marking his place between the pages. It was a volume of Hoffmann's writings.

"How very strange it is," he said, "that you can hardly open the biography of any German author without finding it begin with an account of his grandfather. It will tell you how the venerable old man walked up and down the garden among the bright flowers, wrapped in his morning gown, which is also covered with flowers, and perhaps wearing a little velvet cap on his head. Or you will find him sitting by the fireplace in the great chair, smoking his ancestral pipe, with bushy eyebrows and eyes like bird's nests under the eaves of a house, and a mouth like a Nuremberg nutcracker's. The future poet climbs upon the old man's knees. His genius is not recognized yet. He is thought for the most part to be a dull boy. His father is a stern man, or perhaps dead. But the mother is still there, a frail, saint-like woman, with her knitting-work, and an elder sister, who has already been in love, and wears rings on her fingers;--

Death's heads and similar reminders

Her grandmother and worm-eaten aunts left to her,

"To tell her what her beauty must come to."

"But this isn't true when it comes to Hoffmann's life, if I remember correctly."

"No, not exactly. Instead of the grandfather we have the grandmother, a dignified woman who has long ago turned her back on life's trivial pursuits. The mother, estranged from her husband, suffers from both mental and physical illness, and drifts about like a ghost. Then there is a loving maiden aunt; and an uncle, a retired judge who strikes fear into little boys—the Giant Despair of this Doubting Castle in Koenigsberg; and from time to time the kind face of a respected great-uncle, whom Lamotte Fouqué described as a hero from bygone days wearing a morning robe and slippers, appears at the door with a smile. On the upper floor of the same house lived a poor boy with his mother, who was so mentally disturbed that she believed herself to be the Virgin Mary, and her son the Savior of the world. Wild imaginings would also sweep through that child's mind. He would later encounter Hoffmann elsewhere and become his friend in years to come, though at this time they knew nothing of one another. This was Werner, who has gained some recognition in German literature as the writer of many wild Destiny-Dramas."

"I believe Hoffmann died in Berlin."

"Yes. He left Koenigsberg when he was twenty years old, and spent the following eight years of his life in the Prussian-Polish Provinces, where he held some minor government position; and he developed many bad habits and married a Polish woman. After this he worked as Music-Director at various German theaters, and lived a wandering, miserable life for ten years. He then went to Berlin as Clerk of the Exchange, and stayed there until his death, which occurred about seven or eight years later."

"Did you ever see him?"

"I was in Berlin during his lifetime, and saw him frequently. I shall never forget the first time. It was at one of the aesthetic teas, given by a literary lady on Unter den Linden, where the celebrated figures were fed with suitable refreshments, from tea and bread and butter, up to oysters and Rhine wine. During the evening my attention was caught by the entrance of a strange little figure, with a wild head of brown hair. His eyes were bright gray; and his thin lips closely pressed together with an expression of not unpleasant irony. This strange-looking person began to bow his way through the crowd, with quick, nervous, hinge-like movements, much resembling those of a marionette. He had a hoarse voice, and such a rapid way of speaking, that although I understood German well enough for ordinary purposes, I could not understand half of what he said. Before long he had seated himself at the piano, and was improvising such wild, sweet fantasies, that the music of one's dreams is not more sweet and wild. Then suddenly some painful thought seemed to cross his mind, as if he imagined that he was there to entertain the company. He rose from the piano, and seated himself in another part of the room; where he began to make faces, and talk loudly while others were singing. Finally he disappeared, like a hobgoblin, laughing, 'Ho! ho! ho!' I asked a person beside me who this strange being was. 'That was Hoffmann,' was the answer. 'The Devil!' said I. 'Yes,' continued my informant; 'and if you should follow him now, you would see him plunge into an obscure and unfrequented wine cellar, and there, amid jovial companions, with wine and tobacco smoke, and jokes and witticisms, and quaint, clever sayings, turn the dim night into glorious day.'"

"What a strange being!"

"I once witnessed him during one of his late-night drinking sessions. He sat there in his element, positioned at the head of the table; not completely intoxicated, but warmed by wine, which transformed him into a wildly eloquent speaker, much like the Devil's Elixir affected the Monk Medardus. There, amid the flowing stream of clever conversation, or when quiet, his gray, piercing eyes gleaming from beneath his disheveled hair, observing everything bizarre about the people surrounding him, sat this unfortunate genius until daybreak approached. Then he would make his way home, having, like the souls of the envious in Purgatory, his eyelids sewn shut with iron wire—though in his case it was from champagne bottles. During these hours he composed his strange, fantastical stories. To his stimulated imagination everything took on a ghostly appearance. The shadows of ordinary objects around him moved like spirits through the haunted rooms of his mind; and the old paintings on the walls seemed to wink at him, appearing to step down from their frames; until, terrified by the ghostly crowd surrounding him, he would wake his wife from her sleep, asking her to sit beside him while he wrote."

"No wonder he died in the prime of life!"

"No. The only wonder is that he managed to follow this way of life for six years. I'm amazed it didn't kill him sooner."

"But death finally arrived in a terrifying form."

"Yes; his forty-sixth birthday found him sitting at home in his armchair, surrounded by his friends. But the fine old wine—he always drank the finest—never touched the sick man's lips that evening. His usual humor had vanished. Of all his jokes, his playful antics, his songs, his bursts of joy that used to make the whole table erupt in laughter, not one remained now to mock his own grimacing face—completely dejected. The conversation centered on death and the grave. And when one of his friends remarked that life was not the greatest good, Hoffmann cut him off, crying out with shocking intensity: 'No, no! Life, life, only life! under any circumstances whatsoever!' Five months later, he had stopped suffering because he had stopped living. He died gradually. His feet and hands, his legs and arms, slowly and one by one, became still and lifeless. But his spirit remained alive and active; and throughout the lonely days and sleepless nights, lying in his bed, he spoke his final stories to a secretary who wrote them down. They were indeed strange stories for a dying man to create! Yet he found such joy in dictating them that he told his friend Hitzig he would gladly give up the use of his hands forever if he could just keep the ability to write through dictation. Such was his passion for life—for what he called the sweet habit of existing!"

"Wasn't he the one who, in his final hours, expressed such a deep yearning to see the green fields one more time; and cried out; 'Heaven! it's already summer, and I haven't yet seen a single green tree!' "

"Yes, that was Hoffmann. He died shortly after that. His final moments were remarkable. He slowly lost all feeling in his body, though his mind stayed sharp. Since he no longer felt any pain, he told his doctor, 'It will be over soon now. I don't feel any pain anymore.' He believed he was getting better, but the doctor knew he was dying and replied, 'Yes, it will be over soon!' The following morning he asked his wife to come to his bedside and requested that she fold his lifeless hands together. Then, as he looked up toward heaven, she heard him say, 'We must think of God, too!' Few words more heartbreaking than these have ever been spoken by a human being. A little while later, the spark of life flared up inside him once more; he said he was well again, that he would continue working on the story he was writing that evening, and he wanted the last sentence read aloud to him. Soon after this, they turned his face toward the wall, and he passed away."

"And so a human soul passed away after enduring much self-imposed suffering. Let us walk gently over the poet's remains. For myself, I admit that I cannot bring myself to separate him from the general mass of flawed, sinful humanity and condemn him severely. The little I have witnessed of the world, and what I understand of human history, has taught me to view the mistakes of others with sadness rather than anger. When I consider the story of one troubled heart that has both sinned and suffered, and I imagine the battles and temptations it has endured—the brief moments of happiness—the restless anxiety of hope and fear—the tears of remorse—the weakness of resolve—the burden of poverty—the abandonment by friends—the contempt of a world that shows little compassion—the emptiness of the soul's sacred place—and the menacing voices from within—health lost—happiness lost—even hope, which remains with us the longest, lost—I have little inclination for anything other than gratitude that such is not my fate, and I would rather entrust the wayward soul of my fellow human being to Him from whose hands it originally came."

"even as a little child,"

"Crying and laughing in its childish play."

"You are right. And it is worth a student's while to observe calmly how tobacco, wine, and midnight worked like demons upon Hoffmann's delicate frame; and no less thoroughly upon his delicate mind. He who drinks beer, thinks beer; and he who drinks wine, thinks wine;--and he who drinks midnight, thinks midnight. He was a man of exceptional intellect. He was blessed with sharp humor and cutting wit, and a magnificent imagination. But the fire of his genius did not burn peacefully, with a steady flame, upon the hearth of his home. It was a blazing and erratic flame;--for the branches that he fed it with were not branches from the Tree of Life,--but from another tree that grew in Paradise,--and they were wet with the unhealthy dews of night, and more unhealthy wine; and thus, amid smoke and ashes the fire burned unsteadily, and went out with a glare, which leaves the observer blind."

"This inner fire was like Meleager's burning brand; when it finally went out, he died. And as you mention, evidence of all this is clearly apparent in Hoffmann's works. When I read his bizarre imaginings, I feel the same way I do on a summer night when I hear the wind picking up in the trees, watching the branches bend and gesture with their elongated fingers while voices chatter and taunt through the darkness. A sense of wonder and mysterious fear washes over me. I long to hear the sound of a living voice or footsteps nearby—to glimpse a kind and recognizable face. Honestly, if it's late at night, both the reader and the writer of these supernatural tales would gladly welcome a gentle, calm-eyed wife sitting beside them with her knitting."

Berkley smiled, but Flemming kept talking without acknowledging the smile, even though he understood what his friend was thinking.

The life and writings of this remarkable person fascinate me deeply. Often we can learn more from a person's mistakes than from their strengths. Furthermore, because of the shared feelings we all have as human beings, souls that have fought and endured hardship are precious to me. I gladly acknowledge their kinship. The scars on their faces do not disfigure them so much that they stop being compelling. These marks always show evidence of struggle, though sadly, they too often also reveal failure. Periods of unhealthy, dreamy, unclear pleasure are followed by times of exhaustion and gloom. Where then are the brilliant thoughts that, during the profound silence of night, emerge like stars in the sky of our spirits? Morning arrives, the light of ordinary day streams in around us, and the heavens contain no stars! From the experiences of such people we discover that simple pleasant feelings are not true happiness—that physical pleasures should be consumed carefully and sparingly, as if drinking from cupped hands; and that those who kneel down to drink from these brilliant streams that nourish life are not chosen by God either to destroy or to triumph!

"I think you're being very generous in your assessment. This isn't the typical flaw of critics. Like Shakespeare's samphire-gatherer, they have a terrible profession! And to complete the comparison, they should be hanged for it!"

"I think it would be difficult to hang a man just for the sake of a comparison. But which of Hoffmann's works are you holding?"

"His Fantasy-Pieces in Callot's Style. Who was this Callot?"

"He was a painter from Lorraine in the seventeenth century, famous for his wild and bizarre artistic ideas. These sketches by Hoffmann copy his style. They're filled with humor, poetry, and brilliant imagination."

"And which of them should I read to you? Ritter Glück; or the Musical Sufferings of John Kreisler; or that absolutely exquisite story of the Golden Pot, which depicts the life of Poetry in this ordinary world of ours?"

"Read the shortest one. Read Kreisler. That will entertain me. It's a portrayal of his own struggles at the aesthetic tea gatherings in Berlin, supposedly written in pencil on the blank pages of a music book."

Berkley then leaned back in his armchair and began to read aloud.

Chapter IV. Musical Sufferings of John Kreisler.

"They are all gone! I should have known it from the whispering, shuffling, coughing, and buzzing through every note on the scale. It was like a real swarm of bees leaving their old hive. Gottlieb has lit fresh candles for me and placed a bottle of Burgundy on the piano. I can't play anymore—I'm completely exhausted. My glorious old friend here on the music stand is to blame for that. Once again he has carried me away through the air, just as Mephistopheles did with Faust, and so high that I paid no attention whatsoever to the little people below me, though I'm sure they made plenty of noise. What a rotten, worthless, wasted evening! But now I feel well and cheerful! However, while I was playing, I took out my pencil, and on page sixty-three, under the last system, I jotted down a couple of good flourishes in code with my right hand, while my left hand was struggling away in the torrent of sweet sounds. On the blank page at the end I continue writing. I abandon all codes and sweet tones, and with true delight, like a sick man restored to health who can never stop telling about what he has suffered, I record here in detail the terrible agonies of this evening's tea party. And not just for myself, but also for all those who from time to time might amuse and enlighten themselves with my copy of John Sebastian Bach's Variations for the Piano, published by Nägeli in Zürich, and who find my notes at the end of the thirtieth variation, and, guided by the great Latin Verte (I will write it down the moment I finish this sorrowful account of grievances), turn over the page and read."

"They will immediately understand the connection. They know that Privy Councilor Rödelein's house is a delightful place to visit, and that he has two daughters, whom the entire fashionable society enthusiastically declares dance like goddesses, speak French like angels, and play and sing and draw like the Muses. Privy Councilor Rödelein is a wealthy man. At his quarterly dinner parties he serves the most exquisite wines and richest dishes. Everything is arranged with the utmost elegance; and anyone who does not enjoy himself immensely at his tea parties has no style, no wit, and especially no appreciation for the fine arts. It is with this in mind that, along with the tea, punch, wine, ice-creams, and other refreshments, a little music is always provided, which, like the other treats, is very quietly consumed by fashionable society."

"The arrangements are as follows. After every guest has had enough time to drink as many cups of tea as they want, and punch and ices have been served twice, the servants roll out the card tables for the older and more serious members of the group, who would rather play cards than any musical instrument. To be honest, this type of entertainment doesn't create such pointless noise as other activities, and you only hear the sound of clinking money."

"This is a hint for the younger members of the group to rush toward the Misses Rödelein. A great commotion follows; in the middle of which you can make out these words,--"

"'Beautiful young lady! Please don't deny us the pleasure of hearing your heavenly talent! Oh, sing something! Please, be a dear!--impossible,--terrible cold,--the last ball! haven't practiced anything,--oh, please, please, we're begging you,' and so on.

"Meanwhile Gottlieb has opened the piano, and placed the familiar music book on the stand; and from the card table cries the respectable mother,--"

" 'Sing then, my children!' "

"That's my signal to begin. I position myself at the piano, and the Rödeleins are triumphantly escorted to the instrument."

"And now another difficulty arises. Neither wishes to sing first."

"'You know, dear Nanette, how terribly hoarse I am.'"

"'Why, my dear Marie, I am as hoarse as you are.'"

"'I sing so badly!--'"

"'Oh, my dear child; please start!'"

"My suggestion (I always make the same one!) that they should both start together with a duet is enthusiastically applauded. The music book is flipped through, and the page, carefully folded down, is finally found, and off we go with Dolce dell' anima, etc."

"To be honest, the talent of the Misses Rödelein is quite considerable. I have been an instructor here for only five years, and less than two years with the Rödelein family. In this brief time, Fräulein Nanette has made such remarkable progress that she can sing a melody she has heard at the theater just ten times, and practiced on the piano at most ten times more, right away, so clearly that you immediately recognize what it is. Fräulein Marie picks it up by the eighth time; and even if she sometimes sings a quarter note lower than the piano, it's still very acceptable, especially considering her pretty little doll-like face and very charming rosy lips."

"After the duet, everyone burst into applause! Now solo pieces and short duets followed one after another, and I cheerfully pounded away at the accompaniment I'd played a thousand times before. During the singing, Councilor Eberstein's wife made it clear through her coughing and humming that she was also a singer. Miss Nanette says;

"'But, my dear Finanzräthin, now you must let us hear your beautiful voice.'"

A new commotion breaks out. She has a terrible head cold and can't remember anything from memory! Gottlieb immediately brings two armloads of sheet music, and the pages are flipped through over and over again. First she considers singing Der Hölle Rache, then Hebe sich, then Ach, Ich liebte. In this awkward situation, I suggest Ein Veilchen auf der Wiese. But she prefers the dramatic style; she wants to make an impression, and ultimately chooses the aria from Constantia.

"Go ahead and scream, squeak, meow, gurgle, groan, suffer, shake, and tremble all you want, Madam—I've got my foot pressed down on the loudest pedal, and I'm making myself deaf with the thunderous sound! Oh Satan, Satan! Which one of your cursed demons has crawled into this throat, pinching and kicking and beating the notes around like this! Four strings have already broken, and one hammer is permanently damaged. My ears are ringing again—my head is buzzing—my nerves are shaking! Have all the harsh, discordant notes from some wandering musician's cracked trumpet been trapped inside this little throat! (But this is getting me worked up—I need to drink a glass of Burgundy.)"

The applause was overwhelming, and someone remarked that the Finanzräthin and Mozart had completely set me on fire. I smiled with lowered eyes, feeling quite foolish. I could only admit it was true. And now all the talents that had previously flourished in obscurity were stirring, darting wildly back and forth. They were determined to have an excess of music; tuttis, finales, and choruses had to be performed. Canon Kratzer sings, you know, a divine bass, as was noted by that gentleman over there with the head of Titus Andronicus, who also modestly mentioned that he himself was really only a second-rate tenor; but, though he said it himself, and who shouldn't say it, he was nevertheless a member of several music academies. Immediately preparations were made for the opening chorus from the opera Titus. It went magnificently. The Canon, standing directly behind me, boomed out the bass over my head as if he were singing with bass drums and trumpet accompaniment in a cathedral. He hit the notes magnificently; but in his eagerness he took the tempo about twice too slow. However, he remained true to himself at least in this: throughout the entire piece he dragged along exactly half a beat behind everyone else. The others displayed a most pronounced preference for ancient Greek music, which, as is well known, having nothing to do with harmony, proceeded in unison or monotone. They all sang soprano, with slight variations caused by accidental rises and falls of the voice, perhaps a quarter note or so.

"This rather loud commotion created a widespread sense of tragic dread, a kind of terror that spread everywhere, even reaching the card tables, which could no longer blend harmoniously with the melodramatic atmosphere as they had before by incorporating various exclamations into the music;

"'Oh! I loved—forty-eight—was so happy—I pass—then I didn't know—whist—pangs of love—follow suit,' and so on. It creates a very charming effect. (I fill my glass.)"

"That was the peak of tonight's musical performance. 'Now it's all finished,' I thought to myself. I closed the book and stood up from the piano. But the baron, my longtime tenor, approached me and said;"

"'My dear Kapellmeister, they say you play the most beautiful improvisations! Please play one for us; just a short one, I beg you!'"

"I replied quite curtly that today my imagination had completely wandered off, and while we're discussing this, a devil disguised as a fashionable gentleman wearing two waistcoats had discovered Bach's Variations, which were sitting under my hat in the adjoining room. He assumes they are simply little variations, like Nel cor mio non più sento, or Ah, vous dirai-je, maman, and so on, and he insists that I must play them. I attempt to make excuses, but they all gang up on me. So then, 'Listen, and die of boredom,' I think to myself, and I start playing."

When I reached the third variation, several ladies left, followed by the gentleman with the Titus Andronicus head. The Rödelein family, since their teacher was performing, endured until variation twelve, though not without struggle. The fifteenth variation caused the man wearing two waistcoats to flee. Out of extreme politeness, the Baron remained until the thirtieth variation and finished all the punch that Gottlieb had placed on the piano for me.

"I should have brought everything to a happy conclusion, but unfortunately, this number thirty—the theme—pulled me away irresistibly. Suddenly the quarto pages expanded into a gigantic folio, on which a thousand variations and developments of the theme were written, and I had no choice but to play them. The notes came to life, and sparkled and danced all around me—an electric current flowed through my fingertips into the keys—the spirit, from which it poured forth, spread his broad wings over my soul, the entire room filled with a thick mist, in which the candles burned dimly—and through which appeared now a nose, and then a pair of eyes, and then suddenly disappeared again. And so it happened that I was left alone with my Sebastian Bach, attended by Gottlieb, as if by a familiar spirit. (Your good health, Sir.)"

"Should an honest musician be tormented with music, as I have been today, and am so often tormented? Truly, no art is so terribly abused as this same glorious, holy Music, who, in her delicate nature, is so easily violated. Do you have real talent—real feeling for art? Then study music—do something worthy of the art—and dedicate your entire soul to the beloved saint. If you lack this but have a fondness for eighth notes and thirty-second notes, practice for yourself and by yourself, and do not torment Capellmeister Kreisler and others with it."

"Well, now I could go home and put the finishing touches on my piano sonata; but it's not even eleven o'clock yet, and it's such a beautiful summer night. I'd bet anything that at my next-door neighbor's house (the Chief Huntsman's), the young ladies are sitting at their window, shouting down into the street for the twentieth time with harsh, sharp, piercing voices, 'When thine eye is beaming love'—but only the first verse, over and over again. Diagonally across the street, someone is butchering the flute and has lungs like Rameau's nephew; and in notes of 'linked sweetness long drawn out,' his neighbor is attempting acoustic experiments on the French horn. The many dogs in the neighborhood are getting restless, and my landlord's cat, inspired by that sweet duet, is making certain tender confessions right by my window (since, naturally, my musical-poetic workshop is an attic)—upward through the entire chromatic scale, softly complaining to the neighbor's cat, with whom he has been in love since last March! Until all this commotion is finally over, I think I'll sit quietly here. Besides, there's still blank paper and Burgundy left, and I'll take a sip right now.

"There is, as I have heard, an ancient law that forbids those who practice any noisy trade from living near writers and scholars. Shouldn't musical composers then—who are poor and struggling, and who are forced to transform their inspiration into money to survive—be allowed to apply this same law to themselves and drive away all street singers and bagpipe players from their neighborhood? What would a painter say if, while he was transferring an image of perfect beauty onto his canvas, you held up all sorts of grotesque faces and hideous masks in front of him? He could close his eyes and at least follow the visions in his mind in peace that way. Putting cotton in one's ears doesn't help; you can still hear the terrible racket. And then just the thought—the mere thought of 'Now they're about to sing—now the horn is starting up'—is enough to send one's most elevated ideas straight to hell."

Chapter V. Saint Gilgen.

It was a bright Sunday morning when Flemming and Berkley left the cloud-covered hills of Salzburg behind and traveled eastward toward the lakes. The landscape surrounding them was perfectly suited to inspire their souls toward sacred contemplation. Fields, forests, hills and valleys, fresh air, and the fragrance of clover fields and freshly cut hay, birds singing, and the sound of village church bells, and the gentle breeze moving through the tree branches— no workers in the fields, but villagers making their way to church, walking across the green meadows with roses tucked in their hats—the beauty and tranquility of the holy day of rest—everything in earth and sky touched the soul like a blessing.

They stopped to change horses at Hof, a small cluster of houses perched on the crest of a windy hill, where the church and tavern faced each other across nothing but the dusty road and the churchyard, with its iron crosses and the fluttering tinsel decorations of funeral wreaths. Groups of peasants had gathered in the churchyard and at the tavern entrance, waiting for the church service to begin. They were dressed in their finest clothes. The men wore knee-length pants and tall boots, along with long coats featuring large metal buttons; the women sported straw hats and brightly colored cotton dresses with high waistlines and narrow skirts. They were decorated with an abundance of large, flashy ornaments, and they reminded Flemming of the Native Americans in America's frontier towns. Near the churchyard gate stood a booth filled with bright cotton fabrics; across from it sat an elderly woman behind a table piled high with gingerbread. She had a spinning wheel beside her, where the peasants would gamble a kreutzer for a piece of cake. On additional tables, cases containing knives, scythes, harvesting tools, and other farming equipment were displayed for sale.

The travelers continued their journey without stopping to attend mass. During the morning hours, they suddenly caught sight of the stunning Lake of Saint Wolfgang spread out far below them in the valley. On its banks beneath them lay the white village of Saint Gilgen, resembling a swan resting on its nest of reeds. They appeared to have come upon it unexpectedly, as if they had quietly approached and clapped their hands over it while it slept, almost anticipating that it would unfold its wide, snow-white wings and take flight. The entire scene was one of extraordinary beauty.

They drove slowly down the steep hill and stopped at the village inn. In front of the door stood a magnificent, broad-branched tree, with benches and tables beneath its shade. On the front of the house was written in large letters, "Post-Tavern by Franz Schoendorfer"; and above this was a large sundial, and a half-faded painting of a bear hunt, covering the entire side of the house, and mostly red. Just as they pulled up, a procession of priests with banners, and peasants with their hats in their hands, passed by toward the church. They were singing a solemn psalm. At the same moment, a well-dressed servant girl, with a black straw hat, set flirtatiously on her blonde hair, and a large silver spoon tucked in her belt, came out of the tavern, and asked Flemming what he would like to order for breakfast.

Breakfast was quickly prepared and served at the top of the stairs on an old-fashioned oak table in the great hall, where all the bedrooms had their entrances. At the same time, Berkley requested a tub of cold water, in which he positioned himself while still wearing his coat, with a bedspread wrapped around his knees. He remained this way for an hour, eating his breakfast, smoking his pipe, and laughing frequently. Afterward, he went to bed and slept until dinnertime. During this time, Flemming stayed in his room reading. It was a spacious room at the front of the house, with a view of the village and the lake. The windows had latticed frames with small glass panes, and the windowsills were filled with sweet-smelling flowers.

Finally, the intense heat of midday had passed. The day, like a tired traveler, had arrived at heaven's western entrance, and evening bent down to untie the straps of his sandals. Flemming and Berkley ventured out to wander along the lake's edge. Through the cool, green pathways and lanes, under the bright leaves of the forest, across the sloping hills, in the shimmering patterns of sunlight and leaf shadows—what an invigorating walk! The cool evening breeze by the lake felt like a refreshing bath. They eagerly breathed in the freshness of the moment, and their chests rose with joy and renewed energy after being trapped indoors during the oppressive heat of the long summer day. And there the lake lay as well, so beautiful and peaceful! Didn't it bring to mind, do you think, the lake of Thun?

On their way back home, they walked past the village cemetery.

"Let's go inside and see how the dead are laid to rest," said Flemming as they walked beneath the church's bell tower; and they entered, wandering among the graves in the evening shadows.

How peaceful is the home of those who live in the green villages and crowded cities of the dead! They require no remedy for worry, no protection against destiny. No morning sun streams through the shut windows to wake them, nor will it until the final great day. At best, a wandering ray of sunlight slips through the crumbling wall of an old forgotten tomb—a strange visitor that doesn't stay long. And there they all rest, the blessed ones, with their arms folded across their chests, or lying still at their sides— not sculpted in marble by human hands, but shaped from dust by the hand of God. May God's peace be with them. No one visits them now to take their hand and gently stroke their hair with tender fingers. They no longer care about the sweet words of earthly friendship. They don't need us, no matter how much we might need them. And yet they quietly wait for our arrival.

Beautiful is that time in life when we can say, using the words of Scripture, "You have the dew of your youth." But Death gathers many of these flowers. He places them against his chest, and his appearance becomes transformed into something less frightening than before. We learn to look and not tremble; for he carries in his arms the sweet blossoms of our earthly hopes. We will see them all again, flourishing in a happier place.

Yes, death reunites us with our friends once more. They are waiting for us, and our time here won't be long. They have departed before us and have become like angels in heaven. They stand at the edge of the grave to welcome us, wearing the same loving expressions they had on earth, yet now more beautiful, more radiant, more spiritual! Oh, how well spoken were those words that graves are the footprints of angels.

Death has taken you as well, and you still had the freshness of youth. He has placed you against his chest, and his harsh face shows a smile. The distant land we're all traveling toward feels closer to us now, and the path seems less frightening; because you have gone ahead of us, moving so peacefully to your final rest, that even the end of day itself doesn't fade more gently!

It was during a blessed moment of communion with the souls of those who had passed away that the gentle poet Henry Vaughan wrote those few lines, which have made death beautiful and his own name immortal!

"They have all departed into a world of light,"
And I alone sit lingering here!
Their memory itself is beautiful and radiant.
And my sad thoughts become clear.
"It shines and sparkles in my troubled heart,"
Like stars shining over a dark forest,
Or those gentle rays of light that clothe the hill,
After the sun sets.
"I see them walking in an air of glory,"
Whose light tramples on my days,
My days, which are at their best nothing more than dull and gray,
Mere glimmerings and decays.
"O sacred hope, and profound humility,
High as the heavens above!
These are the paths you follow, and you have revealed them to me,
To ignite my cold love.
"Dear, beautiful Death! the jewel of the just!"
Shining nowhere but in the dark!
What mysteries lie beyond your dust,
Could a person see beyond that boundary!

"Anyone who has discovered a nest with young birds ready to fly may understand,
At first glance, if the bird has already flown away;
But what beautiful field or grove does he sing in now,
That remains unknown to him.
"And yet as angels, in some brighter dreams,"
Call to the soul, when a person sleeps,
So some unusual thoughts go beyond our familiar subjects,
"And into glory peep!"

These were Flemming's thoughts as he stood among the graves that evening in the churchyard of Saint Gilgen. A sacred peace came over him. The burning ache in his heart was soothed. He experienced a brief respite from his suffering and returned to his room feeling calm. Where did this sacred peace come from, this tranquility he had longed for? He couldn't say, yet the place felt blessed. He decided to stay there by the lake, which had become like a Pool of Bethesda for him, and let Berkley continue alone to the baths of Ischel. He would wait for him in the quiet solitude of Saint Gilgen. Long after they had said goodnight, he remained in his room, reflecting on what he had endured, and savored the silence both inside himself and around him. One hour after another passed unnoticed as he sat absorbed in his thoughts. Finally, his candle burned down in its holder, flickered once, and went out with a soft sound. This brought him back to the present.

He walked to the window and looked out into the dark night. It was very late. Already twice since midnight, the great preacher Time had turned the hourglass in his elevated pulpit—the church bell tower—like a minister from the Puritan era, and continued delivering his sermon, booming down to his congregation in the graveyard and throughout the village. But no one heard him. Everyone was asleep in their narrow pews—that is, in their beds and in their graves. Shortly after, the rooster crowed, and the cloudy sky, like the apostle who betrayed his Lord, wept bitterly.

Chapter VI. Saint Wolfgang.

The morning is absolutely beautiful beyond words. The sun's heat is intense, but a gentle breeze keeps the air cool. Birds have never sung more loudly and clearly. The flowers on the windowsill and table—roses, geraniums, and the delicate crimson cactus—are all so stunning that we believe the German poet was right when he described flowers as "stars in the firmament of the earth." Outside, everything is peaceful. Across from the window stands the village schoolhouse. Two espaliered trees spread their branches against the white walls, fastened like the wings of captured kites. That's where the switches grow. Beneath them, schoolgirls sit on a bench by the door, while barefoot children in short pants sound out their lessons. The clock strikes twelve, and one by one they vanish, filing into the building like bees responding to the clang of a metal pan. At the doorway of the neighboring house, a poor woman sits knitting in the shade, with an aqueduct in front of her pouring cool, clear water into a crude wooden trough. A horse-drawn carriage without its horses sits at the inn entrance, where a postilion in a red jacket chats with a blacksmith wearing blue wool stockings and a leather apron. Beyond that stands a stable, and further still, a group of houses and the village church. Workers are fixing the bell tower and its bulbous spire. A bit farther, above the house rooftops, you can glimpse Saint Wolfgang's Lake. Water this brilliant and beautiful rarely exists anywhere else. Green, blue, and silver-white blend together with barely noticeable transitions, like the patterns on a mackerel's sides. Above rise the mountain peaks—some bare, rocky, and cone-shaped, others bold, broad, and dark with pine trees.

Such was the scene that Paul Flemming observed from his window a few mornings after Berkley's departure. The tranquility of the place had brought him comfort. He had grown more peaceful. His heart ached less intensely in the sacred village stillness, just as we naturally lower our voices when those around us speak in hushed tones. He started to feel occasional interest in the simple things surrounding him. The appearance of the countryside brought him pleasure, but even more so the face of the poor woman who sat knitting in the shade. It was a pale, gentle face, with more refinement in its features than was typical among country folk. It also carried an expression of patient endurance. As he watched her, a disabled child emerged from the doorway and clung to her knees. She touched him tenderly. It was her child; in whom she saw her own beautiful features twisted and barely recognizable, like when someone glimpses their face reflected in the curved surface of a spoon.

The child's disability and the mother's gentle care touched Flemming's emotions. The landlady shared some details about the poor woman's story. She was the widow of a blacksmith who had passed away shortly after they were married. However, she lived on to become a mother, much like how in oak trees, right after fertilization, the male flower withers and drops while the female flower persists and develops into perfect fruit. Unfortunately, her child was born with disabilities. Still, she gazed at him with maternal love and compassion, caring for him even more deeply because of his condition. In her heart she spoke, as Mexicans tell their newborn children, "Child, you have come into this world to suffer. Bear it, and remain silent." Though she had little money, she wasn't completely without resources; her husband had left her, along with the disabled child, a lifetime right to a burial plot in the cemetery of Saint Gilgen. During weekdays she worked for others, and on Sundays she worked for herself by attending church and reading the Bible. On one of the empty pages she had written down her birth date and her child's, as well as her wedding day and her husband's death. This was how she lived—poor, patient, and accepting of her fate. Her heart was like a passion flower, carrying within it the crown of thorns and Christ's cross. Her thoughts about Heaven were simple and few. She dismissed the belief that it was a place of endless work rather than rest, and was convinced that when she finally arrived there, she would labor no more, but would always sit wearing a clean white apron and sing psalms.

As Flemming sat thinking about these matters, he found himself paying fresh tribute in his heart to the beauty and excellence of women's character. He thought of those who were far away and those who had died, and said with tears in his eyes;

"Should I thank God for the green summer, and the gentle air, and the flowers, and the stars, and everything that makes this world so beautiful, but not for the good and beautiful people I have known in it? Hasn't their presence been sweeter to me than flowers? Aren't they higher and holier than the stars? Don't they mean more to me than all other things?"

The morning slipped by in quiet contemplation, and in the afternoon, as Flemming was getting ready to head down to the lake according to his usual routine, a carriage pulled up in front of the door. To his complete surprise, Berkley leaped out. The first thing he did was strike the Postmaster, who was standing near the entrance, sharply with his whip. The man who received the blow mildly protested, saying,

"Please, sir, don't; I am disabled."

Berkeley stopped what he was doing and instead began shaking the postmaster's wife by the shoulders, ordering his dinner in English. But he did all of this so good-naturedly, with such a cheerful, laughing face, that no one took offense.

"So you've come back much earlier than you planned," said Flemming, after they had exchanged their initial warm greetings.

"Yes," Berkley replied, "I grew tired of Ischel—extremely tired. I didn't find the friends I was expecting there. Now I'm returning to Salzburg, and then on to Gastein. I'll definitely find them there.

You have to come with me."

Flemming turned down the invitation and suggested to Berkley that he should come along with him on his trip to the lake.

"You'll hear the magnificent echo of the Falkenstein," he said, "and see where the Bridal Tragedy took place; then we'll continue to the village of Saint Wolfgang, which you haven't seen yet except from across the lake."

"Well, I'm dedicating this afternoon to you; tomorrow we'll part ways once more, and who knows when we'll see each other again?"

They headed down to the water's edge without any further delay, and taking a boat equipped with two oars, they rowed across a curved section of the lake toward a barren rock along the eastern shore, where a small white monument gleamed in the sunlight.

"That monument," said one of the boatmen, a sturdy young man wearing leather pants, "was built by a butcher to honor Saint Wolfgang, who rescued him from drowning. He was riding an ox to market one day along the far shore when the animal got scared, jumped into the water, and swam across to this spot with the butcher still on its back."

"And do you think he could have accomplished this," Berkley asked, "if Saint Wolfgang hadn't helped him?"

"Of course not!" replied the man in leather pants, and the Englishman laughed.

From this point they rowed along the shoreline to a low headland, where another monument stood, commemorating a more tragic event.

"This is the place I was talking about," said Flemming, as the boatmen paused their rowing. "The sad and unusual event it remembers happened more than two hundred years ago. There was a wedding party here on the ice one winter, and while they were dancing, the ice cracked, and the entire cheerful group drowned together, except for the musicians, who were sitting on the shore."

They gazed silently at the monument and at the calm blue water beneath which the dancers' bones lay buried, their hands still clasped together. The monument was made of stone, painted white, with a roof that jutted out to protect it from storms. In a niche at the front stood a small statue of the Saviour in a seated position, and below it, an inscription on a marble tablet revealed that it had been erected by Longinus Walther and his wife Barbara Juliana von Hainberg, who had themselves long ago peacefully turned to dust, lying side by side in some cemetery.

"That really broke the ice dramatically!" Berkley exclaimed as they paddled back out onto the lake. Before long, they found themselves floating beneath the towering cliff of Falkenstein—a sheer rock wall topped with a chapel and hermitage where the holy Saint Wolfgang once lived in ancient times. Today, only an echo inhabits the place, so clear and powerful that you might think the saint's spirit still sits there, repeating the voices from below not word by word, but sentence by sentence, as though he were passing them along to the recording angel.

"Ho! ho! ho!" Berkley shouted, and the sound seemed to hit the stone wall like the clanging of steel plates. "Ho! ho! ho! How are you today, Saint Wolfgang! You damned old scoundrel! How is Mrs. Wolfgang!—God save great King George! Damn your eyes! Shut your mouth! Ho! ho! ha! ha! hi!"

And the words were recorded above; and a voice echoed them with terrible clarity in the blue depths overhead, and Flemming felt deep within his soul the stark difference between the sacred heavens, and the mockery of laughter, and the meaningless words, which fall back from the sky above us and do not stain its purity.

Within thirty minutes, they had reached the village of Saint Wolfgang, making their way through a narrow street where the rooftops of charming, old-world houses nearly touched overhead. The street brought them to a Gothic church—remarkably grand for such a small village—which stood before a little courtyard enclosed by Italian-style houses featuring balconies and window boxes filled with flowers. In this setting, an ornately crafted bronze fountain bubbled in the shadows. At its peak stood a statue of the village's patron saint, and along the rim of the water basin beneath, they discovered this inscription written in ancient German verse:

"I was created in honor of Saint Wolfgang. Abbot Wolfgang Habel of Emensee made me for the use and enjoyment of poor pilgrims. They have neither gold nor wine; at this water they shall find joy. In the year of our Lord fifteen hundred and fifteen, this work was completed. God be praised!"

As they were decoding the rough letters of this religious inscription, a village priest descended a tall staircase from the rectory near the church and politely greeted the visitors. After acknowledging his greeting, the eccentric Englishman, without any introduction, asked him how many illegitimate children were born each year in the parish. The question appeared to surprise the good father, but he responded politely, just as he did to several other questions that Flemming considered quite inappropriate, to put it mildly.

"You'll have to forgive our curiosity," he said to the priest, offering an apology. "We're strangers from far-off countries. My friend here is English, and I'm American."

Berkley, however, wasn't so easily silenced. After a few moments of conversation, he burst into the most audacious Latin, in which the only words clearly intelligible were;

"Most reverend, most religious in Christ, and most illustrious Lord, as well as most esteemed friend! Peter spoke thus: 'I have neither silver nor gold, but what I have, this I give to you; rise up and walk.'"

He appeared to be talking about the fountain. The priest responded humbly,

"I do not understand, Lord!"

But Berkeley kept talking rapidly about being a stranger in this land, and how all people are strangers on earth, and expressing his hope to meet the good priest later in the kingdom of Heaven. The priest appeared confused and embarrassed. Through the fog of an unfamiliar accent, he could only make out a familiar word here and there. He pulled out his snuff-box and attempted to quote a passage from Saint Paul;

"As Saint Paul said; he who does good--"

Here his memory failed him, or, as the French say, he had reached the end of his knowledge, and, extending his long index finger, he finished speaking in German;

"Yes—I don't remember so clearly what he actually said."

The Englishman assisted him with a moral saying, and then removing his hat, declared very solemnly:

"Farewell, most learned and revered master!"

And the minister, as if chased by a demon, made a sudden and hasty retreat down a flight of steps into the street.

"There!" said Berkley, laughing. "I defeated him using his own tactics. What do you think of my Latin?"

"I'll say about it," Flemming responded, "what Holophernes said about Sir Nathaniel's: 'Priscian a little scratched; it will serve.' I think I've heard better. But what a strange idea! I thought I was going to burst out laughing."

They were still sitting by the bronze fountain when the priest returned, accompanied by a short man with large feet and a long blue overcoat so greasy that it brought to mind Polilla's coat from the Spanish play, which was lined with slices of pork. His face was broad and calm, but his blue eyes shone with a wild, mysterious, sorrowful expression. Flemming thought the Latin debate was about to resume with more intensity and stronger arguments. He was wrong. The stranger greeted him in German and explained that, having heard he was from America, he had come to ask him about that faraway country, which he was about to sail to. There was nothing unusual in his manner, nor in the questions he posed, nor the comments he offered. They were the typical questions and observations about cities and weather, and crossing the ocean. Eventually Flemming asked him about the purpose of his journey to America. The stranger moved close to him, and lowering his voice, spoke very seriously;

"That holy man, Frederick Baraga, who served as a missionary among the Native Americans at Lacroix on Lake Superior, has returned to his homeland of Carniola; and I have been chosen by Heaven to go forth as an extraordinary minister of Christ, to bring all nations and peoples together in one church!"

Flemming nearly jumped at the unusual intensity with which he spoke these words, and studied him carefully, expecting to see the face of someone who had lost his mind. However, the humble, unpretentious expression of that calm face remained the same; only his eyes held a mysterious glow, as though candles had been lit within his mind to brighten the daylight already present there.

"It really is a noble calling," he responded. "But are you certain this isn't just an illusion? Are you sure that Heaven has actually chosen you for this important mission?"

"I am certain," the German replied, speaking with remarkable calmness and sincerity. "Even if Saint Peter and Saint Paul were to descend from Heaven to confirm this to me, my faith could not be stronger than it already is. This truth has been revealed to me through numerous signs and miracles. I can no longer question it or waver in my conviction. I have already heard the Spirit's voice speaking to me during the night, and I know with absolute certainty that I am an apostle, chosen specifically for this mission."

Such was the quiet passion with which he spoke that Flemming had no choice but to listen. He found himself drawn to this unusual person. There was something deeply moving about the spirit that drove him. After a brief pause, he went on;

"If you want to know who I am, I can tell you in just a few

words. I believe you'll find the story quite interesting."

He then continued by describing the events that are documented in the next chapter.

———————

Chapter VII. The Story of Brother Bernardus.

I was born in the city of Stein, in the land of Krain. My devout mother Gertrude sang psalms and spiritual songs to me during my childhood; and often, when I woke up at night, I would see her still sitting there, working patiently by the stove, and I could hear her singing those heavenly hymns, or praying in the midnight darkness after her work was finished. She was praying for me. From my earliest childhood, I was surrounded by an atmosphere of religious devotion. Later I went to Laybach to study theology; and after completing the standard course of study, I was ordained as a priest. I went out to minister to souls; my own soul was filled with the belief that before long all people would be united in one church. Yet sometimes my heart felt heavy when I saw how many nations there are who have never heard of Christ; and how those who call themselves Christians are divided into countless sects, and how among these are many who are Christians in name only. I decided to dedicate myself to the great work of the one universal church; and for this purpose, to give myself completely to the study of the Evangelists and the Church Fathers. I withdrew to the Benedictine monastery of Saint Paul in the valley of Lavant. The father-confessor at the convent of Laak, where I was living at the time, encouraged me in this decision. I had long walked with this angel of God in human form, and his parting blessing penetrated deeply into my soul. Prince-Abbot Berthold, of blessed memory, was then the head of the Benedictine monastery. He welcomed me warmly and led me to the library; where I gazed with hidden joy at the massive volumes of the Christian Fathers, from which, as from an armory, I would draw the weapons of holy warfare. During the study of these works, my year of novitiate passed. I became a Franciscan friar; and took the name of Brother Bernardus. Yet my way of life remained the same. I rarely left the monastery; instead I sat in my cell and studied those volumes of sacred wisdom. Around this time the elderly confessor at Laak passed away. His death was revealed to me in a dream. It must have been after midnight when I thought I entered the church, which was brilliantly illuminated. The dead body of the venerable saint was carried in, accompanied by a large crowd. It seemed to me that I had to go up into the pulpit and deliver his funeral sermon; and as I climbed the stairs, the words of my text came to mind: 'Blessed in the sight of the Lord is the death of his saints.' My funeral sermon ended on a note of triumph; and I woke up with 'Amen!' on my lips. A few days later, I learned that the old man had died that very night. After this event I became restless and melancholy. I struggled in vain to push away my dark thoughts. I could no longer study. I was no longer satisfied in the monastery. I even considered leaving it.

"One night I had gone to bed early, as was my habit, and had fallen asleep. Suddenly I was awakened by a brilliant and magnificent light that shone all around me and filled me with divine joy. Shortly afterward I heard a voice that spoke these words clearly in the Slavonic language: 'Remain in the cloister!' It was the voice of my deceased mother. I was completely awake, yet I saw nothing except the brilliant light, which vanished when the words had been spoken. Nevertheless, it was bright daylight in my room. I thought I had slept past my usual time. I looked at my watch. It was exactly one o'clock after midnight. Suddenly the daylight disappeared, and it was dark. In the morning I rose, as if reborn, through the magnificent light and the words of my mother's voice. It was not a dream. I knew it was God's will that I should remain, and I could once again dedicate myself to peaceful study. I read through the entire Bible once more in the original text and continued with the Church Fathers in chronological sequence. Often, after the appearance of the light, I would wake at the same hour, and though I heard no voice and saw no light, I was still refreshed with divine comfort."

Not long after this, an important event took place in the monastery. Since the deacon of the Abbey was away, I was chosen to deliver the Thanksgiving sermon for Harvest-home. During that week, Prince-Abbot Berthold passed away, and my sermon suddenly became both a Thanksgiving and Funeral Sermon. It might be worth noting that I was called upon to give the burial address over the body of the last ruling spiritual Prince Abbot in Germany. He was a man of God and deserving of this honor.

One year after this event, I was appointed Professor of Biblical Hermeneutics in Klagenfurt, and left the Abbey forever. In Klagenfurt I remained ten years, living in the same house, and eating at the same table, with seventeen other professors. Their conversation naturally suggested new topics of study, and brought to my attention books, which I had never before seen. One day I heard at table, that Maurus Cappellari, a monk of Camaldoli, had been elected Pope, under the name of Gregory XVI. He was spoken of as a very learned man, who had written many books. At this time I was a firm believer in the Pope's infallibility; and when I heard these books mentioned, there arose in me an irresistible desire to read them. I inquired for them; but they were nowhere to be found. At length I heard, that his most important work, The Triumph of the Holy See, and of the Church, had been translated into German and published in Augsburg. Before long the precious volume was in my hands. I began to read it with the deepest reverence. The further I read, the more my amazement grew. The subject was of the greatest interest to me. I could not put the book down, until I had read it through with the closest attention. Now at last my eyes were opened. I saw before me a monk, who had been educated in an Italian monastery; who, indeed, had read much, and yet only what was designed to strengthen him in the prejudices of his childhood; and who had entirely neglected those studies upon which a bishop should most rely, in order to work out the salvation of man. I perceived at the same time, that this was the strongest instrument for tearing down the walls, which separate Christian from Christian. I saw, though as yet dimly, the way in which the union of Christians in the one true church was to be accomplished. I knew not whether to be most amazed at my own blindness, that, in all my previous studies, I had not perceived, what the reading of this single book made clear to me; or at the blindness of the Pope, who had undertaken to justify such foolishness, without perceiving that at the same moment he was himself lying in fatal error. But since I have learned more thoroughly the ways of the Lord, I am now no more amazed at this, but pray only to Divine providence, who so mysteriously prepares all people to be united in one true church. I no longer believed in the Pope's infallibility; indeed, I believed even, that, to the great injury of humanity, he lay in fatal error. I felt, moreover, that now the time had fully come, when I should publicly reveal myself, and establish in America a parish and a school, and become the spiritual guide of men, and the teacher of children.

"It was at that time, and for that reason, that I wrote my major work on Biblical Hermeneutics in Latin. However, it cannot be published in Germany. The Austrian press censor cannot find the time to read it, although I believe that if I have devoted so many exhausting days and sleepless nights to writing it, this official should likewise find sufficient time not only to read it, but to thoroughly examine all the foundations of my arguments and identify any errors he might discover. Nevertheless, the Spirit granted me no rest, but continuously drove me forward with great force toward the completion of my great work."

One morning I sat writing, under peculiar influences of the Spirit, upon the Confusion of Tongues, the Division of the People, and the importance of the study of Comparative Philology, in reference to their union in one church. I was so absorbed in the thought that I arrived late to my lecture room; and after the lecture I returned to my chamber, where I continued writing until the clock struck twelve. At dinner, one of the professors asked if anyone had seen the star that everyone was talking about. The Professor of Physics said that the student Johannes Schminke had come to him in great haste, begging him to go outside and see the wonderful star; but, being skeptical about it, he didn't hurry, and when they finally came into the street, the star had vanished. When I heard the star mentioned, my soul filled with joy; and a voice within me seemed to say, "The great time is approaching; work tirelessly at your task." I sought out the student; and like Herod, I asked carefully what time the star had appeared. He told me that just as the clock was striking eight in the morning, he had left his house to go to the college and saw a crowd on the square looking at a bright star. It was the exact hour when I was writing alone in my chamber about the importance of Comparative Philology in bringing about the union of all nations. I felt that my moment had arrived. Strangely moved, I paced back and forth in my chamber. The evening twilight came on. I lit my lamp and drew the green curtains across the windows, then sat down to read. But I had barely taken the book into my hand when the Spirit began to move me and urge me to make my final decision and resolve. I made a secret vow that I would undertake the voyage to America. Suddenly my troubled thoughts became still. An unusual joy filled my heart. I sat and read until the supper bell rang. They were discussing at the table a red glaring meteor that had just been seen in the air, southeast from Klagenfurt, and had suddenly disappeared with a dull, hollow sound. It was the very moment at which I had made my final resolution to leave my native land.

Every great purpose and event of my life seemed announced and accompanied by divine messengers: the voices of the dead, the bright morning star shining in the clear sunshine, and the red meteor in the evening twilight.

I now began to seriously prepare for my departure. The room I lived in had once served as the library of a Franciscan monastery. Only a thick wall separated it from the church. In this wall was a recessed alcove with heavy folding doors, which the Franciscans had used as a hiding place for forbidden books. I also kept my papers there, along with my major work on Biblical Hermeneutics. The inside of the doors was covered with terrible caricatures of Luther, Melancthon, Calvin, and other great men. I often looked at them with profound sadness, thinking that these great men had also labored on earth and battled Satan within the church. But they were persecuted, denounced, and condemned to death. Perhaps the same fate awaits me. I thought about this frequently and steeled myself against the fear of dying. I lived in constant worry that the police might search my room while I was away and, by examining my papers, uncover my beliefs and plans. But the Spirit spoke to me, saying: 'Take courage; I will blind the eyes of your enemies so completely that they will never even think to look for your writings.'

"Finally, after facing many hardships and temptations from the Devil, I am heading to America. Yesterday I said goodbye to my closest friend, Gregory Kuscher, in Hallstadt. He appeared to be filled with God's Spirit, and he has remarkably strengthened my resolve. All the armies of heaven watched and rejoiced. The elderly man kissed me farewell; and I climbed the mountain as though angels were carrying me in their arms. Near the top, there was a freshly fallen avalanche that no one had yet crossed. This became my final test. 'Ah!' I shouted out loud, 'Satan has set a trap for me; but I will defeat him with holy weapons.' I leaped over the dangerous snow with greater faith than St. Peter showed when he walked on the waters of the Sea of Galilee; and I descended into the valley while the mountain peaks still glowed in the evening sun. God is pleased with me. I move forward, filled with confident hope. This coming Christmas, I will excommunicate the Pope."

Speaking these words, he slowly and ceremoniously said goodbye, like someone aware of the momentous events that lay ahead of him, and retreated with the other priest into the church. Flemming couldn't smile the way Berkley did; for in the isolated, peculiar zealot who had just departed from them, he recognized only another tragic casualty of loneliness and mental exhaustion; and understood how agonizing it must be to unknowingly become dependent on others' compassion, a sort of helpless beggar seeking the kindness of a good wish or a prayer.

The sun was setting now. They drifted back to Saint Gilgen in silence, surrounded by the cool shadows of evening. The village clock chimed nine o'clock as they reached shore, and since Berkley had to leave early the next morning, he went to bed early. As he said good night to Flemming, he remarked:

"I won't see you in the morning, so goodbye, and may God bless you. Remember what I'm telling you as we part. Don't worry about small things. In this world, a person must either be the anvil or the hammer. Worry killed the cat!"

"I've heard you say that so many times," Flemming replied with a laugh, "that I'm starting to think it might actually be true. But I wonder if Care shaved off his left eyebrow after committing the act, the way the ancient Egyptians used to do!"

"Aha! Now you're chasing impossible dreams! Good night! Good night!"

A tragic event occurred in the neighborhood that night. The widow's child died unexpectedly. "Woe is me!"—this is how the childless mother grieves in one of Greenland's funeral songs; "Woe is me, that I should look upon your place and find it empty! In vain your mother dries the sea-soaked clothes for you!" Though not in these exact words, the grieving mother lamented her child's death with similar thoughts, focusing mainly on the empty space left behind and the daily worries and concerns that come with a mother's love. Flemming noticed a light glowing in her room and saw shadows moving back and forth as he stood at the window, looking out at the starry, quiet sky. However, he had no idea of the terrible family tragedy that was unfolding at that very moment behind those delicate curtains!

Chapter VIII. Footprints Of Angels.

It was Sunday morning, and church bells rang out in unison from every direction. The solemn yet joyful sounds drifted from all the nearby villages, carried through the bright air—soft, gentle, and subdued—blending together into a single harmonious melody that resembled the distant sound of a heavenly organ. Soon the bells fell silent, and the woods, the clouds, the entire village, and even the air itself seemed to be in prayer, so complete was the silence that settled over everything.

Two respected elderly men—who served as high priests and patriarchs in the land—climbed the pulpit steps, just as Moses and Aaron ascended Mount Hor before the entire congregation—since the pulpit steps were positioned at the front and rose quite high.

Paul Flemming would never forget the sermon he heard that day—not even if he lived to be as old as the man who delivered it. The text was, "I know that my Redeemer liveth." The sermon was intended to comfort the devout, poor widow who sat directly below him at the base of the pulpit steps, dressed entirely in black, her heart shattered with grief. The preacher spoke nothing of death's terrors or the darkness of the grave, but instead looked beyond these things, viewing them as mere circumstances to which our imagination gives most of their power. He told his congregation about the innocence of children on earth and the sacred nature of childhood in heaven, describing how the beautiful Lord Jesus was once a little child himself, and how now in heaven the souls of little children walked beside him, picking flowers in the fields of Paradise. What a good old man! On behalf of all humanity, I thank you for those kind and gentle words! And even more than I did, the grieving mother thanked you, and from that moment forward, though she continued to weep privately for her child, still

"She knew he was with Jesus,".

"And she never asked him again."

After the sermon, Paul Flemming walked out alone into the churchyard. No one else was there except for a small boy who was fishing with a pin hook in a grave that was half filled with water. Just a few moments later, a funeral procession came through the arched gateway beneath the bell tower. Leading the way was a priest wearing a white surplice, singing as he walked. Peasants, both elderly and young, followed behind him, carrying lit candles in their hands. A young woman held a dead child in her arms, the body wrapped in its small burial shroud. The grave lay close against the wall, next to the church entrance. A container of holy water sat beside it. The sexton took the child from the woman's arms and placed it into a coffin; as he lowered it into the grave, the woman held a cross decorated with roses above it, while the priest and peasants sang a funeral hymn. Once this ceremony ended, the priest sprinkled both the grave and the gathered crowd with holy water; then everyone proceeded into the church, with each person pausing as they passed the grave to toss a handful of dirt into it and sprinkle it with holy water.

A few moments later, the priest's voice could be heard saying mass in the church, and Flemming watched the toothless old sexton packing the fresh earth into the little child's grave with his heavy boots. He walked over to him and asked how old the deceased had been. The sexton paused for a moment, leaning on his spade, and with a shrug of his shoulders replied;

"Just an hour or two. It was born during the night and died early this morning?"

"A short life," Flemming said. "The child appears to have been born only to die and have its name carved on a wooden gravestone."

The sexton continued his work without responding. Flemming remained among the graves, staring in amazement at the bizarre decorations that people had used to make death frightening and the grave repulsive.

In the Temple of Juno at Elis, Sleep and his twin brother Death were depicted as children resting in the arms of Night. On numerous funeral monuments from ancient times, the Spirit of Death was carved as a beautiful young man, leaning against an upturned torch in a pose of rest, his wings folded and his feet crossed. Ancient poets and sculptors portrayed death in such serene and appealing forms through their imagination. These were people whose souls held a religion of Nature that was like starlight—beautiful, yet dim and cold! It's remarkable that in later times, this angel of God, who guides us with a gentle hand into the "Land of the great departed, into the silent Land," would be transformed into something monstrous and frightening! This is what became of the ghostly rider on the white horse—the ghastly skeleton carrying a scythe and hourglass—the Reaper, whose name is Death!

One of the most popular themes in poetry and painting during the Middle Ages, continuing even into modern times, was the Dance of Death. It appears in almost every language—the vision of the grim specter suddenly interrupting all activities and leading people away into the "remarkable retirement" of the grave. It's written about in an ancient Spanish poem and painted on a wooden bridge in Switzerland. Holbein's designs are well known. The most striking among them shows Death taking one child by the hand from a group of children sitting around a cottage fireplace, leading the child out the door. The little child goes quietly and without resistance, showing no grief in its expression, only wonder, while the other children weep and reach out their hands desperately toward their departing sibling. It's a beautiful design in every aspect except for the skeleton. An angel would have been better, with folded wings and an inverted torch!

And now the sun was climbing higher and growing warm. A small chapel with its door standing open seemed to beckon Flemming inside to enjoy the welcome coolness. He entered. The place was empty. The walls were decorated with paintings and sculptures of the most primitive style, along with several memorial tablets. Nothing there would typically inspire religious devotion, but at that moment Flemming's heart was fragile—as fragile as a child's. He bent his proud knees and began to cry. And oh! how many crushed dreams, how many painful memories, how much wounded pride and unreturned love flowed through those tears as he read through them a strange inscription carved on a marble tablet mounted on the chapel wall across from him;

"Don't look back at the past with sadness. It won't return. Make the most of the present moment wisely. It belongs to you. Move forward to face the uncertain future without fear, and with a courageous heart."

It felt to him as though the mysterious person buried in that grave had parted their dusty lips and spoken the comforting words his soul desperately needed—words that no friend had ever offered him. Instantly, the torment of his thoughts quieted. The heavy burden was lifted from his heart; death no longer lingered there, but instead an angel dressed in white appeared. He rose to his feet, his eyes no longer clouded with tears, and gazing up at the brilliant morning sky, he said;

"I will be strong!"

Men sometimes descend into tombs, driven by painful yearnings to see once more the faces of their departed friends; and as they look upon them, resting there so peacefully with the appearance they had on earth, the gentle breath of heaven touches them, and the features crumble and collapse together, becoming nothing but dust. In the same way, his soul descended for the final time into the vast tomb of the Past, with painful yearnings to see once more the beloved faces of those he had loved; and the gentle breath of heaven touched them, and they would not remain, but crumbled away and vanished as he watched. They, too, were dust. And thus, echoing loudly, he heard the great gate of the Past close behind him as it did for the Divine Poet at the gate of Paradise, when the angel showed him the path up the Holy Mountain; and for him as well it was forbidden to look back.

In everyone's life, there are sudden shifts in emotion that seem almost magical. All at once, as if some wizard had touched the sky and earth, the dark clouds dissolve into thin air, the wind dies down, and peace follows the storm. The forces that create these sudden transformations may have been working inside us for a long time, but the changes themselves happen in an instant, seemingly without enough reason to explain them. This is what happened to Flemming; and from that moment on he decided that he would no longer sway with every changing wind of circumstance; no longer be a toy in the hands of Fate, which we ourselves create or destroy. He decided from then on not to depend on others; but to walk with confidence and self-control; no longer to waste his years in pointless regrets, nor wait for the fulfillment of endless hopes and reckless desires; but to live in the Present wisely, forgetting the Past and unconcerned with what the mysterious Future might bring. And from that moment he was calm and strong; he was at peace with himself! His thoughts turned to his distant home across the sea. An indescribable, sweet feeling grew within him.

"That's where I'll direct my wandering steps," he said; "and be a man among men, and no longer a dreamer among shadows. From now on, let mine be a life of action and reality! I will work in my own sphere, and not wish it were different than it is. This alone is health and happiness. This alone is Life;

Life that will send

A challenge to its end,

And when it arrives, say, "Welcome, friend!"

Why haven't I reached these wise insights and made this sensible decision earlier? Can such a straightforward conclusion only emerge from the lengthy and complex journey of experience? Unfortunately, it's only after Time, with its careless hand, has ripped out half the pages from the Book of Human Life to fuel the flames of passion day after day, that humanity starts to realize that the remaining pages are limited in number, and begins to recall, dimly at first, then with growing clarity, that on those earlier pages of that book, there was written a tale of joyful innocence that one would eagerly read again. Then comes weary indecision, and the unavoidable paralysis of despair; or alternatively the determined commitment to write upon the pages that still remain, a more honorable story than the child's tale with which the book originally started.

Chapter IX. The Last Pang.

"Goodbye, Saint Gilgen!" Flemming said as he turned at the top of the hill to take one final look at the lake and village spread out below him, realizing this was one of the rare places on earth he could leave behind with genuine sadness. "Your magnificent hills have left their mark on my soul like a seal pressed into warm wax. The peaceful beauty of your lake will remain forever in my mind as a symbol of tranquility, purity, and calm, and that inscription in your small churchyard will serve as a lesson of wisdom for the rest of my life."

Before the same sun that had illuminated that beautiful landscape finally set, he was already well on his journey toward Munich. The mountains of Tyrol now lay far behind him, and he gazed upon them one final time in the gentle evening twilight, their lower slopes green with forest trees, and scattered throughout, a jagged rocky peak here and there, along with rounded summits crowned with snow. There they stretched out, their ridges resembling the backs of camels; a vast caravan resting at evening during its trek across the desert.

From Munich he traveled through Augsburg and Ulm on his way to Stuttgart. At the entrances to towns and villages, he noticed large crucifixes, and on the fronts of many houses, he saw crude paintings and images of saints. In Gunzburg, three priests dressed in black were walking slowly down the street, and women dropped to their knees to receive their blessing. There were also many beggars in the streets, and an old man who was making hay in a field beside the road threw down his rake when he saw the carriage approaching and came stumbling over the ditch with his hat held out in both hands, making the most pitiful wailing sound. The next day, the bright yellow jackets of the postilions and the two large tassels of their bugle-horns hanging down their backs like two cauliflowers told him he was in Württemberg, and late in the evening, he stopped at a hotel in Stuttgart. From his room window, he could see the old Gothic cathedral in the bright moonlight, with its narrow, pointed windows and projecting buttresses directly in front of him. Before long, he had forgotten all his worries and sorrows in sleep, and along with them his hopes, wishes, and good intentions.

He was still eating breakfast in his room the next morning when the great bell of the cathedral across the way began to ring, reminding him that it was Sunday. Soon the organ responded from inside, and from its golden pipes poured forth a psalm. The congregation started to gather, and Flemming joined them as they made their way to the house of the Lord. In the main part of the church he discovered that all the pews were either filled or locked; they appeared to belong to families. He climbed up to the gallery and shared the psalm book of a peasant while the congregation sang the magnificent old hymn of Martin Luther,

"Our God, he is a tower of strength,"

"A reliable shield and weapon."

During the singing, a heavy-set minister dressed in black robes, with a white ceremonial vestment draped casually over his shoulders, walked down one of the side passages from under the organ gallery and climbed into the pulpit. When the hymn ended, he read a section from the Bible, and then spoke:

"Let us come together in silent prayer."

And turning around, he knelt in the pulpit while the congregation remained standing. For a moment there was complete silence in the church, which struck Flemming as more powerfully moving than any spoken prayer. The minister then stood up and began his sermon. His topic was the Reformation, and he tried to demonstrate how much simpler it was to enter the kingdom of Heaven through the doors of the Reformed Evangelical Dutch church than through the corridors and penitential staircases of Saint Peter's. He then provided a history of the Reformation, and just when Flemming thought he was approaching the conclusion, he heard him announce that he would divide his sermon into four parts. This brought to mind the resolute old Puritan, Cotton Mather, who after preaching for an hour would calmly flip the hourglass on the pulpit and declare, "Now, my beloved listeners, let us take another glass." He quietly slipped out into the quiet, empty street and went to visit the veteran sculptor Dannecker. He discovered him in his living room, sitting by himself with his psalm book and the memories of eighty years of life. As Flemming walked in, he rose from the couch and shuffled toward him—a dignified elderly man of short height, wearing a loose white jacket, with a face resembling Franklin's, his white hair cascading over his shoulders, and pale blue eyes.

"So you're from America," he said. "But you have a German name. Paul Flemming was one of our old poets. I've never been to America, and I never will go there. I'm too old now. I've been to Paris and Rome. But that was a long time ago. I'm seventy-eight years old now."

Here he took Flemming by the hand and had him sit down beside him on the sofa. Flemming felt a mysterious sense of reverence wash over him as he touched the hand of the kind old man, who sat so peacefully surrounded by the deepening shadows of his advancing years, listening to life's evening bell that rang out with seventy-eight solemn chimes, announcing that the time had arrived when all earthly desires must be extinguished from within, and a person must ready themselves to lie down and rest until dawn.

"You see," he continued in a sad voice, "my hands are cold—colder than yours. They used to be warmer once. I'm an old man now."

"Yet these are the hands," Flemming replied, "that carved the beautiful Ariadne and the Panther. The soul never ages."

"Nature doesn't either," the elderly man said, delighted by this reference to his masterpiece, as he gestured toward the lush trees visible through his window. "This joy remains with me. My vision is still sharp. I can even make out details on the slope of that distant mountain. My hearing remains intact as well. For all of this, I am grateful to God."

Then, drawing Flemming's attention to a beautiful engraving that hung on the opposite wall of the room, he continued;

"That's an engraving of Canova's Religion. I love sitting here and gazing at it for hours at a time. It's beautiful. He created the statue for his hometown, where there was no church until he built one for them. He placed the statue inside it. He sent me this engraving as a gift. Ah, he was such a dear, wonderful man. I've forgotten the name of his hometown. My memory is failing me. I can't remember names anymore."

Worried that he had interrupted the elderly man during his morning prayers, Flemming didn't stay long and left with reluctance. There was something powerful about the scene he had observed—this graceful old age of the artist, sitting beside the open window on that bright summer morning, with life's work complete and having reached that distant horizon where heaven and earth come together, believing it was angelic music when he heard the church bells ringing, though he was now too old to attend. As he walked back to his room, he wondered whether he too might accomplish something that would outlive him—whether he might create something lasting from this rapidly passing human life, and then sit peacefully like the artist in calm old age, folding his hands in quiet contemplation. He pondered how it must feel to grow so old that one could no longer attend church but had to stay home reading the Bible in large print. His heart overflowed with vague yearnings mixed with regrets—yearnings to achieve something meaningful in life, regret that he had accomplished nothing so far but had only felt and dreamed. Just as warm spring days produce passion flowers and forget-me-nots, it is only after midsummer, when days become shorter and hotter, that fruit starts to form. Then the day's heat brings forth the harvest, and after the harvest comes, the leaves fall and gray frost arrives. Reflecting deeply on these matters, Paul Flemming arrived at his hotel. At that very moment, a figure dressed in green descended the church steps and crossed the street. It was the German student from Interlachen. Flemming recoiled as if a green serpent had suddenly slithered across his path. He sought shelter in his room.

That night as he sat alone in his room, having prepared to leave the following morning, his attention was caught by the sound of a woman's voice in the adjacent room. A thin wall with a door separated it from his own. He hadn't noticed before that the room was occupied. But in the quiet of the night, the sound of that voice reached his ears. He listened carefully. It was a lady reading the prayers of the English Church. The voice sounded familiar and immediately awakened a thousand bittersweet memories. It was Mary Ashburton's voice! His heart couldn't be mistaken, and all its old wounds began to bleed again, like those of a murder victim when the killer draws near. His first reaction was pure affection— limitless, overwhelming, wild—just as it had been long ago in the green valley of Interlachen. He waited for the voice to stop so he could go to her and see her face once more. Then his pride stirred within him and scolded this weakness. He remembered his firm decision and felt ashamed to discover himself so fragile. The voice stopped, yet still he didn't go. Pride had gained enough control over his feelings. He lay down on his bed like the child he was. Everything around him was silent, and the silence felt sacred because she was close—so close he could almost hear her heartbeat. For the first time, he understood how weak he was and how powerful his love for that woman remained. His heart was like the altar of the ancient Israelites, and though it was soaked with tears like rain, it was instantly set ablaze by the holy fire from heaven!

Towards morning he fell asleep, exhausted from the intense excitement; and during that hour when sleep draws near to the soul and visions are considered prophetic, he dreamed. Oh blessed vision of the morning, stay! You were so beautiful! He stood once more on the green sunny meadow, beneath the crumbling towers; and she was beside him, with her pale, expressive face and sacred eyes; and he kissed her beautiful forehead; and she turned her face toward him glowing with love and said, "I admit it now; you are the Magician!" and held him in a gentle embrace, so that he "might rather feel than see the swelling of her heart." And then she faded away from his arms, and her face became transformed, and her voice became like the voice of an angel in heaven;--and he awoke, and was alone!

It was broad daylight, and he could hear the postilion and the sound of horses' hooves stamping on the pavement outside the door. At that very moment, his servant entered with coffee and informed him that everything was prepared. He didn't dare remain any longer. However, as he climbed into the carriage, he cast one final glance toward the window of the Dark Lady, and moments later he had departed from her forever! He had consumed the final drop from the bitter cup and now gently set down the golden goblet, knowing he would never see it again!

No more! How magnificently sorrowful those words are! They sound like the howling of wind rushing through a pine forest!

THE END

Thank You For Reading

You've Just Read a Piece of the Greatest Library Ever Rebuilt

Thank you for reading.

This book is one of thousands we're restoring, reimagining, and translating as part of the **Modern Library of Alexandria** — a global movement to preserve and share humanity's most important ideas.

What was once lost to fire and time is now rising again — not just as memory, but as living, breathing knowledge, freely accessible to all.

What You Can Do Next:

- **Keep Reading.**

  Discover more legendary works — in beautiful print, audiobook, or digital form — at LibraryofAlexandria.com.

- **Build Your Own Library.**

  Every title is available as a paperback, hardcover, or collectible boxset — at true printing cost. Craft a personal library worthy of display.

- **Spread the Light.**

  Share this book. Tell others about the movement. Help us translate every timeless work into every language, so no reader is ever left behind.

By finishing this book, you've already taken part in something extraordinary.

Join us at LibraryofAlexandria.com

Together, we're rebuilding the greatest library the world has ever known.

With appreciation,

The Modern Library of Alexandria Team

Visit:
www.libraryofalexandria.com
Or scan the code below:

www.ingramcontent.com/pod-product-compliance
Lightning Source LLC
Chambersburg PA
CBHW011406010726
47495CB00009B/2791

9 781806 680634